SATELLITE
IMAGE

Also by Michelle Berry

SATELLITE
IMAGE

A NOVEL

MICHELLE
BERRY

A Buckrider Book

Published by Buckrider Books
an imprint of Wolsak and Wynn Publishers
280 James Street North
Hamilton, ON L8R2L3
www.wolsakandwynn.ca

Editor for Buckrider Books: Paul Vermeersch | Editor: Emily Schultz
Copy editor: Jamila Allidina
Cover and interior design: Jennifer Rawlinson
Cover image: iStockPhoto/Alex Potemkin
Map image: University of Wisconsin–Madison
Author photograph: Fred Thornhill
Typeset in Adobe Caslon, Times New Roman and Rocinante
Printed by Rapido Books, Montreal, Canada

10 9 8 7 6 5 4 3 2 1

The publisher gratefully acknowledges the support of the Canada Council for the Arts and the Ontario Arts Council. We also acknowledge the financial support of the Government of Canada through the Canada Book Fund and the Government of Ontario through the Ontario Book Publishing Tax Credit and Ontario Creates.

Library and Archives Canada Cataloguing in Publication

Title: Satellite image : a novel / Michelle Berry.
Names: Berry, Michelle, 1968- author.
Identifiers: Canadiana 20240427505 | ISBN 9781998408047 (softcover)
Subjects: LCGFT: Novels.
Classification: LCC PS8553.E7723 S28 2024 | DDC C813/.54—dc23

As always, for Stu.

Satellite images are . . . essentially the eyes in the sky. These images reassure forecasters to the behavior of the atmosphere as they give a clear, concise, and accurate representation of how events are unfolding.
– *"Satellite Images," July 18, 1996, Oakfield Tornado Case Study, University of Wisconsin – Madison*

It was not death she feared. It was misunderstanding.
– *Zora Neale Hurston,* Their Eyes Were Watching God

AUGUST

CHAPTER 1

Ginny hasn't slept well in nine months, since she was attacked in the alley. Matt says her insomnia must be a side effect of the Xanax she was put on for her overwhelming anxiety. It's also too hot tonight and there's still so much packing left to do. Her mind is busy, whirling. Ginny is sitting sideways on the new faux-leather sofa in the living room of their apartment. The lights are off. All she can see is an occasional twinkling out the patio doors down in the city. Her back is against the arm of the sofa, her legs are stretched out. The living room is in disarray, there are boxes everywhere. Some half open, some sealed shut. Ginny's legs are bare and her feet are sticky in the heat. The faux leather squeaks when she moves. The smell of cardboard and sofa chemicals permeate the room. Even with the patio doors open, Ginny can smell it, and also the dust from sealing up their life, from moving everything into the middle of the room, the curry smells from last night's dinner of takeout Indian food, the mouldy smell they never got out of the bathroom. She lies there on the sofa, sniffing. She takes it in, trying to snap a photo of this apartment in her mind, trying to take it with her when they move next week. And trying also to leave it behind. Ginny and Matt have loved living here, they have had some great memories, some great times, but, ever since the alley attack, they know it's time to leave. Ginny needs to leave.

Matt is asleep in the next room. Ginny's laptop is resting on her thighs. It leaves a red mark on her skin, recently sunburned from that last bike ride through the city. She keeps holding the laptop up to cool off her thin, naked legs. The light from the screen makes her squint. She takes off her reading glasses and rubs her eyes. There is a line of mosquito bites on the back of one thigh and she scratches at them ceaselessly. Ginny has been here, in this position, not really moving except to scratch, since 2:00 a.m. The laptop on her thighs, she's been checking on their new house in Parkville. They bought the house in July but it wasn't until tonight that Ginny thought to go on Google Maps. The thought woke her from a light, restless slumber and then her brain started moving and she thought, "Google Maps," and got up to power up her laptop. Matt rolled over, his arms jutting out over Ginny's pillow, his body splaying everywhere, and he snorted. The ceiling fan in the bedroom moved sluggishly and clicked with each rotation, doing little to help with the heat.

Ginny moves her fingers on her laptop down Google Street View. She turns left and right, spins in circles, heading through the town's streets, getting to know their new neighbourhood from above and side to side. A large old tree, maybe maple, here, a neighbour's tulip flag to the left of a red door with the words "Spring into Spring" just visible, a tiny dog walker wearing a bright blue coat, the dog ahead on the lead wearing little doggy shoes, head down sniffing the grass of the passing lawn. She notices that the street sign is missing from the post on the corner just up from their house. She can see a post but no sign. Ginny feels like waking Matt up to show him all of this, but she also knows she needs to let him sleep. The months of her anxiety after the attack, and then buying this house, packing up, and then the stress and uncertainty of Ginny quitting her teller job at the bank is wearing on him. She thinks he might even be getting a cold sore on his lip from the stress.

Ginny continues on. She's enjoying the view. It places her in a space, a direction, even a time. She slides the image timeline back and forth between recent and past – a fall day in 2019 to a grimy, low-resolution 2010 photo. It's spring here now, in this exact image. Even the flag says so.

Ginny stretches and sniffs under her arms. She almost drops the laptop on the floor. She's stinky. Rank. The humidity has been awful and the thought of living outside of the city where breezes can get through, where everything isn't cluttered and tight and close, excites her. She imagines living in the country, in wide open spaces and cut-grass air. A town with no alleys, no lurking strangers. No cackling laughter, or dangerous knives.

Matt tells her, "You're overreaching, Ginny. You're seeing moving to the country as an all-encompassing fix. The actual breeze won't be air-conditioned there. You'll be disappointed."

But Ginny tells Matt it's better to be overly confident about a move as big as this, it's better to think their lives will change for the best, right? They have made a huge decision, uprooting their lives completely. Making a conscious effort to kick-start normality, to stop being so anxious, scared of everything. Getting away from the city, from the anxiety, from the cost of it and jumping into the calm, peaceful, countryish unknown. Ginny would rather be positive about it before she moves and then be disappointed later.

After the attack, when they decided to buy a house, they couldn't find anything in the city that they could afford. There was nothing away from this neighbourhood. Or at least nothing without major problems – termites, asbestos, needing major renovations, crime-ridden locations. Price mostly. Ginny and Matt couldn't afford even the worst shacks. But then they widened their search criteria, extended the search more and more away from the city, more toward rural, they reshuffled their idea of work and thought about creating a family soon, and then they found this house.

Parkville was a place they were familiar with, visiting friends' cottages or just market-shopping when they wanted to get out of the city. They stayed in the bed and breakfast here after their wedding. It has a lake and walking trails – old train tracks converted into wonderful, long hiking and biking trails. And the house is large and has some potential. A few major renovations are needed but that will come with time.

Ginny has been too consumed with packing to think about why she liked the house – everything was happening so quickly – but there was something about its size, about the yard leading into the ravine, about the dining room with ornate, thick trim and a door into the kitchen that swung back and forth. She could see herself carrying dishes through that door to her family someday. She wanted to live away from the claustrophobic, hot, stress-inducing, criminal city, to get a new lease on life. This house felt right. Matt immediately agreed. Having lived in their one-bedroom, tenth-floor apartment with a galley kitchen for two years, Matt felt like this house was akin to winning the lottery. "Think of all the space," he kept saying, his arms spread wide.

"To think that only a year ago all we worried about was what font to use on our wedding invitations," Matt said.

Back then it was a life with relatively no fear. Not in the way fear has thrown a black sheet over them since October.

After Ginny inches her fingers around the laptop, edges around the streets in all different directions, after she studies all the houses around theirs and imagines the neighbours, creates a picture of them from the outside appearance of their houses, after she looks at the sidewalks and the corner store about three blocks away, she clicks on Satellite View and the screen moves quickly out and everything is dark with white lines. Ginny imagines the satellite that caught this shot from space. She has no idea what a satellite would look like, except from movies, but she sees something in her mind that seems right. Like a large drone, grey with black solar panels. She sees it floating there above the Earth taking photos. Ginny's not sure how often the images change, but time has stopped here. Everything is stuck. She uses the trackpad and slowly, slowly travels down to Earth. The mid-size lake at the edge of the town becomes large and Ginny can imagine swimming on hot days like today.

Maybe dipping a baby's toes in the lake. She can see docks with small boats moored to them. Maybe she and Matt will have a boat someday? She can see a few small islands, one of which has a white cabin on it. As she zooms in she can see the streets of Parkville becoming clearer, the backyard pools and roofs are visible. Ginny imagines herself as a bird flying over the town. She swoops around a bit, her fingers flying.

Moving more toward their new house Ginny sees that one of their neighbour's houses has an addition she didn't notice from the ground. It almost doubles the size of their house. The street just over from their house is a dead end, a cul-de-sac, it loops into a U. The leaves are on all the spring trees, but not completely full. It must be early spring. The ravine behind the house looks blurry and empty and sad. A jumbled mess of limbs just waking up from winter. She can't see through the thick trees, the new leaf growth, to anyone on the trail. It's either early in the morning or maybe no one uses the ravine. The neighbours don't seem to use their garages as each driveway with a garage has a car on it. Maybe this is a weekend image, the neighbours tucked inside having breakfast, their cars waiting in the driveways to be used to run errands, the garages full of lawn equipment or boxes of stuff. Ginny scratches her bites again. She yawns. She can hear a car alarm through the patio door going off down in the streets ten storeys below. She definitely won't miss the ever-present sounds of the city. As she expects the air to be cool, like air conditioning, and fresh in the country, she also expects the new town to be quiet. She expects nothing scary or loud to happen when they move to the country.

Ginny's fingers move out again and her screen heads to the downtown core of the new town, walkable from their house. She is curious about the stores, the dumpsters in the back parking lots, the traffic – is there any? She sees a small apartment building and notices the roof has some scaffolding on it.

But back to the new house. Up the street, turn left, turn right, past the cul-de-sac and here she is again. At the house. Ginny and Matt's house.

Ginny feels like she hasn't slept since last October. When she was attacked in the city. The city noises – blaring radios and car horns and alarms – Ginny jumps every time a truck or ambulance or police car whips up and down far below on the spiderweb network of streets in the city. These noises keep Ginny up all night and make it so she can't focus. Noises that add to her stress. And every time something wakes Ginny up she can only picture the attacker's glinting knife, his cackling, strange laughter. Sometimes she hears his laughter in her nightmares.

She is so ready to move.

It was an easy decision to make. Matt wanted a backyard and a rope swing. Ginny wanted a dining room for large family meals. They quickly took out a terrifying mortgage and used the savings they'd been squirrelling away since the wedding for the down payment.

Ginny rubs her eyes again. She polishes her reading glasses on her pink tank top, which is stained with sweat. She knows Matt worries that he'll never be able to stop working. He's worried he's a full adult now. He now has large responsibilities and debts. Matt thought their wedding last year was adulting but now . . . he's a homeowner. That's big. Ginny worries more about leaving her daily routine, her job, about meeting new, trustworthy people, friends, about settling in. And about getting pregnant. But her therapist said she would be happier with a new schedule, that her job and her life in the city, her fears, were making her sick. The therapist said that soon Ginny's anxiety would lead to more serious problems, maybe something autoimmune.

"Stress is as bad on your body as smoking," Dr. Margo said, recommending yoga but refusing to increase Ginny's medication. "In fact, in the country you might not need your pills anymore?"

It is finally time to leave.

The house is slightly bigger and more rundown than they had bargained for. The basement is unfinished and is dusty and stale. The windows all need to be replaced. They were only allowed one showing and no inspection so they had to trust their initial, gut feelings. The real estate agent told them there was another bidder so they had to move fast. They didn't even have time to remember to take pictures. The annoyed agent, bleached hair with out-of-date bangs, orangey lipstick and pink fingernails, stood by the door clutching her phone and watching them rush through. She snapped her gum. She sighed every time they passed her and tapped her pink fingernails on her diamond-studded phone case.

But it's their house now.

White clapboard and brick, a small front porch, a fairly large front lawn and a sheltered car park. There is a stone fireplace and a bay window in the living room. A kitchen with potential (once the wallpaper is removed and new appliances are purchased) and with screen doors going out to the small deck. Ginny imagines sitting in the kitchen with her coffee and looking out to the backyard. Matt says he wants a barbeque just off the porch. And upstairs there are three bedrooms with small closets and a fairly large bathroom with a tub and a shower stall. The attic is half-done – a project started and never finished.

"Not everything has to be done at once," Matt says.

"I'll be patient," Ginny says. She knows she'll need patience when she becomes a mother too.

The attic is unusable now, it needs finished walls and a new ceiling, but it has huge potential. And, yes, the basement and the roof need a lot of work but Matt tells Ginny they can wait on that, do that in time.

At her laptop Ginny's fingers zoom over their roof again, checking out the parts that Matt said look leaky and old. She flies down over the tree in the backyard, a large climbing tree with impressive branches, perfect for a swing or a tree house for their future kids. The backyard is large. All grass, no gardens – she thinks she might try to plant some flowers, maybe a vegetable garden. Zucchinis and sunflowers and tomatoes. There is a gate in the tall fence that encircles the property. The gate opens into the ravine. Matt says he thinks that will be nice for walks. Back at the house there is a small patio off the kitchen that looks slightly rundown, and a basement hatch, one of those old-fashioned things with slanted doors in the ground that open wide and have stairs that head down into the basement. The doors are closed in this image. Ginny doesn't even remember the hatch from when they viewed the house, but it must have been there. She thought that there was no door in the basement to the outside, but she guesses she just missed it. Ginny didn't spend much time in the basement or outside in the back. There is what looks like the roof of a shed up against the house between the patio door and the hatch. Ginny pulls the satellite photo out slightly.

There is something there, just to the right of the hatch in front of the shed. She scratches her ankle and adjusts her glasses. She widens her eyes and rubs them. She looks again. *What is that?* From far out it's just a blotch of white, but as Ginny moves the image closer it becomes clearer and clearer. She's peering. Her hands start to shake. There is no way this is what she thinks it is. It's not possible.

Someone shouts outside on the street and Ginny jumps, startled, and the sofa squeaks and farts where her legs are stuck to it. She sits up straight now, her feet on the floor, and she squints at her laptop. She shakes her head. This is not possible.

Ginny puts the laptop down beside her on the sofa. She gets up quietly and turns on the lights in the living room. Maybe it's just too dark to see anything. Maybe she's too tired and her eyes are playing tricks on her. She looks out at the city lights below the living room window. The lights are twinkling. Her heart is beating wildly. The city is becoming alive below. Waking up. She sees more pedestrians now, people moving about and getting on with their lives. Ginny sits down again and looks at her screen. She expands the image as large as possible until everything is blurred and then back to clear again, and she feels a shiver moving up her back. The image she just saw is still there. She peers and squints. She wasn't imagining it.

CHAPTER 2

"What are you doing up?" Matt says from behind the sofa and Ginny startles and almost falls off. If she wasn't so sweaty and stuck to it she'd be on the floor.

Ginny has woken Matt up with the lights. He is now in the living room, stretching. His unshaven face and dark hair are lost in the shadows. He is wearing his boxer shorts and is shirtless. His chest is shiny, the hair on it wet from sweat.

"It's four a.m., Ginny. Come back to bed."

Ginny looks up at him.

"Matt, what's this?" she says, pointing to her laptop. "Tell me it isn't what I think it is."

"Your laptop, I assume?" Matt yawns. For such a large man he is often surprised his mouth opens only narrowly. He stretches his long, muscular arms over his head and then pulls them behind his back and links his fingers together. He groans.

"What is this, Matt? Come here."

Matt sits down on the sofa next to Ginny. "It's wet here."

"Sweat," she says and unsticks her legs so he can see the sweat underneath them.

Matt moves closer. He looks at Ginny. He studies her. She's wearing an old pair of his boxer shorts that are practically falling off. She's a small woman, almost boyish in figure. None of Matt's clothes fit her but she says they are comfortable and smell like him and so she's always wearing them. Matt often catches her with his T-shirts falling to her knees, his track pants tied up with a belt or rope, his boxers. He always laughs because Ginny's hand is often clutching his clothes to her body, hanging on for dear life, holding everything up. Right now, he smiles and pokes her.

"Nice boxers," he says. "God, it's so hot in here."

"You're the one with the air conditioning rule."

Once they bought the house Matt decided to cut down on costs, including air conditioning, and so they've spent this summer sweating in the apartment. All night. The air is thick and wet. They've been so sticky. And Ginny has complained incessantly about it. But then, Matt thinks, so has he. Even more than her, actually, because he works at home and so can't escape the heat in the day while Ginny basks in air conditioning at work.

"Matt, can you look here?" Ginny points again to her laptop.

"What?" Matt can't see anything. He puts his head closer to the laptop, almost resting it in Ginny's lap. He's tired, not quite fully awake.

"Here, look. What is this?"

"What are you doing here? Are you having more nightmares?"

"This is our new house." Ginny makes the image smaller so he can see it and then she scrolls in closer again. "This is the backyard. A Google Satellite View of it. I was checking everything out."

They stare down at the backyard of their new house together, the house they are moving into in a week. They are sitting in their apartment living room surrounded by boxes, their furniture taken apart around them for the move. And Ginny zooms out, zooms in, zooms out, zooms in.

"The hatch to the basement," Matt says as he squints at the laptop screen. "That's what it is. Was there a hatch? I don't remember that. What do they call it? Storm cellar? Or just hatch? I don't think there is a door out of the basement? And is this a shed? Do we need a shed? Actually, there's no shed part. It's just a roof. I don't remember it being there. But then I didn't go outside much, did you?"

Matt leans into his wife's arm and the laptop tilts and almost falls off her lap.

"No, right beside that, Matt. Between the porch and the hatch, in front of the shed." Ginny points at the screen, smudges it with her fingertip. Scrolls in, closer to it. She points at it again, taps the laptop. "Here. What the fuck is that?"

"Where? Here?" Matt looks again and then he leans back on the sofa and stares out the patio doors at the gradually lightening sky, at the city spread out over a long distance. "I think it's a hatch. Dorothy and Aunt Em ran into one in *The Wizard of Oz* when the tornado came, right?" Matt scratches his scalp. Musses his hair. But then he leans in again, peers at her screen, leans out. He can smell Ginny's sweat. He hears Ginny inhale – she's trying to keep calm. Matt wonders if Ginny should get her eyes checked. Maybe that's it – her eyes are fucked up. Maybe she needs new reading glasses? But then Matt puts his hand over his mouth. The image has finally settled into his brain. He has finally seen what Ginny has seen.

"What is that?" he asks in a whisper, pointing at her laptop. "Ginny, what is that? Is that what I think it is? That's not possible. Are you sure that's *our* backyard?"

Matt's hand hasn't left his mouth. His eyes are wide and have expanded so much that, with his large scruffy face, he feels he might look like a cartoon character. Animated so much he doesn't look normal.

And then, suddenly, Ginny's laptop flickers and goes off. By the time she untangles herself from the sofa, peels off her sweating legs, finds the charger, plugs it in, boots the laptop up again and finds the satellite image, what they saw is gone. It's just a backyard now. A sprinkling of snow on the ground this time. The satellite image has refreshed itself with another image, from another time, another season. The image Ginny and Matt were looking at has disappeared. There are no leaves on the trees now. It is winter. The large tree in the backyard is sparse and evil-looking. It is as if the image went backward or forward in time. There is nothing in the image but backyard and deck and a shed roof and a closed hatch door leading to the basement.

What they saw is not there anymore. There is nothing there. Just some snow. The image is gone. No matter how many times Ginny refreshes her laptop it is not there. Matt tries his laptop too, on, off, on, off – nothing.

Ginny opens her mouth to say something but then closes it. Matt can't think of what to say. He watches Ginny's teeth snap sharply over where he knows the scar is, the ridge in her cheek where her stitches from the attack were and, immediately, he knows she must be feeling pain and tasting the iron flavour of blood.

Ginny's hands shake. Her leg jiggles.

What Ginny and Matt saw in the satellite image on the ground in their new backyard, between the hatch and the deck, was a body. A long, thin body in what looked like winding cloth, a splash of something dark, maybe blood, on the white, lying at an angle that was slightly off, awkward and twisted. It looked broken. A long, thin body that definitely didn't look natural.

Or even alive.

TWO YEARS AGO

CHAPTER 3

Ginny wears a strapless, knee-length, ivory dress and a sheer veil embroidered with flowers. Her copper hair is pulled back and shining brightly under the red and gold leaves of the trees. Matt wears a dark suit and his bow tie matches Ginny's bouquet flowers, orange and red like a robin's breast.

The wedding and reception are under a tent at a small farm. The wind whips through the trees; red, yellow, green, brown leaves fall; the tent shudders precariously but holds. Matt notices that Ginny needs a sweater and her hair comes undone by dinnertime and has to be fixed. He watches her sister, Christine, pin it back up but then it doesn't hold past dessert and so Ginny finally takes it down and shakes it out. She looks beautiful no matter what. Matt and the caterers turn on the outdoor heaters when the food arrives and the guests huddle together to hear the toasts, to watch the first dance, to eat dinner and dessert and drink prosecco. To toast the bride and groom.

Stories about Matt's childhood girlfriend in kindergarten – laughing at table three – and Ginny's love of that line-dancing class in high school. Tales about the babies they will eventually have that will only happen if someone can genetically alter them to look and act like dogs (Matt) or cats (Ginny). A lot of hooting and hollering. Speeches about how Matt and Ginny met in university and how Matt took (and failed) math classes he had no interest in just because of his love for Ginny. Speeches about how Ginny has to still put up with Matt's incessant quoting of famous writers, something he's particularly proud of. How dinner parties in their apartment usually end with something either uncooked or burnt, and how Ginny and Matt have spent several years trying to master cooking but how something always, inevitably, goes wrong.

Ginny shouts, "Matt's usually so busy quoting something that he forgets to turn the burners down," and everyone laughs.

The speeches are long and heartfelt. Ginny and Matt are well-loved by their friends and family. They have essentially been married for years, living together, being together, but today they are officially, legally united.

"To Matt and Ginny."

When all of this is over Matt and Ginny get in their car and drive down the dirt road of the farm toward the small town of Parkville, toward the bed and breakfast they've booked on the outskirts for the night. One night here to rest up and then they have to drive back to the city, to the airport, to go on their honeymoon. Greece. Temples and ruins and warmth and blue sea and white buildings.

The guests at the wedding scatter quickly back to the city, rubbing their hands together, holding their sweaters tightly across their chests. As everyone leaves, a sudden rain begins and several cars get stuck in the damp field. It is a fast, cold wedding, a windy wedding, with a wet conclusion. But Matt and Ginny are in love and the blustery, rainy day doesn't bother them. They've been waiting and working for this wedding for what seems like a long time. They happily twirl their white gold wedding rings and look into each other's eyes and are just glad the whole thing is finally over.

Too much annoying planning, Matt thinks. Too many arguments with the mothers and the stepmother-in-law and Ginny's sister. What kind of cake? How much prosecco? Will people want chicken or fish? Or maybe tofu? Discussions about what to do if it rains (and it did). But, funnily, no discussions about wind or cold (which it was). Whose unfortunate friend will sit with Aunt Berta – is there someone else just as annoying? Where will Matt's divorced parents and their spouses sit? How far apart? How close together? And, in the last week before the big day, Ginny tells Matt she is worried that she won't be able to breathe in her dress. She says she's been stress eating and the dress is now feeling slightly tight.

Matt thinks Ginny should have worried less about her dress and more about her spiked heels. The narrow points stick in the ground and she spends all night pulling them out of the dirt with rapid jerks of her legs. By the end of the night the white heels are brown and she says her leg is sore from the twitchy pulling. In Greece Matt knows she will be limping up and down the hills. Whose idea was the farmer's field? Whose idea was the tent – whose idea was outside? Why outside in the early fall far from the city and how did they not know the temperature would quickly drop when the sun disappeared?

But it's over now and Ginny and Matt have showered together, soaped each other and giggled prosecco giggles, they have made tired love and now they are sitting on the living room sofa in their bed and breakfast, the heat from the gas fire making them even more drowsy. They are in their warm matching pyjamas that say "Just Married" on them, a wedding shower gift from Ginny's sister, Christine. Even though they thought she was crazy buying them they both kind of like the pyjamas right now, although Matt will get rid of his when they get back from Greece. But right now the pyjamas are warm and comfortable. Matt and Ginny are sipping red wine and talking about the day and evening over the muted TV, which shines scattered blue light all over the room. They smile at each other.

"Finally," Matt says.

"It's over," Ginny adds.

"I don't think I can take another phone call from your mom panicking about something."

Ginny's lips and tongue and teeth are stained red. She tells Matt she's definitely tipsy but feeling only really sleepy, not drunk.

"I won't be sick tomorrow, but I've had enough to blur my mind and relax me."

Matt picks at his pyjama top. "Amazing that Christine got us the right size."

"She called me," Ginny says, "to ask what your size was. I guess at her wedding Helen gave her the wrong size and so John got to wear his, but Christine was out of luck."

Matt laughs. "Is this a thing? Matching PJs?"

"Everything's a thing now, Matt. Ten bridal showers, matching jammies, tropical stag holiday, Nashville bridal hen parties . . ."

"Hey, I didn't have a tropical stag holiday and you didn't go to Nashville. We didn't go anywhere."

"Believe me, you wouldn't have wanted to have one with your groomsmen. That would have been a disaster. You're lucky they didn't know about the tradition. And Nashville? No thanks."

Matt nods, yes, Ginny is right. There would have been a lot of video game playing and Shakespeare quoting.

"The new traditions," Ginny continues. "That's the thing about all this. All these rules. When my parents got married there weren't all these new rules. You had a stag. You had one wedding shower. You got married. Just like that."

And there, Matt thinks, is one of many reasons he married this woman. Practical, confident in her own skin and mind, not one to fall prey to every little trend. In fact, Ginny wanted to elope until her sister talked her out of it. She wanted to elope one morning at City Hall and then go for a bike ride in the country in the afternoon.

But now Matt's glad they did the wedding. They enjoyed themselves and were happy to celebrate with their families. It was a big party with the people they love.

Of course, Matt thinks he'll never get married again. In fact, planning a wedding is a sure guarantee against divorce. That is, if you make it to the wedding day. He's exhausted and he knows now, without a doubt, that he doesn't love planning weddings. But it's over. He's tired and feeling the effects of the wine.

"Did you see Christine slip?" Ginny asks.

"No, when?"

"Over by the head table. She tripped on her purse on the ground. Went straight down." Ginny laughs. She tells Matt she loves when her older sister makes a fool of herself. Which is often. "My mom tried to help her wash the dirt off her butt with a bottle of water, but she just smeared it. Poor Christine. Muddy butt."

"Poor Christine." Matt laughs. "I didn't notice."

"It's done, all over." Ginny pours herself more wine, tops up Matt's glass.

"All over," Matt says. He yawns, he pulls Ginny close to him on the sofa. "Nothing more to do."

Ginny and Matt look at the TV, they watch the muted news, the weather tomorrow is supposed to be sunny and unseasonably warm. No wind. No rain. Perfect weather.

"Of course," Ginny points at the TV. "Fuck. Tomorrow is supposed to be perfect."

Matt laughs. "Just our luck."

"We have no luck," says Ginny. "Figures."

"I have lots of luck," Matt says. "I married you, didn't I?"

"Sweet." Ginny pokes him with her toe.

They sit in silence, sipping, snuggled together. They watch the news some more and then Matt turns the volume on so they can hear. There are rains and floods in Europe. Some forest fires. A few distressing wars. The bus drivers back in their city are thinking of going on strike. And the politicians are arguing about immigration and health care. As usual. Housing prices in the city are rising every day and there was a murder a day ago down the block from their apartment. Ginny purses her grape-stained lips and tsks. She sounds like her mother, Matt thinks.

The wine is finished, their glasses rest on the coffee table, the couple slowly sink into the sofa. Exhausted. Clean. Warm. Done.

And then Ginny says quietly, almost as if she's talking to herself, "Now that the wedding's over, now that that's all done, do you think we'll be bored? What will we have to do now? What if nothing big like this, nothing all-consuming, ever happens to us again? What's next?"

Matt says, "I'm ready for nothing to stress about anymore, aren't you?" He looks at Ginny. She's fallen asleep tucked into his chest, her "Just Married" pyjamas twisted around her legs so high they almost look like shorts.

ONE YEAR AGO

CHAPTER 4

A year after Matt and Ginny's wedding Ginny is on her way home from work. A tall man covered by a black raincoat, his face enveloped by the shadow his hood makes and the encroaching dark and rain, follows her off the bus she is taking home. But she doesn't notice. Because it is cold. Because she's irritated and in her own head – Ginny's employers kept her at work longer than necessary tonight, a new system is being implemented at the bank. Ginny is one of the only ones willing to help set it up – or at least one of the only people without a kid to get home to. Ginny and Baxter, he stays too. But he leaves at 6:30 p.m. and Ginny hangs back to power everything off. It is around seven o'clock when she locks up her office, when she says goodnight to Peter, the night guard, and hops on the bus toward home. The rain pours down.

She doesn't notice anyone out of the ordinary on the bus, everyone looks like they just want to get home for dinner. They are gazing at their phones and staring out the darkened windows. But when Ginny steps off the bus she hears heavy footsteps behind her. She doesn't think anything of it, until she has walked a little way and still hears footsteps following her down the empty, rain-soaked road toward their apartment. She knows Matt is there, probably making dinner, and she keeps walking but she speeds up, faster and faster. She has no umbrella. She is soaked. She can smell the man as he gets closer, a heavy, thick cologne. She looks behind her twice and the man keeps walking forward, ignoring her. Ginny's heartbeat speeds up.

And then the sounds of his footsteps disappear. Is he tiptoeing? Did he leave? Turn down another street? She looks back and, suddenly, the man reaches out, it is inevitable, just as Ginny turns the corner. She can see her apartment building up ahead, a glowing beacon of light and warmth. But he reaches out then and grabs her arm. He pulls Ginny back, she almost falls. This isn't someone needing directions or asking a question, this is pure force. Strength. She looks up into his face and can only see his forehead, wrinkled, as if in anger. She can see no defining features. She has no sense of age or race, there is nothing obvious. Ginny offers the attacker her red purse, her laptop in its case, her wedding and engagement rings, her smartwatch, the change in her coat pocket. She looks around frantically to see if anyone is on the street, watching, to see if anyone can help.

But there is no one on the street. It is still and quiet, only the patter of rain and then the eventual screaming, Ginny's mouth open wide. The weather, the dinner hour. It is a Wednesday in October. A darkened wet sky. The man pulls her toward an alley and she slides on her heels down the street behind him. She screams on and on but he quickly reaches into his pocket with his left hand and brings out a knife. He slices at the air around her; he punctures the wind. Ginny shuts up. And then the man lets her go and punches her twice on her cheek with his right fist. Ginny tastes a wave of iron, blood, where his blow crushes her teeth into her cheek. The knife in his left hand has fallen to the ground.

They say that at times like this you see your whole life pass before you. But all Ginny can see is the shadow of his face and his lined forehead, and all she can think about is why is he so angry at her? What did she do to provoke this?

He grabs her again and when they are both in the alley, when he has dragged her far enough, he stops.

And then he lets her go.

She stands there. Shocked. Paralyzed. Wet. What is she supposed to do? He has picked up his knife again somehow and he shows her it again and then he starts to laugh. A deep, throaty laugh, a roll of phlegm, a cackle. And he spits, saliva shooting out of his hood. Cufflinks from his shirt sleeves glint on his wrists as the knife moves.

But Ginny turns quickly and she runs. She runs hard, through deep puddles and off curbs, straight to her apartment building and she runs up the stairs to the tenth floor. She can't wait for the elevator. She can't stop running.

The attacker didn't take her purse or her laptop or her soul or her life. He didn't rape her or hurt her too much. Ginny's face is swollen for a few days and she needs some stitches inside her cheek, but she recovers. Most of all he didn't kill her. He let her go. He laughed. It was a game for him. And Ginny made it home, straight into Matt's open arms.

And so, almost overnight, after the police reports, after the hospital visit, they go from a newly married, carefree and happy young couple to a couple where one of them is suffering from extreme stress and anxiety.

For months Ginny won't go out anymore and then she won't walk the same streets by herself. She asks Matt to drive her to work and to pick her up. In the time it takes for the stitches in her mouth to heal she goes from an independent, confident woman to a shell. She sits in the apartment most evenings watching Matt mark his school papers from the online English high-school classes he teaches and watching the cars and pedestrians below.

"Do you think you should see someone?" Matt asks. "It's been months."

The therapist Ginny finally sees puts her on Xanax.

"Ginny, you need to change your life somehow, change your

routine, meet new people. You need to remember that strangers can be trustworthy and good. You might feel safer if you did that," Dr. Margo says.

"She has a point," Ginny says to Matt.

They are in their small galley kitchen weaving in and out around each other, carrying pots and pans and trying hard not to bump into things.

"This kitchen is too small," Matt says, as he always does. "I wish we had a bigger kitchen."

Ginny turns toward Matt. She is holding a chopping knife in her hand. She looks at it and remembers the man slashing the knife all around her in the alley. She shivers.

"What if we moved," Ginny says.

Matt stops draining the noodles and looks over at Ginny. She used to feel ferocious and wild, constantly talking, laughing, but ever since the attack she's been quiet and reserved, scared of loud noises.

"Move? Where?"

"What about if we bought a house? We have some savings for a down payment and the prices are good right now." Ginny pauses, she holds the knife in the air as if conducting an orchestra. "What if we, I don't know, also started trying for a baby."

"A baby and a house?" There is a shine in her eyes. Matt swallows. "A baby and a house."

SEPTEMBER

CHAPTER 5

A few weeks after Ginny and Matt move into their new house they are having a dinner party for their new neighbours, a kind of meet-and-greet on a beautiful, warm, almost muggy evening. Might as well start off well, Ginny had said, even though there was still so much to do here, with their dining room, with the fact that they don't have much furniture yet.

Matt is down the table from Ginny, sitting on a plastic storage box instead of a chair. On Ginny's left are Pierre and Ruby from next door, the house toward the park. Michael and Pat are on the right, from the house on the other side, closer to town, the one with the huge addition. And then there's Rain, the hippy, young, single woman from directly across the street. She's down by Matt.

"And then I guess the satellite image on Google Maps suddenly changed pictures," Ginny says. "Just at that exact moment. Matt and I were stuck there, literally. On the sofa, in shock. It was so hot." Ginny smiles around the table. Her mouth feels large and she's definitely sure her teeth and tongue are stained with red wine. She is also definitely a little drunk. She's nervous, plus she hasn't had much to eat yet, as she's been so busy serving everyone.

This has been a conversation Ginny has been waiting to have for two weeks now. After she talked herself out of the shock of seeing the satellite image and then talked herself into believing that she never saw the image, convinced herself that it was never there in the first place, Ginny decided to have a dinner party. She's been so busy unpacking that she goes through periods of time not remembering the image. Here she is, though, telling all the new neighbours about it as they eat spaghetti in Ginny and Matt's sparsely decorated dining room, surrounded by unpacked boxes. There are no pictures on the walls yet, Ginny hasn't gotten around to hanging them and Matt has been working. School is in full session now. He has no time. There is so little furniture too that hanging pictures seems pointless. Where would she place them?

Last week Ginny swallowed her fear and went out and knocked on all their doors. She left a note if they weren't there. She invited them all to the house. Ginny's first dinner party here. She's actually quite proud of herself. She was ready to make some changes when they moved here, ready to deal with her increasing anxiety from the attack, and to make new friends, and this dinner party is her first challenge. Ginny now has to wean herself off her anti-anxiety medication if she's going to try to get pregnant and this is a start. She can't remember the last time she even wanted to make new friends. But here they are, sitting in the dining room of a house they own, with all new people. With strangers. Just like Dr. Margo told her to do. Ginny smiles sloppily at Matt and he smiles back. He's proud of her, she can feel it. Plus she didn't burn the meatballs so the party is off to a good start.

Since the attack Ginny only wants to go back to normal. She wants Matt to stop tiptoeing around her, to see her the way he used to see her, full of energy and with an infectious personality. He's been shuffling around her since last October, looking at her sideways, afraid to say anything, afraid to make a noise.

"But what did you see?" Rain asks, twisting her dry spaghetti up. Rain has long, knotty hair, almost like dreadlocks but less successful and not intentional. Rain didn't mention she was vegan when Ginny asked about allergies in the invite and so Ginny's meatballs and Parmesan cheese are kept out of her bowl. She says she occasionally eats cheese if she has to, so she's not full vegan, but she doesn't like Parmesan. "It smells like barf," she says and laughs. Ginny could see Matt agreeing, he's never liked Parmesan either. She offers to cook something else for Rain but skinny, pale Rain says, "No, I don't really eat dinner anyway." Why did she bother coming then, Ginny wonders? To a dinner party? Rain twirls her noodles around with her fork and spoon and occasionally takes a nibble. "There's a group of us in town," Rain says. "A lot of us. Clean living, I guess. Everyone calls us crunchy but we're not really. We're just vegan." Ginny smiles politely. Matt rolls his eyes. The rest of the neighbours avoid each other's eyes.

Ginny jiggles her leg. Rain's refusal of food makes her a bit nervous. But Rain smiles and takes small bites like a mouse with her long hair draped in front of her face like curtains. Ginny has this strange urge to brush her hair, or at least wash it and tie it up behind her head. Rain is wearing layered floppy clothes, a tunic top and baggy cotton pants. Although she's completely covered up, Ginny does think she looks like she feels the coolest of all of them in this September heat. The patio door in the kitchen is open and a light breeze is coming through, but the air barely reaches the dining room. The house has retained the heat from the day and, in her summer dress, Ginny is still hot.

Ginny has decided that she really likes the neighbours who have done the addition, Michael and Pat. They are interesting and kind and polite and laugh at everything. They make her feel at ease, they take away her nervousness. They both work in town. They own an antique furniture store called Truth and Beauty. Ginny has a hard time guessing ages but she would say they are in their fifties. Michael might be a bit younger than Pat, he is slim and tall and athletic, but his bald head makes Ginny unsure. They've been married for ten years, "This year!" Michael shouts. The men hold hands under the table. Pat is on the heavy side with greyish hair and smiling eyes. He eats all his spaghetti and half of Michael's.

They trade bowls surreptitiously and are willing to keep the conversation going even when everyone else at the table stops talking. Ginny can tell that Matt likes them too. He smiles from his low perch on the plastic box and sips his wine.

And then there are Pierre and Ruby. Hard to read. Ginny can't figure them out. And why Pierre? Is he French? He has no accent. When she was cooking in the kitchen, finishing off the spaghetti noodles and stirring the sauce, everyone else came in to keep Ginny company. But not Pierre and Ruby. They stayed in the living room with the cheese and crackers, whispering and looking around. At what, Ginny doesn't know. There's nothing in there to look at but their faux-leather sofa, two chairs, a coffee table and a lamp. Everything worth looking at is still in boxes. The pictures, odds and ends and art books. If you want to know anything about Ginny and Matt you'd have to open their boxes up.

Ginny tried speaking loudly and she called out to Pierre and Ruby from the kitchen in order to include them in the lively conversation, but they stayed out in the living room, huddled on the sofa nervously. And Matt kept whispering to her to keep her voice down. Was he embarrassed by her?

Pierre wears a dark suit; his lanky frame looks uncomfortable in it. His black hair is greased back and he sports a small moustache, something Ginny hasn't seen on a man in a long time. No one in the city, at least no one she knows, has just a moustache like this – lots have soul patches or some scruffy growth. It reminds her of the real estate agent with her bleached hair and severe bangs; the people of Parkville seem to have come from a different era. Like they haven't caught up in time yet. Rain is the hippy from the 1960s, Pierre and Ruby are from the 1970s. Pat and Michael, with their enthusiasm over their marriage, seem to be stuck in the early 2000s. Ruby also has black hair, just like Pierre's – do they both dye their hair? – hers is curly and short. Ginny half-wonders if it's permed, do women do that anymore? Perm hair? Ruby is wearing a tight black skirt and a short-sleeved blouse. She looks like she's going to work. She might even have nylons on. In this heat. Her lipstick is too bright for her skin tone. From what Ginny can gather from their conversation they both work at home, or at least Pierre does. He does something with the internet and Ginny finds his description of it so boring and complicated that she has a hard time listening.

"Linux," Pierre says. "That's the way to go." This stopped all conversation. "Open-source hardware . . ."

Pierre's slow, methodical talking puts Ginny on edge.

"Blah, blah, blah," Ginny hears and her nervous, rapid-fire conversation stalls. She can't think of what to say and she finds it hard not to help him finish his sentences.

Ruby expressly says, with force, "My job is motherhood." It seems odd, coming out of her mouth so strongly when the rest of the night she's been quiet and meek. But Ginny admires that because hopefully, someday soon, motherhood might be her main job too. Ruby seems to mostly take their kids to school and then pick them up after it's over. Elton and Erin. They are ten and fifteen so Ginny's not sure why they would need their mother to walk them to school and back (is this what they do in the country?), but who is she to judge? Ruby does make lunches too, she did firmly say that. And does laundry, of course.

Ginny's mind is spinning. She's gone back in time.

Ginny takes a bite of spaghetti and looks down the table at Ruby and smiles. Ruby looks back at her with anxiety in her eyes. She's shy.

"Well," Ginny continues. "You wouldn't believe it. We both weren't sure we saw it at first. It was late or, well, actually four in the morning, so early? Is that late or early?" Ginny looks at Matt. He nods and shrugs. "And Matt had just woken up and I had been up for a while and was really tired. Maybe we misinterpreted what we saw? But, no, when we ran over it in detail and asked each other what each of us had seen it was exactly the same thing."

She looks around the table, pausing for effect. It seems to

Ginny suddenly that everyone knows what she's about to say. Or as if everyone can just anticipate it, that it confirms something to them. She can read slight anxiety and every single person here, except Matt, seems to be hanging on her words, prepared for what is to come. She's suddenly the centre of attention. You can hear a pin drop. And Ginny's not sure she likes this feeling.

Matt listens carefully to Ginny talk about the satellite image as he refills the wine around the table. Rain puts her thin hand over her dry, empty glass. She doesn't drink either. She doesn't eat dinner and she doesn't drink. Matt asked her if she wanted water but she said no. She said, "I don't really hydrate after five o'clock," which Matt thought was interesting.

Then Michael says, quietly, "It's because of the fluoride," and Pierre and Ruby nod. Rain says, "No, I'm not like them," but Matt doesn't know what he heard so he ignores them and continues being polite.

When they bought this house Ginny and Matt had a long conversation about all the things they were going to do differently here and one of the biggest things they were going to change was their incessant judging of other people. "That's a city thing," Ginny said. "Cutting everyone up. Feeling superior." Both Ginny and Matt decided that once they moved they were going to just accept the people they met. "Within reason," Ginny had said. "I'm not going to be accepting of racists or fascists or anti-vaxxers or homophobes or . . ."

And the list went on. But Matt knows what she meant. And someone who is vegan and doesn't eat much or drink water after five o'clock was certainly not on Ginny's list. Matt is going to just accept Rain as she is and get to know her. Same with Ruby and Pierre, who are certainly odd. So stiff and quiet. He does like Michael and Pat a lot, though. There's nothing about them he has to force himself to enjoy. Michael even said he is looking for a running partner. It's been years since Matt has jogged but when he was in university he would go out every day. Matt said he'd love to run with Michael and they set a date.

Another thing Matt is going to help change is Ginny's fear. Watching her tonight Matt thinks she's already made big strides. Walking the neighbourhood this week and inviting strangers for dinner is a huge step. As is carrying on this kind of conversation, controlling it, being patient with the story, creating a story. Ginny usually blabs out anything she's thinking rather quickly and then spends the rest of the night feeling awkward and worried. She usually goes to bed saying, "What did I say wrong?" He's proud of her tonight.

She used to be so confident. But after the attack Ginny became so nervous and stressed and, although he expected it to get better, it got worse over time. Matt has spent the last year driving her to work and picking her up every day. They would pass the alley where the attack took place and Ginny's whole body would begin to shake. He's looked up PTSD and Ginny definitely has it. So when Ginny decided they should move, have a baby, change their lives and start looking in the city for a house, he got excited, hopeful. But then they quickly realized they couldn't afford anything they liked in the city, they couldn't afford the right areas. When she suggested they buy in the country, it made sense to Matt. And Ginny jumped on it. And see, Matt thinks, they are out of that area, away from that alley, not having to go back and forth to the bank. It seems to be working. Things are changing.

Ginny is halfway through her story and everyone is rapt. Matt watches her animated face, her little jagged front tooth, the way she moves her arms around as she speaks. He loves her so much that sometimes it hurts. She's been falling apart around him for awhile, but she still makes his life interesting and exciting. She makes him laugh. And he feels an intense need to protect her. He's settling in here, on his plastic box, a glass of wine in his hand, and he's thinking that they made the right decision. Staying in the city in their apartment would have been a huge mistake. But here they can grow together, they can get a hold of Ginny's fears and worries and start anew.

It wasn't a good start, however, with the satellite image, but Matt thinks that's behind them now. It was obviously not a real image. They never found it again. A trick of the imagination, a flicker of an image.

Matt and Ginny have rehashed what they saw, or what they think they saw, in the satellite image. They've been over and over it, trying to figure out if it had something to do with the light or darkness of the room, of the laptop, or if the image had blurred over another image from somewhere else at the exact same time. It's not possible that it was real, but still . . . They both saw the same thing. And it freaked them out.

When they first moved in, the first night, with the cardboard boxes scattered everywhere, the furniture in pieces, a pizza box on the kitchen counter, a prosecco bottle beside it, Matt was locking the back patio door and he stepped outside onto the deck and looked down at the grassy spot where they saw it. There was nothing there, of course, no dead body, but the memory was still distinct. The wind was strong and he could hear a moan and some creaks coming from the ravine behind the house as the trees ricocheted back and forth. He was creeped out and he scurried back inside the house and locked the doors. Even with his height and muscle there are things that still frighten him. There are times he still feels like a small boy. He looked at the old roof of the shed just standing there beside the house. The roof of what was once a shed, attached to the side of the house, with thick wooden poles holding it up. Just the roof. Maybe a barbeque shelter? Matt can't imagine why the previous owners got rid of the shed but left the roof. He looked at that and sighed.

The day they moved in they met the sellers. An older couple, probably in their late seventies or eighties (Ginny and Matt both agreed that age becomes impossible to guess the older you get).

Marina and her husband, Charles Smythe.

"Mr. and Mrs. Smythe are moving into an apartment, aren't you?" The lawyer said, snapping her briefcase closed. "Downsizing." She looked almost proud of the word, as if she'd just come up with it.

Charles said nothing. He looked sullenly at the floor. Marina smiled shyly and stared at Matt and Ginny. Matt felt she wasn't blinking and he stared at her eyes until he saw them move. Charles looked angry. He was tall and had greyish skin. His skin colour was off like he was malnourished. His overall appearance was grey, in fact. Even his clothes were grey, as if faded from one too many washes. A short-sleeved faded black T-shirt and military-style blackish baggy pants with lots of pockets. There were dandruff flakes on his shoulders, Matt could see this from across the room. His movements were jerky. His eyebrows were so bushy that Matt thought they looked like caterpillars. Charles looked furious all through the meeting and kept looking down at the floor. Until he stopped looking at the floor and looked straight at Matt. Matt noticed his hands were twitching and there was a mothball smell about him. It was sad. Matt tried to talk to Charles but couldn't get an answer from him. Not a word. Just a few grunts.

Marina was only slightly different. Greyish, small, both soft and strong. Matt could see her legs were swollen and thick. She gave the impression of having come straight from a farm somehow. From a farm located somewhere in the past. Like Charles, she was faded-looking, washed out, dusty or sun-faded. Even her hair, sprinkled with grey, looked as if it was dusty. It was as if there was no definition in either of them, as if they were blurry or foggy, peering out of a mist. And, strangely for the month of August, she had big boots on. Marina was wearing a ratty floral dress, as unwashed-looking as Charles's clothes. A holey, grey cardigan. Matt thought she looked like she had just stepped out of *The Grapes of Wrath* and he selfishly thought that, after all the money Matt and Ginny were paying them for their rundown house, the Smythes might have tried to look a little better. Especially since they were downsizing a lot. Matt asked them what their plans were for the future, was the apartment in Parkville or somewhere else? Was it smaller and more manageable, he asked? Did they have kids? Marina smiled slightly and nodded a lot for yes and shook her head for no, and Charles ignored everything. He grunted something to Marina about not wanting to move. "I told you," Charles hissed and Marina shushed him. She looked tired of him and frustrated and nervous.

"Malnourished?" Matt asked Ginny later, as they were unpacking boxes. "I thought they looked unwell."

"I have no idea why they were so empty of emotion or life," Ginny said. "I wish we never met. Now my opinion of the house is tainted with thoughts of them inside it."

Matt agreed. "It does look slightly different now," he said, tidying up their pizza box, flattening a packing box. "I'm sure, though, that will change as it becomes ours." He then imagined Marina and Charles in his house, creeping around in their faded clothes, not talking to each other – silent, unhappy ghouls.

The lawyer that evening had them all sign the papers and then Marina and Charles left. They didn't turn around to look at their old house at all, they didn't stop on the street to take one last glance before getting into their truck. Marina sat in the passenger seat looking straight ahead and Charles started their truck and they drove off. Matt had turned away from watching them at the front window and looked at Ginny, who had popped open some prosecco. They drank out of the bottle, giving their one unpacked glass to the lawyer, who had never heard of prosecco and kept calling it "bubbly" – and then she gathered all her papers and left too. On the way down the front lawn she pulled up the large, red Realty Plus sign and stuffed that in her car. "I'll drop it off with your agent," she said. The smell of perfume followed her out the door.

"Funny," Ginny said after she left, "she called the espresso I offered earlier 'expresso.' And she didn't like it. She took one sip and gagged. Said it was bitter. And she also called our chimney a 'chimbley.' We're going to have to learn a new language in this town."

Matt and Ginny spent the rest of that first night moving their furniture in from the rental truck out front. For such a small person, Ginny was strong when determined. Matt manoeuvred the large things himself or put towels under some furniture to drag. A lot of their furniture needed to be reassembled, but that could be done in stages. And in a few weeks the new things they ordered to fill the house would come.

And now Matt is perched on a plastic box at the dining-room table with their first guests, the neighbours, listening to Ginny tell the satellite image story and suddenly noticing that everything around him feels charged and off. Everything feels suddenly cold. He shivers. As if a wind has passed through the house. Something feels different. It feels like someone has come into the house and moved through the room.

Matt gets up from his box, just as Ginny gets to the description of the body in the yard. "It was white. There was a stain of blood on the side of the stomach," she says, and Matt goes into the living room, nothing; then into the kitchen, still nothing. But he can feel something moving. Wind? Air? Is a window open? Matt checks the front door, closed, and the patio door (he avoids looking out at the body's place off the porch). The patio door is open, the screen closed, but there isn't much of a breeze out. And whatever breeze there is is warm, not cold. Matt notices the gate to the ravine behind the house is slightly open, but that shouldn't make a difference to the feeling in the house. He knows there are no other windows open. There can't be. Most of them won't open, they are all painted shut or they have heavy storm windows. In fact, Matt and Ginny have been missing September air and cool breezes. The window at the top of the stairs, in the upstairs hallway, is actually the only one that opens and Matt knows he closed it in case of rain before the dinner party. There was that feeling of rain earlier. And that's the feeling he has now, like a cool breeze, like rain is coming.

But when Matt looks up the staircase he can see the window at the top is open. Wide open. The latch must be broken. He walks up the stairs and shuts it and looks around. The hallway is dark, so is their bedroom. Matt shrugs and heads back downstairs. He's thinking of using a quote to everyone in the dining room, one he read recently when his class was studying Dickens – "For the night-wind has a dismal trick of wandering round and round a building of that sort, and moaning as it goes; and of trying, with its unseen hand, the windows and the doors; and seeking out some crevices by which to enter" – but when he re-enters the dining room everyone is sitting completely still. No one is moving at all. Pat's spaghetti fork is paused in mid-air. Ginny has finished the story and is smiling, mouth open wide, as if she's just told a joke. Her eyes, though, look scared and confused. But no one seems to understand the joke and they all at once turn and look at Matt as he enters, and he knows that the expressions on their faces isn't humour, or even surprise at what Ginny has told them about the body on the ground in the satellite image. It is fear.

CHAPTER 6

And then everyone starts talking again and moves into the living room.

"I love this room," Ginny says. "But we aren't sure if the fireplace works."

"Get it looked at," Michael says as he and Matt carry chairs in from the dining room. "I've got a guy. I'll give you his name."

Rain sits on the floor in lotus position. Ginny recognizes this from the few yoga classes she took in the city before the wedding, when she quickly realized that yoga wasn't for her, it just made her bored and sleepy.

"All the stretching and concentrating and breathing," she told Matt over a beer one night after class. "And thinking about your breathing. That's the worst. My mind always wanders. If I think about my breathing I stop breathing."

Pat and Pierre and Ruby are jammed together on the sofa. Ginny thinks they all seem to know each other fairly well, but it looks like they've probably never been so physically close. She watches Pierre squirm and squeeze closer to Ruby.

"I mean, we knew them only slightly," Pat says. "Charles and Miranda. But no one was really friendly with them. In fact, this street . . ." Pat pauses. "No one really hangs around."

Ginny watches everyone nod guiltily. They seem to be holding something in, not saying what they are thinking. As if someone is hiding something. Or all of them are.

Pierre moves farther away from Pat. He is practically sitting on his wife, Ruby.

"Marina, like boats," Michael says. "Not Miranda. It's Marina."

"Oh, yes, right, Marina." Pat giggles slightly, sips his wine. "She was an odd duck. He was so in control of everything and she was so nervous, skittering around."

"But we didn't really see them," Ruby says. "Just their packages at the end."

Everyone laughs.

"Packages?" Matt asks.

Everyone ignores him.

Rain, still looking shell-shocked from Ginny's mention of the body in the yard, moves out of the lotus position and stretches her legs out on the floor. Ginny wonders if she'll go into corpse pose – that would be appropriate. Rain says, "She didn't like me. They both didn't like me at all. In fact, no one on this street has ever liked me."

"What? We've always liked you," Ruby says. "Remember when you first moved in and I brought you banana bread? I didn't know you didn't eat wheat."

Everyone nods.

"They didn't like us either," Pat says. "Not at all. Charles thought Michael and I were an abomination. Unnatural."

"Were they religious?" Ginny asks.

Everyone shrugs.

"Not in the way you'd think," Pierre murmurs.

Again, Ginny gets a feeling they are hiding something. The mood in the room is off. Everyone seems nervous.

"Definitely homophobic," Michael says quietly. "But then a lot of people here are, so that's nothing new."

"I think," says Pat, "that they just liked to keep to themselves.

They both didn't talk to anyone. Whenever Marina was out in the front yard Charles would rush out and bring her back in if he saw anyone approaching. They both seemed mistrustful of everything. Especially Charles. He gave me the creeps."

Rain nods. "Charles would grab Marina and they would scurry back in so quickly. And any loud noise, a car backfiring, say, and Charles would jump out of his skin. I would watch him from my front window. He got worse too, as time went on. He was definitely the most anxious. It started with the packages, I think."

"What packages?" Matt asks again. And again no one answers him.

Pierre says, "Especially after he retired. Before that he would just ignore everyone. Go to work and not even wave good morning to all of you getting into your cars."

"He was a real estate agent," Michael says. "But I never saw his signs anywhere."

"And really," Ruby finally speaks up, "if you think about it, neither of them was ever out front that much. They didn't garden and rarely cut the grass. It would grow so high. I was afraid of ticks."

"Yes," Rain suddenly shouts and everyone jumps. "Ticks. God, I'm afraid of ticks too."

"Too?" Ginny says. "What else are you afraid of?"

"Just too as in 'as well,'" Rain says. "As in I also don't like ticks. Or snakes. I hate snakes. I'm not really keen on spiders either."

Ginny thinks of her unfinished basement and thinks Rain wouldn't want to go down there. It's infested with spiders. Webs draped over the exposed beams and wires, scurrying tiny spiders and large ones. Ginny shivers.

There is silence for a minute and then Pierre pulls his phone out of his pocket. He fiddles with it for a bit. "There's nothing there on Google Satellite," he says. "Just the backyard, no dead body. There's snow on the ground. You said it was a white image? Maybe you just saw the snow bunched up or something?"

"No." Matt looks at Ginny. He shrugs. "The image was of

spring when we saw it. But it immediately changed to winter. We weren't sure we saw it. But we did, we –"

"We both saw the same thing," Ginny interrupts him. "We described it in detail to each other after it disappeared."

"So odd," Rain says. "Really strange. I've always thought something was going on here. The packages. Lots of them. Maybe six or so trucks a day. But I guess we didn't ask any questions." She stretches her arms out to include everyone in this. "So I guess anything could have been happening." Rain lies down and, yes, she gets into corpse pose, on her back with her arms and legs out from her sides. As if she's been shot. Eerie. And then it occurs to Ginny that there must be a yoga studio in this town. Maybe she'll retry.

"But you'd think we'd know if we had killers living next door." Pat laughs. "Right? We'd know. I'm sure of it."

"You always used to say Charles could be a serial killer," Michael says. And then he laughs.

Pat says, "I rarely saw them. Not in the stores, or on the street. And then I would see them and it would startle me because I had forgotten they even lived there."

Ruby, suddenly animated, says, "You never know. You read those stories about people keeping girls in their basements for years and no one knows. I just heard a podcast about a girl kept in a coffin-like box underneath the bed of the husband and wife who kidnapped her. Only taken out occasionally. They even had kids and lived a fairly normal life with this girl stuck in a box under their bed. There were pictures of the box, it was really small." Ruby's eyes light up. "She lived in the box for years."

Rain, from her position lying on the floor, puts her hands over her ears. "La la la," she whispers.

Ginny says, "Didn't anyone hear her in the box?"

Ginny thinks of the odd noises she's been noticing in this house in the night, the creaking of the house, the furnace sounds like someone breathing. The wind moans. There are clicking sounds, like a cat with long nails moving slowly. The occasional bump, all of this is normal. It's a large house, an unfamiliar house. And compared to the sirens in the city, the fire trucks and police cars and ambulances and people talking on the street, the fights and shouting and laughing, this is nothing. The laughter always woke Ginny in the city, especially after the man in the alley. She couldn't bear to hear someone laughing as they walked down a city street. But here this is just a large house, a large, holey, windswept, noisy house. She thinks the quietness of the area takes some getting used to, that's all. It's obvious that the quiet here makes every noise seem louder and scarier. You notice every single thing. There is also the size of the house compared to their old apartment. So much more space for sounds to creep around and wake her up.

Matt leaves the room to get a bottle of wine for the guests. He's given up asking about the packages. Why bother? He thinks about how there are a few things he has noticed in these two weeks since they've moved into the house that don't make sense to him.

First there is the heavy lock on the back side of the basement door in the kitchen. As if someone was living down in the basement with the spiders and dust and needed privacy? It's not on the side of the door going down to the basement, which would make more sense in case someone broke in through the basement; it's on the side of the door coming into the kitchen. You'd have to be down there, on the stairs, in order to open or lock it.

There's also the entrance from the hatch out in the backyard that used to lead down into the basement. It's been oddly bricked off now so the hatch is still there, the stairs are there, but there is no entrance into the basement anymore. The stairs end in bricks. The only way you can get into and out of the basement is through the kitchen. Which makes no sense, especially considering the placement of the lock on the door. So if someone was living down there and needed a lock for privacy they couldn't get into the basement from the outside? And why would someone need to lock the basement door to the kitchen? Who locks themselves in a basement? And isn't it against the building code to have no exit to the outside from a basement? Why would Marina and Charles have bricked up the outside door? For what purpose? Matt's head spins.

Then there are all the locks on the kitchen cabinet doors. They didn't notice these when they looked quickly at the house but they look like they've been there for years. Was someone locking their food in? These are key locks. Someone had to have a key to open the kitchen cupboards? And now the cupboards look jimmied open, as if someone lost the key and needed to get in. Odd, but maybe someone was kind of weirdly childproofing? Matt doesn't know anything about childproofing. Did Charles and Marina have kids? Matt isn't sure but it didn't look like they did. They are old enough that, if they had kids, they would have moved out a long time ago. None of the rooms have any "kid feeling" – no measurements on door frames or crayon scribbles made years ago by a small child. But maybe they put the locks on the cupboards when the kids were young and then lost the keys later and had to jimmy them off? Matt's creating the scenarios in his mind, trying to figure out the lives that lived here.

The hatch being bricked up is the weirdest, Matt thinks. What's the excuse for that? Why get rid of the entrance to the basement? Unless you are keeping something dangerous in the basement? An animal? Snake, tiger, bear, dinosaur? Why seal up your whole basement? And why would you lock yourself down there with it?

Or were they trying to barricade themselves in, create a hiding place to protect themselves from something (or someone) that (who) was coming after them?

His imagination runs wild. Imagine what Ginny's mind would do. Her hands would start shaking and she would fall into that panicked stillness where she can't focus on anything or even say anything. Maybe it's just a matter of the basement door leaking, of needing to brick it up to stop the leak? But then again, maybe not?

He hasn't told any of this to Ginny. She's been so busy with the move and he hates making her more stressed. With not enough furniture, with a limit on their funds, with quitting her job, with getting to know new people and feeling untethered to society, with weaning off her medication, with thinking about starting to try to get pregnant, it's all become too much for her. And the backyard fiasco, the body on the satellite image – that's made her quite nervous, she won't even go down into the basement, says she hears noises down there, so Matt does all the laundry himself now. They used to share the job in the city. Matt would take the laundry down to the laundry room in the apartment basement, and Ginny would go down later to change it over to the dryer. He would go back down to pick it up. But lately he's been doing it alone here. So if he told her what else he's noticed around here, well, he worries that will break her apart. And him. He'll be doing everything and she'll be stuck in a fetal position in one room, unable to move.

Ginny did tell Matt that she noticed a few odd things when they moved in – like that Charles and Marina had taken all the light bulbs. Every last one of them. From all the light fixtures. Ginny and Matt spent the first night carrying the standing lamp they had brought with them from room to room as they carried in their furniture. They used their phones to light things up until their batteries went dead. They didn't notice this when they were signing the papers as it was still light out. The next day Matt went to the hardware store in town and bought about fifty bulbs.

And Ginny did notice, of course, the silver-foiled room under the staircase. A room that probably used to be a closet covered in aluminum foil, top to bottom. Were the previous owners trying to build a sauna? A grow room? For pot? Or plants? Matt and Ginny can't figure it out. Right under the staircase. What did they need that reflection for? There is a plug in there too. Ginny said it would be for a grow light. The closet is only big enough for one person to stand in.

Matt wants to fix up this house and make it their own, make it not as odd. The size of the place is so great and the old, large baseboards and trim, the potential hooked him right away. The house has so much history. He wants to take out all the stuff, fill up the holes from the locks, he wants to get rid of those things that make him stop and question what was going on here. He wants to put the house back to its original self, make it exude family. And he wants to do that before they have a child, which they're about to start working on. As soon as Ginny gets a family doctor in town so she doesn't have to commute to the city for appointments. There are a lot of midwives in this town, but Ginny decided she'd go with an obstetrician for her first time. But she needs a family doctor to recommend an obstetrician. And then they can start trying.

When they finally have a baby there is no way Matt wants it to grow up in a house haunted by the oddness of the previous owners.

⊗

The dinner party ends and the guests go home. Rain skips across the street, her mess of hair flopping up and down.

"How does she have the energy?" Matt says. "She didn't eat anything."

Michael and Pat hold hands and go down the front walk and onto the sidewalk and then back up their own walk. Ginny notices they don't cut across the grass. Ruby and Pierre walk quickly across the lawn but then circle back and stand next to Michael and Pat on their front walk for a while talking. Matt and Ginny can see them looking back at the house.

"What are they talking about?" Ginny asks. "Us?"

"Maybe the packages?"

Ginny looks at him, confused.

"Probably your story. Probably either hiding what they know, getting their stories straight or –" Matt stops talking.

"Or what? Talking about how they think I'm insane?" Ginny glares at Matt. Then she looks back out the window. Pierre is there, standing in front of Ruby. It doesn't look like she's saying anything. Pierre is pointing up to Matt and Ginny's attic window. Ginny wonders what they are talking about. All the lights are on in Pat and Michael's house and also in Pierre and Ruby's. In the city everyone turned off all the lights when they left their apartments. But Ginny guesses that utilities might be cheaper here and she's about to ask Matt when she sees the four neighbours quickly split up and move toward their individual homes. Pierre and Ruby open their front door, cascading light on the lawn, and then they disappear inside. Michael and Pat slide into their house. They've taken their shoes off on the front porch and they carry them inside.

Ginny turns from the window and walks into the kitchen and starts cleaning up. The house smells like coffee and oregano. Matt pushes his plastic box–seat back into the living room and starts to clear the dishes from the dining room. Ginny scrapes the plates and puts them in the dishwasher.

"So," Matt says. He's putting the leftovers in the fridge. "What did you think about everything?"

"I think it went well," Ginny says. And suddenly she thinks this feels like the Ginny and Matt of old. Gossiping in the kitchen after hosting a party. They did this all the time before the wedding, before the attack in the city, back when, Ginny thinks, life was pretty normal. "I had fun. What about you?"

"Yes, it was fun. I especially liked Michael and Pat but I thought everyone else was nice too. Rain's food issues are weird. And Ruby looks afraid all the time. Plus Pierre?" Matt looks at Ginny. She nods.

"Lack of communication skills?" Ginny smiles.

Matt laughs. "That's a nice way to put it."

Ginny wipes down the countertop. The dishes are all done. The dining-room table is cleared. The food is put away. Matt and Ginny stand and look at everything. At their new kitchen. A bit shabby, but it'll do for now. Ginny can't wait to get their new furniture. Their new appliances. She can't wait to put their photos and books out and their paintings on the walls.

"There'll be the right number of chairs the next time we have a dinner party," Matt says.

"No more plastic boxes."

"My back is killing me from that thing. And I was way too low. I felt like I was shovelling the food directly into my mouth from the table."

"Oh, sorry about that. I should have taken that seat. I'm shorter anyway. The new furniture will be here in a week. I keep imagining the living room and dining room in my mind. I want a rug for the living room and a loveseat."

"Slow down," Matt says. She can tell he's thinking about her non-existent job and the mythical baby and the number of renovations needed on the house.

Ginny reaches up and touches Matt's face. He reaches down and kisses her and then leans back.

"What did you think about their reactions when you told the satellite image story? What do you think that meant? The way they acted?" Matt throws his dishtowel down on the counter. He crosses his arms and leans on the wall. Ginny looks at him. She forgets how handsome he is with his dark hair and complexion, with his height, his curious eyes. When he's thinking she can see his brain moving.

"I'm trying not to think about that," Ginny says. "Let's not talk about it. It's dark outside now and I don't want to think about the backyard or the satellite image or the body, or anything to do with the feelings I get in this house, or the feelings about the neighbours. Not before bed. I've had just enough wine to dull all those fears."

Matt is staring at Ginny. She can tell he doesn't want to upset her, that he's careful with his words and actions. He's changed so much since Ginny was attacked. It's obvious he doesn't know what to do. Like her, Matt must feel as if everyone at the dinner party knew about the satellite image already. Ginny knows that couldn't be true. But she felt as if the story wasn't a surprise to them. The way no one looked at each other, they only looked at Ginny as she talked. As if they were worried they would give something away through eye contact with each other if they looked around. And then they met outside after the party, talking low, in whispers. Ginny knows this is ridiculous and she's just being anxious and paranoid, but . . . "I felt," she continues, "as if they all knew something we didn't know."

"Me too!" Matt almost shouts. "I felt this wasn't a new story for them. That they knew something weird was going on in this house before we moved in."

"Or at least if they didn't know anything about this, as if it didn't shock them or anything. As if the Smythes could have done anything and it wouldn't have shocked them. Why would they think that?"

"Yeah, it was strange," Matt says. "Makes you wonder."

He stares at Ginny and she stares back. The house is still and quiet. Ginny feels odd about how big the house is when she's standing here in the kitchen. It's above and below her. The house is everywhere.

"They did say that Charles and Marina weren't very sociable, right? No one seemed to know much about them. And what's with all the talk about the delivery trucks? They didn't look like they had many things when we saw the house," Matt says.

"True. They weren't very happy people when we met them. But why would you then accept that the body in the image had something to do with them? Just because they kept to themselves?" Ginny leans forward and wipes the already clean counter with a sponge again and again and then she wrings it out and throws it in the sink. Her hands start to shake.

And then, suddenly, there is a noise, a dull thump, from the second floor. And then a squeak. As if a door has opened. And then a sharp bang and Matt and Ginny jump. Ginny gasps and Matt runs up the stairs.

"It's the hallway window," Matt shouts down. "It blew open again. Nothing to worry about."

It isn't until later, in bed, the lights out, Matt asleep beside Ginny, that she begins to think about the window. How could it have blown open? Didn't Matt latch it earlier? And why isn't this window sealed shut like all the other windows? Why is this the only window in the house that opens? And there is no screen. She rolls toward Matt and looks at his sleeping face.

She thinks, it isn't even windy out. It is a still night. Not even a small breeze.

After about an hour Ginny finally begins to fall asleep. Matt is snoring beside her. But then she wakes. She hears it again, that sound. The window again? A wind has picked up now and is moaning through the trees outside. Is an appliance downstairs shuddering? Are those footsteps on the basement stairs? She listens and listens. There is a creak, like someone shutting a door over and over. It's coming from outside, Ginny thinks. She gathers all her strength and courage and walks down the hall toward the bathroom. She passes the window and it is open again and Ginny looks outside. The gate leading to the ravine is open. Just enough to smack back and forth in the breeze. That must be the sound she's hearing.

Ginny stares, she tries not to jump or shout or cry, she stands still, willing herself not to see a dark figure she thinks she sees at the gate. She blinks twice, slowly. And then the shape is gone. She shuts the open window again and latches it as tightly as she can. And then she turns back to the bedroom and sees, there on the floor, a small shape. It's twitching.

"Matt," she calls loudly down the hall. "Matt."

He comes out, his hair sticking up, his boxers baggy and loose at his waist. "What? What are you doing?"

"There was someone out there." Ginny points to the ravine, the gate. "And look." She points down at the floor, at the twitching shadow huddled up against the baseboard. "A bird."

"Where?" Matt follows her gaze. "I don't see anything." And then the bird moves again. "Oh, poor thing."

"Came in through the open window," Ginny says.

Matt reaches over Ginny and opens up the window again. "I'll get him out. He just looks in shock, not injured."

Ginny and Matt spend an hour chasing the bird out the hall-way window. When it finally flies off they shut the window and Matt turns the latch again. They watch the bird fly over to the fence and then fly away.

OCTOBER

CHAPTER 7

They are sitting together in the dining room drinking the last dregs of their wine from dinner.

"I can't believe we've been here over a month," Ginny says. "I just feel settled."

"When the furniture arrived," Matt says. "That's when I finally felt settled." Matt doesn't want to say it, but he also began to feel more settled when he convinced himself that the only reason Ginny thought she saw a figure out by the back gate after the dinner party was because she drank too much wine. The Xanax mixed with wine wasn't a good idea.

A couple of weeks ago they worked together shuffling the new furniture around the living room trying to figure out the best combination of recliner/sofa/coffee table and lamp. And then they opened their boxes and hung the pictures on the walls and stacked the books on shelves.

"We definitely need more," Ginny says. "We need lamps. It's still too dark in here. Yesterday I stubbed my toe on the sofa while stumbling around. And all the lights were on."

The shadows cast on the walls in each room give an eerie feeling to the house as soon as the sun sets. Ginny sips on the last of her wine. Matt plays with his fork. The new dining-room table, now with enough chairs, fits right in the middle of the room but they need to get a new light fixture here too.

"It's like we're living in a cave," Ginny says. "Everything's so dark. I'm going to ask Elaine for a light fixture for Christmas." Elaine is Matt's stepmother. Ginny always says it's hard enough having one mother-in-law, but two?

"For all I can say about her that is bad," Matt says, "at least we know she has good taste. She made my dad's house pretty nice when she married him."

Over the month they have done a few things. They've sent off the old table with the delivery company to a charity shop in the city that Ginny's mom told them about. And they have done a few renovations. Like peeling that aluminum foil wallpaper off the room under the stairs and making it back into a hall closet for coats. Ginny thought it must have been a room for growing pot. She found some soil under the carpet. Matt wasn't sure what he thought but he wanted to get rid of it. After the aluminum foil came off they cleaned the panelled walls and then Ginny spent a day painting them white. Matt thinks it doesn't look too shabby now. Because of the outlet in there they didn't even have to hire an electrician, they just wove the cord of a dangling Ikea light around the back of the closet and up the wall to the ceiling and plugged it in.

"Voila," Matt said after turning on the light, and Ginny smiled, her red hair splattered with paint.

"Slowly things are coming together," Ginny said.

But now they sit in the dining room and stare at each other silently in the dark.

"Candles?" Ginny jumps up and heads through the dining room door to the kitchen. "Do we have candles?"

Matt watches her leave the room to search for light. "I've been thinking about the attic," he says loudly. "About working with my students online in the guest room . . . and I've been thinking we should fix up the attic as an office when we have the money. I want to make that an office. What do you think?"

"We'll talk about that later," she says. "There's just too much other stuff."

Rifling through the kitchen cabinets looking for candles, Ginny thinks about how she thought she would be missing her job at the bank, missing talking to her old friends and colleagues, but she's actually relishing the silence around her. She thinks about how there is no more cackling laughter coming from alleys, no more car horns and sirens in her life. No more shouting on the street just when she's finally fallen asleep. She loves walking to the town on Wednesdays for the fall outdoor market that Ruby and Rain told her about. She's also enjoying trying new recipes and figuring out the best placement for her new furniture. After she tackled the closet, she stripped the kitchen wallpaper and painted the hallway and the trim, her headphones on, listening to true crime podcasts.

"Is it the healthiest thing to listen to these?" Matt asked when he passed her in the hallway that day and heard a tinny talking sound coming from her ears.

"I found the podcast Ruby mentioned at the dinner party about the teenager hidden in a box under the bed of the kidnappers," Ginny said. It was horrifying. After that she couldn't sleep for a week. "It was so gruesome. The couple would bring the girl out every couple of days to 'play' with her and I couldn't stop thinking about what that means, about all the connotations of 'play.'"

Matt rolled his eyes. "You might want to avoid listening to that kind of stuff."

The house now smells like acrylic paint most days and Ginny feels accomplished and tired most nights.

She finds the candles, "Ah ha!" and holds them up to Matt as she enters the dining room. She lights them and they sit longer, looking out the dining room windows into the black night. Trying to see past their reflections.

But Ginny can't always sleep these days. When she does finally sleep she is woken by sounds moving all around the house.

She wakes to hear scratching in the walls. Another bird? But it sounds different. The sounds move around inside the walls in the upstairs hallway. She wants to wake Matt, pull at his arm, but she knows he won't hear it, and he'll give her that sympathetic look, mixed with frustration. So she lies in bed, petrified, afraid to move. But then Matt wakes and when he hears the noise he says, calmly, that it must be squirrels in the walls.

"You are right," Ginny says the next morning when they are both crouching down looking at a hole in the wall just at ankle level.

As they watch, a brown squirrel sticks its head out and looks at them. Ginny jumps and screams. Matt seals up the hole, hoping the squirrel will escape backwards, creep back to where it came. But every night for a while they both hear the scritch-scratching as the rodent moves in the walls trying to get out. This noise leads to more nightmares and Ginny dreams of snakes in the walls, of cats, of more birds, some flying over her head, pecking at her eyes. She dreams of a baby stuck in the wall, kicking out at his enclosure, trying to break the wall to get free. And when the baby finally gets out he stands on his pudgy baby legs at the end of Ginny's bed and watches her.

She wakes in a sweat most nights. And those are the good nights, when she finally does fall asleep. The nights she doesn't sleep she lies there afraid to close her eyes, afraid of seeing something emerge from the walls. The squirrel eventually disappears. Or maybe it dies? Ginny is unsure but can't smell anything and so she hopes the squirrel made it out alive.

⊗

"I visited Rain at her booth," Ginny says, biting into a grilled cheese sandwich as they eat lunch one day.

"Her booth?"

"Yeah, she sells essential oils at the market. Little bottles of smelly oil stuff that you drip onto things. I think. I'm not really sure."

"Is that her only job?" Matt spears a pickle.

"I don't know. She has this booth that is pretty decked out. Golden bells and mirrors. The whole booth rings and smells." Ginny laughs. "The scents are overwhelming, lavender mixed with eucalyptus, mixed with berries and sweet vanilla and ginger. Honestly, I couldn't stay long. It almost made me gag. I didn't buy any oils, but I guess I should? Maybe your mom would want a bottle for Christmas? Although what do you do with essential oils? They look so odd. Little bottles filled with oily liquid and sealed with different coloured bows. I'm not sure what people use them for?"

Matt shrugs.

"Rain smiles and nods each time I see her and she seems to be getting more comfortable talking to me but there's still something off. Although today I think I figured out what kinds of things she might eat. Seems it's mostly garlic, onions and beans."

Matt rolls his eyes, stuffs the end of his sandwich in his mouth and waves to Ginny. "I've got a one o'clock class," he says. "See you at dinner." And he disappears up the stairs for his online session after he puts his plate in the dishwasher in the kitchen.

Ginny sits there, at the dining table, watching him leave and she thinks about how different her life is now. How Matt just walks out of rooms and leaves now, how in the apartment in the city he had nowhere else to go and so would spend time talking to her, how at the market today she almost screamed when a man accidentally grabbed her elbow, thinking she was his wife. Ginny used to feel invincible. Now she's sometimes lonely and always scared.

⊗

At the outdoor market Ginny wanders purposefully from booth to booth. She knows her way around it now, knows where to get the best vegetables and fruits, where the butcher's van is, where the flowers are the freshest. She can smell the pierogi booth from a long way away and loves to watch the cotton candy machine and the kids lined up in front of it. In the distance Ginny sees a man who she thinks is Charles Smythe. She barely remembers him, but there is a tall, lean, greyish man standing down one row of stalls. He is listening to a few bearded men who are holding motorcycle helmets. He has his hands in his pockets. He's wearing the same T-shirt and pocketed pants she saw him in before. Even with his friends, who are talking and smiling and smoking, he seems angry and distant. She gathers her courage and begins to head toward him, wanting to ask him how he is and maybe ask some questions about the house, but when she gets close she can hear the others.

"Influenced by what she sees on TV," one man whispers. "She tried to go to a doctor." The bearded men standing together shake their heads. "Heartburn, I told her. Chew ginger."

"Apple cider vinegar," one of the men says. "Don't want to pollute your body." Charles nods. Ginny gets closer.

"Tums," she hears another man say. "Big Pharma."

Everyone nods. But then Charles sees her and ducks out of the group and is suddenly gone. As if he was never there. The other men look at her, they stop talking and scowl. For a minute Ginny doubts she saw him. She doesn't know where he went – into that booth? Around that corner? Into the doorway of the hockey arena? Matt told her that Charles and Marina still lived in town, but she forgot. She assumed their apartment was elsewhere.

Ginny's been trying to forget about all the stuff in the house, but she thinks that maybe being able to talk to Marina and Charles would answer some of her questions. She's weaning herself from her anti-anxiety medication and is almost done but each week her mind still seems to obsess on something new. This week she's been thinking too much about the image of the body in the backyard and the sealed-up door in the basement (and the podcast about the girl in the box under the bed). All of this is consuming her. She keeps seeing a white-clothed human splashed on the ground, legs akimbo, every time she looks out the back patio doors. If Matt catches her focused on the backyard he pats her head, like a cat, to calm her and speaks slowly and softly. Lately he's been trying too hard to calm her down. He's been reading up on the side effects of weaning from her meds. And he's been trying to solve everything. She gets it, she wants her life back too, but it's frustrating and demeaning.

Big Pharma, she thinks. Where has she heard that before?

"If we hadn't seen that satellite image you wouldn't even be worrying like this," Matt had said.

But we did see it, Ginny wanted to shout. And she can't stop thinking about it.

What if the body was buried somewhere back there just after the satellite photo was taken? What if it's in the ravine right now? Ginny has this constant headache lately that just won't go away.

She has no idea who or what Marina and Charles are. And she doesn't really care, does she? Ginny sighs. She is paused at a booth in the market that sells hand-stitched baby clothes. She is rifling through everything – tiny knitted booties and hats, soft velvety sleepers with feet, toddler dresses and slippers. Matt and Ginny have tried twice now. Two times without a condom during her fertile window. It was thrilling at first, the first time in her life without protection, but now she's a little nervous. There is so much they have to do with the house. There are so many things just plain wrong and creepy and weird.

Ginny's become a worrier. She's always worried now, but at bedtime it seems to be the worst. Her thoughts spill out everywhere and that's when she begins to hear the creaks and thumps, to feel the breezes and think about the backyard, about the ravine, about the satellite image. That's when she always begins to question her choice about moving away from the city. There are also big, loud trucks, or motorcycles revving on the streets here that wake her continuously through the night. And in the day the noise of lawn mowers and leaf blowers rattle her. She can't seem to escape loud sounds. Lately, she wants to roll into Matt and squeeze him hard. But she's become afraid to touch him. He gives her this look these days, like he's frustrated and annoyed with her constant worry and fear, like he's tired of protecting her. She's skittish, jumpy.

Rain comes up to Ginny at the baby booth. "Are you pregnant? You don't look pregnant."

"Pardon me?"

"A baby?" Rain points to the tiny clothes in Ginny's hands. And then points at Ginny's stomach as if Ginny doesn't know where babies nest.

Ginny says, "Someday I'll get pregnant, I guess." The last thing she wants is for everyone in the neighbourhood to be asking her about her baby-attempts. One thing Ginny has learned in the time she's lived here is that if someone knows one thing about you, then everyone knows that one thing about you. The mail carrier now knows that their window flies open most nights in the upstairs hallway. Just because Matt told Michael about it when they went out for their first jog together. Michael then ran into the mail carrier at his store. And then, after putting Ginny's mail in the slot in her door, the mail carrier knocked and told Ginny about her own window, as if she didn't already know.

Sometimes Ginny feels as if everyone at the market is looking at her because they've seen her trash. They've noticed how many bottles of wine were in the recycling bin, how many bottles could have been taken to the liquor store for a return, and then they think she's lazy for putting the bottles in the recycling bin instead. Or maybe they think she's rich. Who wouldn't need the return money? But Ginny just never gets around to returning the bottles and they pile up. Especially after a dinner party. Besides, the bottles she puts in recycling get picked up around dinnertime each week by a man with a cart blasting his music from a boom box balanced on the handlebars. He rolls up and down the streets and collects the bottles and Ginny feels a little bit like she's just given something to charity. A noisy charity. So much noise.

Rain nods and moves back to her booth. "It's good when you think about having a baby. When you plan ahead. Not just have one by accident," she says. This hits Ginny hard. Did Rain have a baby? She doesn't know what to say, but Rain continues, "Oh, I should tell you, the outdoor market ends on Thanksgiving. Then we move inside on Saturdays. And if you want to order your turkey you should do that now. Booth eleven is taking orders."

Ginny nods, "Thanks," and wonders about Rain and a baby. And if Rain had a baby, where is it?

"Where's the inside market?" Ginny asks.

"The old mall downtown that's boarded up. You know. They just take the boards off the windows and open it for the winter market. They were going to tear it down but then the market committee thought this would work."

Strange, Ginny thinks. If not odd. Why not just tear down the building and make it an indoor market all year round? "Got it." There seems to be no preplanning in this town. Ginny's been here two months and she's already noticed that stores close and then open as something else with no renovations in between. So the doughnut store still looks like a laundromat. There are bubbles on the sign.

Ginny watches Rain head back to her booth and talk to a customer. She keeps looking back at Ginny as if she wants to say something else, but then she stops looking and focuses on her customer. Then Ginny becomes distracted by another booth and walks toward it. Cheeses. Goat cheese and even vegan cheese. Cashew cheese? And then she catches another glimpse of Charles. This time he starts walking quickly toward her, as if he's going to run her over. She backs up.

"You stole my house!" he shouts and waves his fists. "It's my house." But then he is gone. Everyone in the market around her has stopped talking and is now staring at Ginny. Her hands start to shake, she looks around. They don't know her and they think the worst. What did she do to that older man? She feels cold, a sudden chill, and wraps her arms around her body. She shrugs and tries to smile as if to say, "Who, me?" Yet her face is burning. Her heart beats hard. She needs to go home.

But where is that? Where is her home really?

CHAPTER 8

Matt, decked out in running gear, heads out the gate at the back of their property and down the slope to the path, or what he assumed was a path but now realizes is more mud and damp than path. The ravine is dark and the ground is covered with leaves. The trail is overgrown. There used to be a path obviously, but it's mostly gone now. There are several large apple trees on the ravine's side of his fence and a bit farther down. He wonders if, in the fall, they'll be able to pick apples for pies and jams. And then he wonders if Ginny knows how to make pies or jams. He certainly doesn't. Matt notices that none of the other neighbours along the ravine have a gate in their fence. He guesses no one else comes down here.

There is some garbage scattered along, but other than that (and the mud) Matt thinks it could be pretty down here in the summer. He kicks at a hypodermic needle. There is a smell, a decaying odour. He assumes that's from the dying leaves. He looks back at his gate, getting his bearings, taking note of what it'll look like when he comes back. And then he moves on. An owl hoots. The trees creak above him. His feet stick in the mud, slurp out, stick in. It reminds him of their wedding, when Ginny was fighting each step with her high-heeled shoes. He smiles, remembering the wedding, remembering how different Ginny was before, how any given day of the week she would call him from the movies or from a bar or a restaurant or a minigolf course and say, "Get down here." Just because she was walking home from work and felt like a movie, a drink, a burger, a game of minigolf. How she would bike the ravines around the city in the rain or jog down at the water in the snow by herself because she loved how no one was around to get in her way. Before the attack, before their world changed so drastically. When he reaches where the path used to be he begins to jog, jumping over the fallen branches and puddles and overgrown areas.

He hears something from the bushes at the side of the path. An animal in the bush? A snap of dead wood, was that a slight cough or a groan? A hiss or a rattle? He must have startled a bird? A squirrel? He speeds up.

She's inside now, Ginny, making their dinner. Matt told her he would help but she wanted to pour a glass of wine, blast the music and create something new. Try a recipe she found online. "One I won't burn," she laughed. She said Matt can do the dishes after and she told him to go for a jog.

"Soon it'll be too cold to want to go outside," she said, reaching up to kiss him. He knew she meant for him to jog on the roads and when he headed out the back patio door he could see her gaze fall nervously on the backyard. He saw as she peered suspiciously toward the ravine. He saw her swallow, hard.

So Matt is outside, squelching through mud and leaves and jogging down the "path" toward what would be the end of his street. So far he has not yet had the time, nor inclination, to go into the ravine. This is the first thing he thought he would do when he moved here, the idea of having a ravine right out back excited him, but time has gotten away from him. That and energy. For some reason he has been so tired lately. Probably from the move, maybe from the overload of fresh air. Maybe because Ginny keeps waking him up at night. But it's true his lungs aren't used to the country air in a small town, away from the pollution of the city. He's also worried about Ginny, of course, about trying for a baby, about this house. Not only is it a creepy house that seems to tell a story, but it needs a lot of work. Every weekend he does work. Work he wasn't expecting. Painting, lawn mowing, cleaning, raking, moving furniture, trips to the dump or recycling boxes, renovations that seem to come out of the blue and make every weekend disappear quickly. Last weekend he vacuumed all the spiders out of the basement, got rid of their webs. He knows they'll be back.

When he turns around, he can suddenly smell a fire. Maybe someone's fireplace? He looks up into the sky but can't see any smoke up toward the road. But when he turns his head deeper into the ravine he sees what he thinks is a puff of grey smoke in the woods. Someone smoking? It doesn't smell like cigarette smoke, more like woodsmoke. Is there someone with a campfire, living down here? He can't hear anything, just the crack of sticks under his rapidly speeding up feet, just the moaning of wind through the trees. Matt is alone, he thinks, there's no one around, but he isn't exactly sure of this. He feels like he's being watched and after a time runs quickly back toward home.

He shakes his head and tries to summon up some energy, tries to think about how he can sleep more. The noises at night are so different here. And he has so many worries about the mortgage and the renovations that are needed on the house. The fucking hallway window, it's always banging open. Ginny is tossing a lot now as well, and occasionally she kicks out at him when she has a nightmare. Matt thought moving out of the city would solve a lot of problems, a lot of fears. But it has opened up a snake's nest of new issues. Like the cold air from the open window, the heat he now pays for because the window opens every night.

All of a sudden, up ahead on the path, there is a man walking. Startled, Matt slows down. It's been so silent here, only the moan of the wind through the trees. The trees are almost empty of their leaves, the ground is a carpet of them, the birds are quiet. Nothing. Where did this person come from? He cuts a dark figure, up ahead, walking quickly, too far ahead for Matt to see clearly and the sun has almost gone down. Matt realizes he really can't see the ground clearly and he might trip. It's one straight, overgrown path through the ravine, but there's something about the light and the setting sun that makes everything look blended and confusing. The path disappears and comes back again. Matt runs one foot in front of the other. He can feel his heart in his jaw and realizes he's grinding his teeth. He's sweating. The man up ahead is going forward and is almost at Matt's gate. Maybe it's a neighbour? In this light Matt can't even really tell if it's a man or a woman or a teenager. This makes him suddenly think of the satellite image and how he couldn't tell what size or gender the body was. Matt moves forward carefully. He fumbles in his pocket for his phone, making sure he has it in case he has to use it. Yes, he does have it, and he holds it tightly like a lifeline in his pocket and then flashes on the memory of Ginny, after the attack, telling him that if she ever has to go out at night now she carries her keys woven through her fingers so she can punch someone with force if they strike. And then he notices that the smoke smell is gone and the decaying smell is stronger, as if the dark brings out the mould. The darkness is bothering him – it happened so fast, the sun just fell, the ravine is tucked into the earth and feels like it's going black too quickly. He never used to be nervous but something about this place has made him incredibly anxious.

The man has now passed Matt's gate and continued on.

Matt hopes Ginny's anxiety isn't rubbing off on him. Her attack last year messed both of them up, but he thought he handled it well. He's been supportive and calm. Matt's brain moves rapidly as he thinks, as he runs faster and faster. But Ginny's getting better now. Isn't she? And her fears of this house are justified, right? He thinks, the open window, what the hell is with that? And she said she saw a figure standing by their gate into the ravine, right? Maybe it was just this man here, in front of him, going for a walk? There are obviously people using the ravine. Matt looks up again, not just at his feet, and there is no sign of the man, he is suddenly gone. Matt slows down. He shakes his head.

Matt stops at his fence, recognizing it from the large apple trees, and then he sees the gate, which he rushes through in the encroaching dark. As he comes into his yard he sees Ginny in the window of the kitchen, lit up and glowing. And then he thinks that the light on the body spilling out from inside the house is perhaps why it looked to be glowing, why it looked so white. Even in the daytime the kitchen light would shine on the outside. Light from inside the house blanketing it as it lay there. Ginny thought it was wearing really white clothes but maybe that was a trick of the light. Surely it wasn't even there – it was nothing, a mistake, a computer glitch? He can hear movement on the street in the front of the house, sounds like kids playing, shouting and laughter. Then he looks up at the second floor of his house and sees the upstairs hall window open again.

"Damn," he says. He whispers to himself, "Even through the shut windowpane, the world looked cold," and can't remember who said that. Was it Orwell? There is no screen on the window and it's quite large, big enough for a human to get through, or animals. Like that bird, a raccoon or a squirrel could get in next and wander through the house. Bring in disease and fleas. He'll have to first try fixing the latch and then, worst-case scenario, board it up if he can't fix it. This weekend he'll climb up and see what's happening from outside, climb up the side of the overhang – the roof that used to be on the shed. It should be easy to climb on. It should be no problem. He doesn't have a ladder yet and was hoping to put off getting one until the spring. It's not that far up and there are plenty of places for his feet and hands, plenty of places to climb to the window. Which is another reason to fix this window soon. Not only animals can get up, he realizes suddenly, but definitely people too.

From the kitchen window Ginny doesn't see Matt standing there at the end of the yard looking up and she begins to dance slightly, stirring something in front of her – and singing. She's belting out some tunes and Matt watches her. He can't hear her but he can see her mouth moving. It's kind of funny and it slows his beating heart. Even the changed Ginny somehow always slows his heart. He walks through the yard and takes his running shoes off on the back patio. He'll clean the mud from the ravine off them later. He glances at the hatch and the area where the body lay again and then he enters the kitchen, which is full of smells, garlic and spice, and roasting chicken, full of warmth and noise, the stereo is turned up to full volume. Nothing is burning. Ginny hands him a glass of red wine.

"Did you have fun?" she asks and stands on her tippytoes to pull down his face and kiss his nose. "What's the ravine like? As scary as it looks?" She smiles widely, buzzed on wine and happy. The music is loud. Matt steadies his wineglass in his hands. Ginny stops moving, stands still, and looks out the back window. "Look," she says and Matt looks out the back window at the gate.

"What?" He turns and looks at Ginny and then out at the backyard again.

"That man, that figure," she points.

But Matt sees nothing.

"He's gone now," she says.

Matt turns again to the window and as he's turning he spills his wine, a drop of it on the floor. Dark red, thick. Like blood.

CHAPTER 9

Ginny has organized another dinner party. Michael and Pat are the first to arrive. Exactly on time. Six thirty. A faint smell follows them inside but Ginny thinks it must be the garbage in the kitchen. Then Pierre and Ruby. Then Rain comes in and the smell of essential oils (eucalyptus? Cumin? An odd smell) covers the garbage stench. Ginny gathers the garbage up anyway, and she puts it out in the cans on the back porch. She sees Matt's old running shoes out there from his jog in the ravine the other night. He must have forgotten to clean them and put them away. What's new? Matt touches Ginny's shoulder when she comes in to thank her for doing the garbage and then pours wine for everyone but Rain. Ginny has created a few vegan dishes based on what Rain told her at the market. It seems vegan cooking consists mostly of garlic. It's making Ginny a bit queasy. But even the smell of garlic isn't covering up the other lingering smell.

The conversation is much more casual this time. Everyone is feeling less uncomfortable, less like brand-new friends now. There have been moments outside – Rain at the market, Michael and Matt jogging the streets, Ginny once ran into Ruby in the grocery store – these appearances are making the neighbours more familiar with each other. And Matt has a chair this time. In fact, everyone has a chair that matches this time. Ginny takes everyone into the living room and dining room to show them all the new furniture, the paintings on the walls. She sees it from their eyes, a little barren, but getting there. Ginny feels flushed and slightly proud. She's never had real house furniture before, she's mostly had Ikea. This makes her feel more like a married adult and less like a terrified, anxious person who recently left the city. She takes a deep breath and lets it out.

"I love this chair," Pat says. "I get to sit in it after dinner." He laughs.

But there's still that smell? Everyone sniffs a bit. It seems to be following Pat and Michael around. Oh god, Ginny suddenly thinks, did one of them step in dog shit? It smells like dog shit. There's a woman from up the street who lets her little dog shit on their front lawn, Ginny has seen this happen a few times. The old woman pretends to bend down and pick up the poop – she even takes out a poop bag and opens it and looks around smiling as if she's doing such a good thing. But Ginny has gone out later and has seen that the woman actually leaves the poop there and walks off carrying an empty bag, swinging it as if it's full. She might even stuff it with grass or leaves or something so it looks like it's full. Ginny keeps waiting to see this again so she can run out and confront the woman. Or at least that's what she hopes she will do.

"Shit," Ginny says. It just comes out of her.

Everyone stops talking and looks at her. They are all back from the furniture tour, gathered in the kitchen again, drinking wine and talking politely.

"What's shit?" says Michael.

Ginny feels herself turning red. Matt looks at her. Her whole face darkens and flushes. She's sure it matches the red shirt she's wearing.

"What's up, Ginny? Did you forget something?"

"No, I . . ." She doesn't know how to mention it. She looks at

Pat and Michael. "I think someone has something on their shoe," she says. "Sorry."

"What?" Everyone starts looking at their shoes. They bend, fold themselves in half, and peer at the bottom of their feet. Pierre leans on the kitchen counter and takes off his shoes to look at the bottoms. He's not flexible and he tips slightly and almost falls.

"Oh crap!" Michael shouts. "Literally! Pat, you've got dog shit on your shoe!"

Pat's face whitens. He looks panicked. He immediately hops and limps to the front door, not letting his shoe touch the floor. "Oh my god, I'm so sorry." He hops out the front door and down the front walk. Everyone watches him. He almost falls several times. "Oh god," he keeps saying, over and over.

Ginny rushes to his side and takes his arm to balance him. He won't step on the foot that has the shit on it. She holds him while he jumps over to his house where, he says, he'll leave the shoe on the front porch and go inside and get something else to wear. Ginny waits. She looks back at her house, at the front door wide open and the light spilling out. She sees everyone in the kitchen looking out at her. And she starts to laugh. Inside she sees the others start to smile. Matt is behind the others, on his hands and knees with a paper towel and spray Lysol, cleaning up any remnants.

And, just like that, any tension or wariness between the neighbours seems to disappear.

Pat comes out of the house with new shoes on and sees all of them laughing. "I'm so, so sorry," he says. "We always use the sidewalk, not the grass. But this time we took a chance and used the grass. I'm going to have to throw those shoes out now." And Ginny laughs again, thinking he is joking.

But he isn't. Michael whispers to Ginny later that, if he could, Pat would cut his foot off. He's a germaphobe, apparently, and Michael says he has nightmares about stepping in dog poop.

"Well," Pat says as he enters the house, "at least that smell wasn't your food. I was worried for a minute that you were serving something really horrible. Maybe for Rain?" he jokes.

Pierre laughs. He snorts and giggles. Rain looks insulted. But then, watching Pierre, she starts to laugh too.

"Vegan food sometimes smells bad, I give you that," Rain finally says. "But not like dog shit."

And everyone settles in. Ginny thinks it's wonderful that a little dog poop can settle the nerves.

⊗

After dinner the conversation comes back to the Smythes and to the dead body on the satellite image, almost as if they've picked up where they left off at the last party.

"I've been thinking about it," Pierre says. "It might have been a Halloween prop, a decoration, or even just a glitch in the satellite's software."

"But the Smythes never celebrated Halloween, remember?" Michael says. "They turned off all their lights and their blinds were always shut tight, remember? No pumpkins even. They hid from all the kids."

"What?" Ginny says. "What did they have against Halloween?"

Pierre nods. "That's true. So then a computer glitch. One image from somewhere else overtop of another image."

"They did decorate last year," Ruby says.

"Oh, Jesus. I forgot," Pierre says.

"'It's Okay to Be White' signs. Remember?"

"God, yes, the 'My Life Is My Own Choice' flags."

"That has nothing to do with abortion," Rain whispers.

"What?" Ginny says. What were they saying? Did she hear what she thought she heard? She looks around at all her white neighbours, at the two gay ones, at the white one with dreadlocks, and she wonders what she is supposed to think of all this. She thinks about how she really hasn't seen any BIPOC in this town and how it bothered her at first – the city they lived their whole lives in is so diverse – but now Ginny's getting almost used to it here. Or if not used to it, she doesn't notice it anymore. Ginny feels ashamed.

"But the hatch," Matt says. "And the porch? And the overhang? All are in the image. It's our backyard. And there was no blurring." He looks at Ginny who still has her mouth open and is staring.

Pierre looks down. "One of those blow-up sex dolls then?" he says quietly, touching his moustache.

And everyone giggles. Ruby looks horrified and smacks her husband.

Pierre glares at her. "What? You never know what Charles was up to?"

"What do you mean?" Matt asks. He's leaning back and drinking another glass of wine, his long legs stretched in front of him.

"They were old," Rain says. "He was strange. Let's change the subject."

Ginny thinks, *he* was strange?

"They didn't do anything. They never went out."

Everyone nods. Ruby says, "I tried at the beginning to be friendly, when we first moved here. Marina was nice at first. But that Charles –"

"So," Ginny says, "you all don't think something suspicious went on here? In the backyard?"

"There was nothing going on," Michael says. "Nothing more than the rest of this town. They were just reclusive."

"And sexist and racist and –" Pat mumbles.

"But the body," Ginny interrupts. "And the noises we hear."

"It's a creaky old house," Pat says. "Ours is too. The body was just a glitch."

"What about the locks and the constantly opening window?"

"Old house," Pat says again. "Think how many years of owners with their own quirks and ideas. We had a back staircase in our house that was sealed over at one time. When we found it, we put it back."

Ginny sits back and stares at Matt. She stares at everyone.

Something doesn't feel right, she's sure of it. Not just the fact that the Smythes were reclusive and strange. Something's not right in this house and she doesn't know what.

"What about the packages?" Matt throws out.

Everyone is silent as they think about this. Matt clears his throat, watching Ginny. She can feel her cheeks flush. Maybe this time someone will say something?

When they don't, Ginny says, "I saw him at the market. Charles Smythe."

"You saw him?" Matt asks. "I forgot they live here. I always think they left Parkville. Did you talk to him?"

"Their apartment," Ruby says, "is right downtown." She says this as if it is something that everyone should know.

"I didn't talk to him," Ginny says. She thinks of the old man attacking her with his voice, shouting at her. She thinks of the words she heard him utter.

Matt raises his eyebrows.

"I didn't say anything. He just kept disappearing. And he screamed at me."

"What? So now he disappears too? A dead body and a disappearing act?" Pierre smiles. He's had too much wine already.

"Okay, so, well . . . I saw him, twice actually, and once he yelled at me and the other time he was gone by the time I tried to make my way through the crowds to talk to him."

"Crowds?" Rain laughs. "When are there crowds at the market? I wish there *were* crowds there. Maybe I'd sell more."

Ginny feels like she's back in high school, like everyone is in on something and ganging up on her. Even Matt. She glares at him. He doesn't look at her.

But slowly the conversation returns to other topics, to the market and Thanksgiving and everyone breaks up into several separate conversations.

⊗

When everyone leaves and the dishes are done Matt says, "That wasn't bad."

Ginny is wiping the counter and biting her cheek. She plays with the bit of a scar on the one side where the man punched her in the alley in the city. It's not healing well – it has ridges and bumps in it. When he knocked her teeth into her cheek that rainy night she needed stitches, and now there's this ledge she just can't ignore. Especially when she's nervous. "Do you think so? Rain didn't eat anything again. Well, a few nibbles."

"I think there's nothing you can feed her that would please her."

"True."

"Although whatever you made did stink. Worse than Pat's shitty shoe."

Ginny smacks Matt with her towel and then hangs it up and heads upstairs.

She can hear Matt turning off the lights in the kitchen and hallway on the way up. At the top of the staircase Ginny stops. She's about to turn left toward the bathroom when she feels a chill and sees that the hallway window is open again. Just a bit.

"Damn. Why does this keep coming open?"

Matt scooches past her and jiggles the window. He plays with the latch.

Ginny heads into the bathroom first to wash up and brush her teeth.

"I keep forgetting to fix the latch," Matt says from the hall. "But it feels solidly locked when I jiggle it. I don't get it."

Ginny says from the bathroom, her mouth full of toothpaste foam, "Maybe I'll just call someone in to fix it." She's learning, since they moved here, that Matt has a tendency to just talk about fixing things and not do anything. Or he'll start a chore and never follow through. Ginny will find tools all over the house or the yard. He never cleans up, puts anything away.

"I'll fix it," Matt says, grumpily. "I just need to figure it out, what keeps pushing it open. And I need to find more of my tools in the basement. I still haven't unpacked a lot of those boxes."

Find more tools, Ginny thinks. Why not use the ones he's left everywhere?

Ginny shivers when she hears the word "basement." She hates the basement so much. Every time she's in the kitchen there are sounds coming up from there that make her cringe. The furnace, sure, maybe the hot-water tank gurgling, but sometimes she hears creaking sounds, as if someone is down there. And then she starts thinking that yes, someone is down there, and she wants to lock the door. If the bolt was on the right side she could seal it tight. She could lock that door forever and never go down and Matt could deal with whatever is hiding in the basement. Her teeth are clean, her face is washed, she moves into the bedroom and Matt is there and he pulls her onto the bed.

"Should we try again tonight?" he says, as if nothing just happened, as if the window wasn't open again, as if everyone at the dinner party wasn't talking about the unhappy, rude couple who lived here before, as if they didn't sink all their money into this frightening house.

Matt tries to kiss her and Ginny pushes him away.

When Ginny finally sleeps she dreams of boxes under her bed, shaped like coffins, with children in them. Babies and teenagers. She hears sounds in her dreams, crashing noises and squeaks and knocking coming from under the bed and out in the hall. Twice she wakes up suddenly and can't get back to sleep. Matt snores beside her.

At one point she half-wakes and imagines she sees a large figure at the bottom of the bed. She doesn't know if she's dreaming, awake or asleep. She can't seem to move so she must be dreaming. Matt is gone. She turns her head to look down the hallway. The bathroom light shines under the door. The figure is sitting on her side, near her knees, he is touching her leg with one finger. A dirty finger. But she can't see his face. She can't move although every part of her wants to run. She wants to scream. Everything about the figure is in shadow and even though the light shines from the bottom of the bathroom door down the hall, he is completely blacked out. And then she wakes fully, startled, and the figure is gone and there is a chill in the house. Ginny can feel pressure on her leg, a remnant of his finger.

Ginny turns in bed toward the hallway and, under the windowsill on the carpet, she can see a small circle of dirt. She rolls toward Matt's body, but he is still gone.

CHAPTER 10

The next day Matt wakes early and heads downstairs to the kitchen. The window is open again. He shuts it. Today he's going to try to fix it for good. In the kitchen he heats up the espresso maker as he unloads the dishwasher. He looks out the patio doors and notices that his running shoes from the jog in the ravine the other day are gone.

Next door Pat looks out his front door in the morning for his shit-covered shoes. But they are gone.

"Kids," Pat tells Michael and Michael agrees. "I was going to throw them out anyway," Pat says. "I can't abide by dirt or mud or shit. Especially shit. You know this. It bothers me so much. So I'm getting a bit of a chuckle thinking of the kids who stole them finding out there's shit on them."

But Michael thinks later, what do teenagers want with old man loafers? Why would kids steal them? And then he thinks about last summer and all the thefts that were going on in the neighbourhood. Clothes from the line, patio cushions, planters, lanterns, any glasses or plates or bowls you left out overnight. He chalks Pat's shoes up to that – it's happening again. But he doesn't say anything to Pat because, if a little shit on your shoes can make you paranoid, imagine what this knowledge will do.

Ginny lies in bed touching her stomach, petting it. When she woke earlier she went to pee and took a pregnancy test. Just in case. Why not? Why not know if her entire life is going to suddenly flip, change, modify? Will her life get better? Get worse? Her body will swell, her life will shrink, the dynamics of the house will distort. Last night she felt peculiar, like something, or someone, was passing through her.

The test read positive.

Ginny moulds herself into a fetal position and smiles slightly.

$\otimes$

Matt doesn't remember weather like this in the city; all of fall just seemed the same. Leaves fell, wind blew. He thinks that when you live closer to nature maybe you notice it more. But now, it seems like all of October is crazy. The weather is hot, then cold, then hot. It's windy and frosty and dry and raining and sunny. The clouds scudding across the sky, the smell of decaying leaves in the air, the wind picking up dust on dry days and shooting it wildly along the streets and sidewalks. Matt sits in his second-floor office during the cold days dealing with grumpy students, but he listens to Ginny rumbling around him, moving throughout the house. She isn't outside as much lately.

The hallway window seems to be staying shut for now. It hasn't opened up for a while. Matt spent a weekend fiddling with the latch. Jiggled it and screwed it tighter. But he still sometimes finds it swung open, and on a couple of days he finds the patio door off the kitchen slid open too. He slides it shut and reminds Ginny to make sure it's locked. She says she locks it – and she doesn't like to go in the backyard anyway – but Matt is sure she just doesn't remember. He's been noticing some of his clothes are missing too and he still hasn't found his running shoes and he wonders what Ginny is doing with everything. A few shirts, a sweater, a pair of pants and some socks he just can't find. An old belt. Ginny says she did nothing with his shoes or clothes, but he's sure she just put them somewhere and then forgot. In the city Ginny used to give his clothes to charity, the ones she didn't like, but he thought she had stopped doing that. And she used to tell him when she was doing it too, she would ask his permission, holding them up for him to judge, and she would take the unwanted clothes out to the charity bins and dump them inside. Sometimes Matt wonders if he's losing his mind. He doesn't seem to be able to focus anymore and tiny bits of anxiety are creeping into his daily life. He doesn't remember being anxious like this in the city. Or forgetful. Or worried all the time. He wants his city brain back. It's like he's turning into Ginny. There is just so much to worry about when you own your own home. Especially when you own a home that needs so much work.

And then, "I'm pregnant," Ginny whispered that morning after the dinner party, as he came from the bathroom into the bedroom. She was lying in bed and staring at the stick she held in front of her. Matt was just starting to head downstairs but he sat down immediately and smiled at the wall. And then life ratcheted up considerably.

They were lucky it happened so fast. Unbelievable, really. And they lucked into getting a doctor because Matt's mother called her doctor, who took pity on them and referred them to a family doctor in Parkville who then recommended them to an obstetrician. Ginny's so thankful as half the people in Parkville don't even have a doctor. There is a shortage of doctors and long waiting lists. Matt doesn't have a doctor and has been told it'll take years to get one.

It took them only two months after leaving the city to conceive. They are due early July. Matt is pretty proud of himself, as if he's solely responsible, and he's also pretty terrified. Even though the hall window is stable right now and hasn't opened in the middle of the night for a few days, he's still not sleeping very much. Neither is Ginny. They both look up at the ceiling from their bed and worry. Ginny says she's mostly stressed about the house, the creepiness of it, the creakiness of it, and the fact that she's so far from her mom. Matt says she knew she would be far from her mom when they chose to live here and, besides, Ginny's sister, Christine, is due with her baby a couple of months before theirs so Ginny's mom will be occupied with that.

"That doesn't help, Matt," Ginny says. "Are you saying my baby won't be as important as Christine's?"

The house has infected their feelings. When they lived in the city, before Ginny's attack, life was all about everything outside of the apartment, the restaurants and shops, the bike lanes and boardwalks, but in this small town, with their big, rundown house, everything has now become about the structure they live inside. About the need to fix things up, update things. About the sounds in the night and the open windows and doors. The chilly breeze even when a window isn't open, as if there are holes in the walls. The trees in the ravine moaning and creaking and cracking in the wind.

On weekends now Matt fixes things (like the hallway window) and does chores. Drives to the hardware store for every little thing. Ginny wanders the rooms trying to figure out which room would be the best nursery and she helps him out. Hands him tools when he needs them, rushes up and down the stairs for coffee or water. Paints rooms. He notices she rubs her belly a lot. She's slightly nauseous off and on.

⊗

They go to Home Depot and Walmart and they once take a trip into the city without telling anyone to visit Ikea. Even though Ginny wanted to avoid Ikea she's finally beginning to realize that they will need a lot more furniture and odds and ends that they can't afford. Ginny thinks she'll ask her family for baby stuff for

Christmas presents but then she thinks that might be premature. She'll only be two and a half months pregnant then. But there is so much to do, so much to buy. She wonders often if quitting her job was a good idea. She's scared about not having enough money now.

Ginny says, "How will we afford a stroller? Or mobiles? Or a diaper changing table? What about diapers? Or university someday? I'm beginning to wish we had begun our family with a dog or a cat instead of a baby. Was this" – she points to her stomach – "the right thing to do right now?"

Even though her stomach is still flat she's constantly aware of something going on in there. Cells moving and swimming and floating and growing.

Is her anxiety affecting the baby? Ginny feels her stress is affecting Matt, he's different now, and so she is trying to keep it bottled up. But the stress comes out around every corner, every room, every step she takes in this place. And now Matt and Ginny aren't talking to each other as much, keeping everything inside. Does Ginny really see a shadow in the attic window when she drives home after shopping, or a man crouched on her bed when she's sleeping, or is there really a noise in the basement?

She immediately touches her stomach, rubs what will soon be a baby bump.

It's October 30, a blustery cool day, and the leaves are falling rapidly. Halloween is tomorrow. Their first real Halloween, not apartment Halloween, since Ginny and Matt were kids. Ginny opens the front door in the early morning to put the final touches on decorating the house. And there, on her doorstep, is Marina Smythe. Marina didn't knock or ring the bell. But she is standing there smiling a bit when Ginny opens the door carrying the crashing-witch decoration she bought at Walmart. She screams slightly and drops the witch. Ginny was going to put the witch on the front door so the witch looks like it has taken a wrong turn.

"Oh, you startled me. Hello?"

"Hello," Marina says and stares at Ginny. The space between the silence seems too long. Marina says nothing for a full minute. Ginny's mouth opens slightly as she thinks of what to say.

Marina finally speaks, "Have you seen Charles?" and Ginny feels suddenly disoriented. Does Marina mean, has Ginny seen Charles at the market? Ginny hasn't been back to the market since September. And how would Marina know that Ginny saw him there? That he screamed at her there? Or does she mean has Ginny seen Charles just now? Is he in the neighbourhood? Ginny picks up the witch from the ground and looks around. She can see two people across the street walking their dog, a car drives past slowly, a baby somewhere cries.

Marina is peering around the door into Ginny's house.

"Sorry, no," Ginny says. "I haven't seen him. Is everything okay? Oh, you see we painted, took off some wallpaper. Hope you like it? Would you like to come in and see?"

"No, thank you," Marina says. "Have you seen him in the ravine, maybe?"

"The ravine?"

"He used to like to walk in the ravine when we lived here."

"No, I haven't even been down there yet. Matt goes down there sometimes to walk or jog but he hasn't mentioned seeing Charles. He says there really is no one in the ravine. The occasional man walking. But mostly Matt's alone. He smelled smoke the other day, but he didn't see where it was coming from, and he has tripped on some garbage, that kind of thing . . ."

Ginny is rambling, she's tapping her foot, she's nervous in front of this older woman. They are about the same height, but Marina is thicker. Ginny feels small but healthy beside her. And she can't stop thinking about all the bizarre stuff in the house and is imagining this old woman living here.

"Is everything okay?" Ginny asks. "Is something wrong with Charles?"

Marina starts moving away from her, down the front walk. "Have a nice day." She's almost shouting at Ginny by the time she reaches the sidewalk. Her voice is strained, odd, she seems almost scared.

"Are you sure you wouldn't like to come in? Sit down? Have some tea? See the house again?"

Marina pauses. She is intrigued, Ginny can tell from the way her shoulders straighten up. But then she says, "No, I shouldn't. Thank you, though." She keeps walking and turns and moves quickly away. She doesn't have her truck. She's just walking down the street alone. She's a little off-balance and Ginny has the urge to drive her home. She starts to say something but Marina turns the corner and disappears.

Ginny feels sad for her. As she's hanging the witch on the door she thinks about Marina's overall demeanour. She seemed confused and was worried about Charles. Marina was still wearing a flowered dress under her ratty coat. It didn't look warm enough. Her hair wasn't brushed. Grey hair. She had boots on, but no tights. Her legs must have been so cold.

Ginny hangs some red lights in the entranceway around the witch. She looks around at the neighbours' decorations, put up weeks ago. She tries to copy some of their looks and stretches out some spiderwebs and places a few plastic spiders in them. Ginny wants to fit in. The whole time she decorates, she thinks about Marina and Charles. About aging. She imagines Charles and Marina living in this house, and tries to picture what their lives were like. A nervous old woman and an angry old man. Ginny begins to worry about her old age, she begins to worry about Matt's old age – what if he was an old man lost in the ravine? – she begins to really worry about Charles. And then she worries about the state of the world. She needs to call her mother, text her sister. She's losing touch with everyone.

"Are you crying?" Matt comes outside to see the decorations. "Ginny, are you okay?" He puts his arms on her shoulders and turns Ginny toward him.

"Hormones," she says. "I think. I'm just predicting the future. Or, at least, thinking about it."

"Hope those are happy tears then?" Matt says, as he kisses her head and admires the decorations.

"Do you like the decorations?"

"Yeah, they're great," he says. "But isn't the house scary enough without all this?" He laughs but Ginny knows he's not joking.

The next morning Ginny opens the front door and the witch is gone. Matt finds her later attached to the backyard gate on the ravine side. When he opens the gate there is the witch, crashing into the wood. She's been hung there purposefully, Matt tells Ginny, her cape spread out, her hat askew.

"There is a small nail that holds the broom to the gate. What kind of Halloween revellers, punks, carry a hammer and a nail to create chaos? Wouldn't they just throw the witch down the ravine?" he grumbles.

Ginny immediately thinks of the dark figure of her dreams, the dark figure she thinks she sees by the gate at night, and she can picture him in her mind as he nails the witch up. Her green hair, her broomstick, her black cape and hat. The witch has no face, she is just clothing and a broom. Striped socks and pointy shoes. He's crucified her on their gate.

Matt goes out to pry the witch off the gate. He looks worried.

"There is weird stuff going on around here," he whispers to himself as he pulls the witch off and comes inside, dragging her behind him, her green hair picking up the leaves, her broom snagging on the grass.

⊗

On Halloween night all the neighbours are outside. There are sounds coming from most of the houses, mixing together – howls and shrieks and loud music, cackling witches and meowing cats. Matt has never seen a neighbourhood so decorated. They didn't do this when he was a kid and they certainly don't decorate like this in the city. At least not where he and Ginny lived. He looks at his house with the spiderwebs and spiders, with the red light. Just enough, he thinks. Rain is across the street, her house howling and lit up, flashing lights, creepy music, she's handing out homemade organic gluten-free bars. She brought one over to him a minute ago. He thanked her but told her to save them for the kids. "Chocolate," he can hear her telling the trick-or-treaters, but she told Matt it was carob. Such a gruesome creation, carob. Matt thinks it probably ruined many kids' lives in the 1970s. He knows it traumatized him the first time his mother, during a health kick, gave him some. He remembers feeling cheated; instead of the chocolate, something else coated his tongue, something he spat out quickly. Matt knows the bars will all be in the garbage tomorrow morning.

Ruby and Pierre have left a bowl of candy on the porch with a sign that politely says, "One only please." Matt saw them go out trick-or-treating with their own kids. Erin was a unicorn and Elton was his namesake, Elton John, with huge glasses and a wig. Matt wonders why they are so protective of their teenagers, but it's not his business or his judgment call. Of course their bowl was empty in about ten minutes and now kids are avoiding their house as if it's common knowledge that it's dry. Michael and Pat, next door, are taking turns answering the doorbell and the "Trick or treat!" One after the other. Matt watches as each one opens the door and shouts, "And what are you tonight?" Matt smiles.

A couple of angry-looking men pass by wearing dark clothing. Matt watches them. Are they costumes? He doesn't think so. They are too old to dress up. They all have beards. One guy looks right at him for a long time, too long. He looks like he's going to come up the front walk but he moves on by. Matt feels uncomfortable. The kids on the street ignore the men and pass by them with no comments. The men ignore the kids too.

Ginny and Matt haven't had many kids come yet but he knows that will change as the night goes on. Plus, if what everyone says is true, this wasn't a common house for visiting in the previous years.

Matt and Ginny have to build up the house's reputation. The parents stay way back on the sidewalk scowling and carrying pillowcases to hold the overflow candy. Matt watches them tip pumpkin-shaped bins into pillowcases and hand them back empty and then their kids move on to the next house. Matt waves but no one is really that friendly. They are just wandering in hordes and talking to their companions. Matt sees that a lot of people are dropping kids off at the start of the dead-end road and then heading off in their cars, probably going down to the town to have coffee or a drink. These are the kids being driven into the town from the country in order to pick up the best loot. "Meet me back here at eight o'clock," one loud woman shouts from her truck. She throws her cigarette out the window and turns up her music and drives off.

In their apartment in the city Ginny and Matt gave out, on average, ten chocolate bars each year. Full-sized ones. To the ten children who lived in the building. But that was it. Here Matt purchased about two hundred pieces of candy and small bars at the local hardware store. He hopes he has enough for when Michael and Pat's predicted hordes start to arrive.

Matt ducks back into the house during a lull to refill his bowl and sees Ginny standing in the hall looking back at the kitchen. She turns to him with a haunted expression on her face. She's quite still. Doesn't move. He knows this look. She's having an anxiety attack.

"You okay?" Matt asks. He walks to her and puts his arm around her.

"There's someone in the backyard," Ginny says. "Someone down by the gate. It's too dark to see who it is."

"What?" Matt drops his arms and heads to the kitchen at the back of the house. He sees the back sliding door is open. "Why is the door open?" He shuts it.

"I was looking out," Ginny says, she's right behind Matt.

"But why didn't you close it if you saw someone out there? You have to get used to locking the doors, Ginny. For heat, if nothing else."

"Don't yell at me," Ginny says.

"I'm not yelling."

There is a knock on the front door. Ginny jumps. Then a ding-dong. Then another harder knock. Then "Trick or treat" from what sounds like hundreds of kids.

"Just a minute," Ginny shouts. "Over there, by the gate, do you see?" She points. Matt sees nothing.

"I see nothing."

The front doorbell keeps ringing. Sugared up, these kids are wired and impatient.

"I'll go," Ginny says and she leaves the kitchen and goes to the front door.

"Trick or treat!" the kids yell.

Ginny says, her voice one tone, she's obviously trying hard not to panic, "Oh, I like that costume. What are you supposed to be?"

He hears her shut the door. "Do you see?" she calls down the hall to Matt.

"Nothing," he says, still staring into the backyard. And then, suddenly, he sees a tall shape moving down by the gate. "Oh wait, yes, I see someone."

"It's a man." Ginny is squinting out, trying to see who it is. She has come back to the kitchen and is holding herself tightly, her hands wrapped around her chest. It looks like she's actually squeezing herself so hard she's almost buckling over. Matt touches her arm. "Who is it? Can you tell?"

Matt opens the sliding door. "Hello?" he calls out. "Can I help you?"

The man stops moving and stands completely still. Matt flips on the backyard light and turns to Ginny and says, "I always forget we have a light back there."

Ginny looks horrified. Her mouth is open. She's looking out when the light goes on and Matt turns and sees a person move quickly toward the house, run toward them, and then turn and run back toward the gate and then head through the gate down to the ravine and disappear. It looks almost like a military drill, as if the person is running through a hail of bullets, ducking and dodging. As if he was running through bullets but then he changed his mind and ran away. Ginny screams. Matt jumps.

"What the hell was that?" Matt says.

"You mean *who* the hell was that?" Ginny says. Her voice is shaking. Matt looks at her, looks back at the yard. "What is going on?" Ginny asks.

"Who was it, Ginny? Did you see who it was? I couldn't tell."

The doorbell rings again. "Trick or treat!"

"Charles Smythe," Ginny says. "It was Charles Smythe. And he was running toward us fast."

"What the hell?" Matt runs his hands through his hair.

NOVEMBER

CHAPTER 11

Matt enters Truth and Beauty. The bell jingles over the door as he looks around. The store is so jumbled with odds and ends that, for a minute, Matt doesn't realize Michael is at the back desk until Michael moves and waves. The movement startles Matt.

"Hello, Matt."

"This is incredible. All this stuff."

Michael adjusts his glasses and starts the long weave from the back of the store to the front, around furniture and pillows and lamps and statues. He doesn't knock anything over.

Matt is astonished. "That takes skill," he says and laughs. Everything Michael passes is gold-coloured and shiny, with dangling silk ropes and chandelier glass twinkling. Everything looks breakable. Matt blinks hard and smiles back.

"What are you doing here? Coming in to buy something?"

"No, just to say hello," Matt says. He shakes Michael's hand. "I was downtown and just thought I'd drop in. See if you'd like to try another jog someday soon? And I've never seen your store."

Michael nods and smiles and pats Matt on the back. "Take a look around. You'll love the stuff."

Matt wanders as far into the store as he can, afraid to knock anything over. His backpack is full of vegetables he got from the indoor market, carrots and kale poking out of the top.

"I'm afraid to turn around."

He heads carefully through the store to the back, trying hard to show some interest. He picks up a few items scattered around, a butter dish on a mahogany desk, a pen holder on a mirrored side table, a glass paperweight shaped as a cat, and then he backs out again to the front door when he thinks he's shown enough interest in the store. He stands by the door. He looks out at the street. It's empty.

"See anything you like?" Michael asks.

Matt shrugs. "Ginny's the buyer of our household stuff," he says. "I don't have any taste. Put a poster on the wall of the Eiffel Tower or a cat hanging off a screen door and I'm just fine." He laughs, hating that he's claiming to leave interior design to his wife, but also knowing that this is how you can get out of an awkward situation sometimes.

Michael looks disappointed. After all, there is no one else in the store, it must be pretty lonely and depressing. How many people in Parkville buy antiques on a good day? Matt looks out the front windows again, it's cold out and there is no one shopping on the street, just leaves scuttling past. Then he sees a few men wearing black and standing about in a huddle by the garbage can. It looks like a meeting of some sort. They weren't there before, were they?

Matt is about to say something about the men when Michael clears his throat and directs Matt's attention to a table by the front, to pamphlets about a performance from a theatre company up from the city, to pins and buttons and a donation box for cancer. By the time Matt looks up again the men near the garbage can are gone.

Matt blinks twice and says, "I was thinking we could jog in the ravine before we get snow. What do you think? We're always jogging on the sidewalks around the back streets and keep within such a small radius of our houses. We're always doing the same loop. I thought it would be more interesting to jog the ravine this time together?"

"I'm not sure about that," Michael says, turning back to his desk at the rear of the store.

"Oh? Why?"

"It's just that I don't go in the ravine."

"What? Why not?"

"No one goes in the ravine anymore. Have you been going down there?"

Matt pauses. "Sure, yes, I've gone for the occasional run when it's not muddy."

"Well, you shouldn't," says Michael. "I wouldn't recommend it. Pat and I stopped going down there about a year ago."

Matt stares at Michael.

"We just kept finding things. Garbage and stuff, of course, but other things."

"Like what?"

"Lots of dead animals."

Matt opens his mouth.

"It's just that there always seemed to be dead animals down there. Raccoons and squirrels and rabbits and birds. Mostly rabbits. It was disgusting."

"What do you mean?"

"Well, we'd see a lot of bones. Not as many full animals, to be honest, but some. But when it was the whole animal it was rotting and smelled disgusting and . . ." Michael pauses. "God, I hate to think about this again. We just stopped going down there. There was also so much garbage. Like it was being used as a garbage dump. No one goes down there anymore. Pierre and Ruby don't. I don't think Rain does either. It's all overgrown now. And then last summer we had all those thefts so Pat and the others all got rid of the gates."

"I haven't seen anything dead down there," Matt says. "And only a bit of garbage really, mostly cigarette butts. And I haven't seen any people. The occasional walker. But it's really empty."

"Well, you'll see the dead animals eventually. I'm sure of it." Michael looks away.

Matt does notice the odd decomposing smell when he's down there. But he thought it was the rotting leaves and the mould on the soil. Fall smells. And he does occasionally smell smoke.

"Well, yeah, I get it. Let's not go into the ravine then. Definitely not."

"Sorry to burst your bubble," Michael says. "We were like you when we came back here. We thought everything would be perfect in our small, quaint town too." He smiles, shakes his head. "When we were kids everything was much better here." He pauses and fiddles with a letter opener on his desk.

The knifelike look of it reminds Matt of Ginny's attack in the city. At least, he thinks, this place is better than the city.

"Let's just go on the regular neighbourhood loop tomorrow morning if it's not raining," says Michael.

"Sure," Matt says. "That sounds great." Another thing not to tell Ginny about, Matt thinks. She will never go into the ravine if she hears about this. Matt is starting to get so stressed about not making Ginny stressed, about watching what he says, that he has started wondering if he should take her leftover anti-anxiety pills. But he knows that's ridiculous. He shakes his head and leaves the store.

As Matt walks out the door he notices more people around. Regular people, in all different clothes. Not that much black. It's getting near lunch and the workers are coming out of their stores, their offices. He looks toward the garbage can and beyond and suddenly sees Marina down the street. She is hunched over, looking through her handbag and seems consumed with worry. He starts to walk toward her but she looks up and sees him and turns quickly and walks away at a clipped pace. Matt doesn't want to run to catch up, that might scare her, a large man lumbering toward her, although he'd like to talk to her about Charles coming into their yard on Halloween night. But Marina turns a corner, ducks between two stores, rushes down the alley and is gone. She walks fast for someone her age, Matt thinks. And Charles ran so fast on Halloween night it was startling. If anything, for all their oddness, Matt thinks, the two of them are at least in fairly good shape.

⊗

It's a cold dark night. Matt and Ginny have decided to go for a walk before bed. They are bundled up and they head out the front door. They walk quickly, heads down; the wind is piercing. Ginny can hear it moaning through the trees behind the houses. A few kids try to get one more basketball shot in before bed. They are in hoodies and sweatpants and even with the exercise they look cold, stamping their feet, blowing into their fists. Matt and Ginny head around the corner past the parking lot that is attached to the park that leads into the ravine.

"Too bad we can't walk in the ravine. There should be lights," Matt says.

"Even with lights I'm not sure I'd go down there at night."

Matt sighs.

"What? I wouldn't. Just because we're out of the city, Matt, it doesn't mean life isn't still dangerous."

"I know, but what could happen?"

Ginny looks at him. "A person with a knife. And he'd laugh. And —"

Matt puts his hands up, shuts up, says, "Sorry," as he realizes his mistake. They walk on.

They turn another corner through the streets and loop around to head back. Past the ravine entrance again. Ginny looks toward the path and sees something beside a large maple tree. A figure? A shadow? She can't tell. It's too dark. But then it moves and Ginny clutches Matt's hand and points. He follows her finger.

"What?"

"There's someone there."

"Where?"

"By the bottom of that tree." The street is suddenly quiet, all the basketball kids have gone inside. And then the figure moves again and it is someone. A person crouching. The figure stands suddenly, straightens up, and turns and walks back into the ravine. Dressed all in black.

Ginny's heart is beating hard, she's squeezing Matt's hand.

"You saw that, right?" Ginny whispers.

"Where?" Matt says. "I didn't see anything, Ginny. You're probably seeing shadows from the streetlights." Matt peels her hand off his. He shakes his hand out. "Ouch, you were holding tight there." He takes Ginny's hand again, loosely. He kisses it. "Let's go home."

That night Ginny goes to bed and dreams again of the figure in black, like a shadow — no definition to his face — as he slides through their bedroom. He slides up the walls and down the hallway and Ginny follows him in her dreams. He's huge and sinister, a snakelike, liquid form, sliding everywhere. He disappears down the basement stairs and Ginny wakes with a scream. Matt comes running. Ginny is in the basement. She's walked in her sleep. She's sitting on the basement stairs. She doesn't know how she got here. Every corner looks sinister, dark, there are shadows and shapes everywhere.

"Where am I?"

"What are you doing down here? What's going on?" Matt looks panicked. "I woke up and you were gone and then you screamed."

On the way back up the stairs to bed Matt says it must be her hormones, he says it must be the baby. He says it must be post-traumatic stress. He says it must be the attack and their move. On and on. And Ginny thinks, what if it is the baby, do they want a baby who does this to her? Matt climbs into bed, exhausted. He turns away from Ginny. He sighs. Is he mad? Ginny touches his shoulder.

"Go to bed, Ginny," he says. "Everything will be okay." And Ginny lies there, all night, eyes peeled open, staring at the ceiling.

⊗

Ginny is trying new recipes, Ginny is lonely, Ginny is bored.

They have a November dinner party. Seems like a once-a-month thing now. Before everyone comes Matt feels slightly tired of this. Same old wine, same old conversation. Michael and Pat will get tipsy and talk about the "good old days." They are only in their fifties – what good old days? Rain doesn't eat or drink anything and she giggles a lot, awkwardly. Pierre is now comfortable and snorts often and talks loudly and drinks too much. He doesn't really let Ruby say much, but when she talks it's always about how scary life is – diseases, murders, crimes, anything that makes life precarious. Or her children. She talks about them a lot. About how they don't do anything bad. Matt wants to snort. All teenagers do things they shouldn't. None of these people talk about anything but themselves. And it seems to Matt as if no one is interested in anything but the local news. No discussion of international news, or history or books they've read or art. He's a high-school English literature teacher, doesn't anyone read novels or poetry anymore?

But Matt knows he's just in a bad mood. There are birds in his eavestroughs and the incessant pecking and wing-flapping fights are driving him crazy. He can hear the noise throughout the whole house, a howling, violent sound, as if they are preparing to peck each other's eyes out. Also, his students were ridiculous today, not paying any attention, moving all over the place on his computer screen, freezing suddenly. Teaching over the internet always gives him such a headache, but when everyone is moving and jiggling it's even more annoying. These are the problem kids too, the ones who can't sit still in a regular class and who attack other kids for no reason, the ones who scream and challenge their teachers physically – sometimes with compasses or pens or chairs or tables in real life. The violent ones. They have been put into online learning because no one wants them in the classroom anymore. Matt finds it hard enough keeping them engaged – in English literature, no less – but when it's cold outside, cloudy and dark, it's near impossible. He can see the ravine from his window and feels full of pent-up energy, like his students, with nowhere to put it.

Wasn't that the point of moving here, Matt thinks. Jogs in the ravine? The great outdoors? The sudden country surrounding the town? These days, ever since his conversation about the ravine with Michael, he has mostly been going for walks and jogs around the block to relieve stress. But that's boring and doesn't give him the space or tranquility of all the trees in the ravine, of the silence. Even though the ravine is frightening and muddy and full of unknowns, it's still the wilderness. The ravine sometimes feels like noise-cancelling headphones to him, it cocoons him and swallows him up, makes him feel completely alone. But then, of course, Ginny is worried about the ravine. And Matt can't stop thinking if what Michael said is true – is it really full of dead animals? He hasn't seen any dead animals. What else is in there? Who else is in there? Matt rubs his eyes. He misses the romantic idea of the ravine, the one he thought it was when he moved here. But now, with Michael's words in his head and Ginny's wide-open frightened eyes and the early fall darkness, everything has changed.

CHAPTER 12

Ginny notices Matt looks distracted during this dinner party. She tries to give him jobs to do in the kitchen, filling up the coffee machine, getting out the dessert forks, and, during dinner, filling wine and water, so that he doesn't seem so dour for the guests. She pokes him under the table. He should have said something if he didn't want the dinner party tonight. She could have cancelled.

Carrying in the salad before the main course Matt meets Ginny in the kitchen. She reaches up, puts her hand on his shoulder.

"You okay?"

"Just tired," Matt says. Ginny pats him and hands him the forks.

Michael comes in to see if they need help. He mentions the theatre company coming to Parkville next summer and hands Matt a pamphlet from his store. He says they put on Shakespeare in the park.

"We're getting tickets now for all the plays. Would you and Ginny be interested in joining us?"

Ginny leaves the men in the kitchen just as Matt's face lights up. She can tell he's thrilled. She smiles at him and nods "yes" on her way out to the dining room. They'll bring the baby. She glances at the kitchen patio doors and sees her reflection gazing back at her.

She's been so off lately, confused and wary and anxious, and she knows her behaviour is rubbing off on Matt. Their relationship has become tense and strained. And Ginny wants to tell someone about their baby but there is no one here in Parkville to tell. Not yet. She called her mother, of course, and her sister, but although they both seemed happy – her sister, in particular, was excited their babies would be the same age – they also seemed busy and distracted. Christine is continually shopping in the city for all kinds of baby things and their mother joins Christine any chance she has. Neither of them offers to come up to Ginny's house to visit and Ginny doesn't want to leave Matt without their car all day to go into the city. She could do that, of course, but if she's honest with herself she doesn't want to leave Matt. Even if half the time Ginny is mad at him, she would rather be with him here, really, and what if he needed the car for something? At least that's her excuse. Maybe she really doesn't want to see her mom or her sister?

"We'll come see you when it's been three months," her mother said.

"Really, Mom? Really?" Ginny knew she was shrill, but her mother now planted the thought of losing the baby in Ginny's mind. It felt like an ice pick in her heart. She worried about this in the beginning but now she's trying not to stress about anything. The thing about worrying though, as Ginny is finding out, is that when you try not to worry you worry more about not worrying. It's a vicious cycle.

"Honey, you know it's a possibility. You really shouldn't tell anyone yet."

"Should I not have told you and Christine?"

"No, no, we're fine. We're family. But don't tell your friends. Not yet."

Ginny doesn't understand this logic. Wouldn't her friends want to be there for her if she miscarried? But then she realized that since they've moved here Ginny doesn't really have any great friends anymore. Not yet. She knows she will eventually, but it will take time to establish tight bonds. Rain, Ruby, Michael or Pat. Ginny doesn't think she will tell them before the time is safe. They aren't really friends yet. There's something strange about them and Ginny knows she keeps inviting them to dinner parties to figure out what it is. Sometimes she thinks they are hiding something from her, as if they all know something she doesn't know. She watches their eyes, the way they look at each other. Sometimes she thinks she's imagining things and she is just new and different. After all, she and Matt grew up in the city. And Ginny's friends from the city are mostly from work and they still talk about the bank all the time and are not interested in anything Ginny tells them about Parkville. She's losing touch with them rapidly.

"How quaint," they say now when she talks about anything in her life. "How adorable."

Ginny knows what that means. She used to say that to people who had moved away. Before Ginny and Matt moved, one of her banking colleagues actually took her aside at work and said that everyone in small towns is inbred. They are all related, he said. "It's like a cult." And Ginny felt like punching him.

Ginny sometimes wonders if Pat could be her best friend here. He's funny and kind and happy most of the time. He giggles a lot, uses his arms when he speaks and is contagiously satisfied. Ginny knows she could use a little of that. But he's busy at their antique store and, well, there's nothing really to do here that they could do together – no opera, no playhouse, no shopping, no symphony. Only one good restaurant in Parkville and it's really not that great according to Michael and Pat. Matt and Ginny haven't gone out for dinner yet. When Pat said, "How many times can you have fried chicken and mashed potatoes cooked in different sauces?" Matt and Ginny decided not to spend money there. There isn't even a movie theatre in Parkville, that's in the next town, about half an hour away. It's a small cinema with only one movie playing at a time. There is a drive-in but it's forty-five minutes away in a farmer's field and only operates in the summer. Besides, Pat and Michael seem to have a never-ending supply of friends so they really don't need any more. Ginny often sees a lot of men and women walking up their front path, so what would Pat need with Ginny? Ginny has a feeling that if you didn't grow up in Parkville you'll never be someone who really fits in.

Pat and Michael tell Ginny and Matt that they lived in the city for a while but grew up here, in this town. They moved away for a bit of their lives but came back. They have history here. Family. Nieces and uncles and nephews and cousins. They share memories of high school with other Parkville birthers, summers at the lake, new buildings coming and old buildings going. Ginny sometimes sits through half an hour of dinner party conversation she can't figure out. Where everyone at the table here knows what everyone else is talking about except for Ginny and Matt.

Michael and Matt are back in the dining room and everyone is digging into dinner.

"Pass the red sauce, please," Rain says and that knocks Ginny right out of her thoughts. Rain's eating?

Ginny made a beetloaf with a ketchupy kind of sauce. Lots of garlic. No one else is touching it. It smells awful. But Rain is digging in. It's dripping off her chin, actually. Ginny hands her a napkin. Seeing this makes Ginny happy. Three dinner parties and Ginny has finally found something Rain will eat. She'll eat loads of garlic, it seems. Or maybe Rain finally got hungry. It's hard to be in such control, Ginny thinks. Sometimes you just give up.

Everyone else at the table is watching Rain, judging her. Michael and Pat are smiling. Ruby looks at Pierre and sighs. "Baby steps," Ruby whispers to her husband.

The roast beef is going down well with everyone else. No one is complaining. And Ruby brought a dessert that looks amazing. Some sort of cake, it's sitting on the counter in the kitchen right now. Ginny has been craving sweets lately so she can't wait to dig into this.

"I thought I would have a Christmas dinner party. Does that sound okay? Or will you all be too busy with the holidays?" Ginny suddenly asks, interrupting a conversation between Ruby and Rain about the indoor market and how it'll have to close soon because the heating is broken and the town can't afford to replace it. Everyone looks at her.

"I'm not doing anything for the holidays," Rain says. "I'm in."

"We have a few things booked, but let's plan the dinner now so it's set in the calendar," says Pat. Michael nods.

Ruby and Pierre nod. "If you feel like having another one? We find this very nice."

Ginny smiles. "Wonderful," she says. "How about the middle of the month, that way we'll have the tree up? I'll get my phone in the kitchen and put this in the calendar and send you all a text." Everyone nods.

Matt continues handling the conversation in the dining room as Ginny gets up and walks into the kitchen for her phone. For a man who started tonight wishing he wasn't here, he's switched, with a few glasses of wine, into quite the host. He watches the swinging kitchen door smacking back and forth.

"Maybe we can cook for you guys sometime too," Michael says. "Or maybe we can all bring something to the next dinner?"

Pierre says, "Maybe Rain shouldn't cook."

Ruby smacks her husband lightly. "Pierre," she warns. "Too much wine. Stop."

"I can bring . . ." Rain stops, she doesn't know what she could bring. "Bread?" Rain says she has been meaning to start making sourdough bread, she says the idea is intriguing to her. Everyone at the market is making sourdough these days.

Matt is smiling to himself, contemplating what Rain would poison them with if she brought a dish and then thinking about sourdough starters and how hard they are, when Ginny suddenly screams from the kitchen. The sound of a crash carries into the dining room.

Everyone at the table looks at each other and then they all push back their chairs and run into the kitchen, all cramming through the door at the same time, getting trapped, stuck, pushing through.

"What is it?" Matt shouts. "Are you okay? Ginny?" He rounds the corner into the kitchen first and sees Ginny. She is standing by the back patio door, which is open, the sliding glass is frosted as if it has been open for a few minutes, letting the cold into the heat of the kitchen. Ginny is pointing.

Pat takes her arm and squeezes it. "Are you okay? What happened?"

Matt rushes to close the back door. The heat is escaping. He is trying to show sympathy and calculate how much that will cost at the same time.

Ginny turns to Pat and looks over his shoulder to Matt. "He was here again. Standing on the patio. Looking in," she says.

"What?" Everyone is confused. Except Matt.

"Charles?" Matt says. But for just a moment he wonders if it is the man, the dark figure, she says she sees in her dreams.

"Yes. He was standing on the patio when I came in. I didn't see him at first. I dropped the dessert when I saw him." Ginny looks at the floor, everyone follows her gaze. The plate is smashed on the tiles. The cake is on the floor in pieces. "I dropped the dessert. Ruby, your plate, I'm so sorry. He ran away."

"What was he doing here?" Matt asks.

"I don't know. I don't know." Ginny shakes her head. "He ran, Matt. So fast. I've never seen anyone move that fast. Just like before."

"Charles Smythe?" Michael says.

"You broke my plate," Ruby says. "That was my mother's plate." She's had too much wine and has become a bit weepy. "My plate. And the cake." They all look down at the floor where pieces of cake are mixed with ceramic.

"I'm more sad about the dessert," Pierre slurs. "You'd made such a good cake, Ruby. My favourite. But your mother's plate was ugly."

Ginny holds up her hands. "I'm so sorry."

"We've been having problems," Matt says to the others. "Charles is bothering us. We don't know what he wants, but he's been hanging around our house. Hey, maybe he's the one who stole my running shoes?"

"*Your* shoes were stolen? My shoes were stolen too," Pat says. "Remember the shit shoes, Michael?"

Michael says, "It's happening again. Like last summer. The thefts."

Everyone nods. And groans.

"What's happening again?" Matt asks. He is confused and persistent. "What's happening?"

"Does Charles say anything?" Pat asks. "Anything at all?"

Ginny shakes her head. She puts her hands down and stares at the broken plate on the floor.

Matt tilts his head to the patio doors. "What happened last year, Michael? What thefts?"

"You should get curtains," Pierre says. "That would be better."

Ginny nods. Yes, curtains, definitely.

"And get rid of your gate, like the rest of us did last summer, or put a lock on it," Ruby says.

"Before you two moved in we all had some trouble with theft." Pierre is holding his wineglass, tipping it slightly. His eyes are drunkenly unfocused.

"Yes," Michael says. "Our patio cushions were stolen one night."

"Lots of things were stolen," Pierre says. "Someone was sneaking through our backyards and stealing things. Laundry on the line, patio cushions, like Michael said."

"This was before Charles and Marina moved out," Ruby says.

Ginny and Matt didn't think they had to protect themselves from the backyard, from the ravine, but, yes, they will get curtains. They won't take away the gate, however, not that. Someone could just climb over the fence anyway. A missing gate might dissuade some people, but Ginny doesn't want to be the kind of person who gives in to fear. They moved from the city to escape fear. This place was supposed to be so different. They won't go that far yet.

⊗

Later, after everyone has left, Ginny stares out the patio window toward the gate, her arms crossed over her chest, while Matt does all the dishes. He keeps looking at her. She feels his eyes on her back.

"What's going on here, Matt?" Ginny says.

And Matt sighs heavily. He says nothing.

Ginny turns from him. She means what is going on in general? With everything. The house, the town, the people, the strange feelings she gets living here. She walks up the stairs to their bedroom. She lies on the bed knowing fully she won't be sleeping again tonight.

⊗

In the morning Ginny is in the bedroom making the bed. She's thinking about her hormones and how they are making her angry and she knows she's more frustrated at herself than at Matt. She gets that on one level, but on another level everything is Matt's fault. Sometimes Ginny thinks she's going crazy. She knows she wasn't like this before the attack in the city. Everything makes her jump now, makes her worry all night. She hasn't slept soundly in so long. Sometimes she lies in bed and wonders if there really is anything strange about this house – maybe the attack in the city just made her so anxious that she now sees everything as a threat? Maybe it's a normal house, a normal town, nothing to worry about?

But the hall window unlocks occasionally still, Matt can't seem to fix it and even when he thinks he's fixed it, it pops open again, and Charles is in the yard, and even the patio door somehow opens up now on its own. And the figure she keeps seeing. Matt can't see him. How is that possible?

Ginny thinks everything is so goddamn creepy here. And Matt

keeps quoting things to her. Yesterday, when she closed the hallway window again and swore loudly, it was something from Aesop, "Those who enter through the back door can expect to be shown out through the window." She's sick of it. He used to do this all of the time in the city but she thought he'd grown out of it. Now that he's a homeowner. It was an affected way of talking in university, it was pride, he was bragging: "Look how much I know." He should not be fucking quoting things anymore, Ginny thinks.

And now she's really worried about losing the baby too. Ginny never feared that until her mother and Christine and Matt all started saying, "Stay away from stress or you'll lose the baby," and of course that makes her so stressed she can't breathe. She's turning in circles.

Ginny walks past Matt's office. She can hear his students rattling away about something and Matt saying, "How do you feel about that?"

Why does he never ask Ginny how she's feeling about anything? There was a dead body in her yard, there is a creepy, dark ravine out the back, there is an angry, strange old man rushing at her, a window that won't stay shut, lots of unexplained locks everywhere, a figure on her bed, and why was there a grow room where there should have been a coat closet? Why does no one ask Ginny how she's feeling?

When they finally meet for lunch Ginny asks him again about the window.

"I'll call someone to fix the window," Matt says. He has a break for fifteen minutes so Ginny makes their lunch and Matt wolfs it down, talking to her quickly all through the bites. "I tried but I can't get it to latch properly." He pauses and then holds up a book he had in his lap. He says, "Listen to this. Virginia Woolf wrote a nice thing about windows. 'The light struck upon the trees in the garden, making one leaf transparent and then another. One bird chirped high up; there was a pause; another chirped lower down. The sun sharpened the walls of the house, and rested like the tip of a fan upon a white blind and made a blue fingerprint of a shadow under the leaf by the bedroom window. The blind stirred slightly, but all within was dim and unsubstantial. The birds sang their blank melody outside.'" He puts the book down.

Ginny looks at him. Her mouth is wide open. She wants to scream. She wants to take the book out of his hands and bash his head in with it. "Are you kidding me? Virginia Woolf? Are you kidding me?"

Matt blushes and shrugs. "I don't know. I just liked that and thought I'd share. You don't need to shout."

Ginny clears her throat. She looks down at her plate and makes a conscious effort to keep her mouth firmly closed. She can't believe him. His damn quotes. She steadies her voice. "That would be great. Call someone. We can't do everything ourselves, Matt."

"I will. This afternoon. I really tried it myself, Ginny, but I couldn't fix it."

"You could have asked Virginia Woolf to help you," Ginny grumbles. "Has it occurred to you that maybe someone is coming in through the window? Maybe that man I keep seeing? Maybe he's coming into our house."

"We'd hear. And we haven't had anything stolen, have we? If someone is getting in, what are they doing in the house? And we're always here."

Ginny thinks of Matt's running shoes but they were outside.

"We're always home when that window comes open. Who would take such a risk? Climb in when we're home? In bed? Asleep?" he asks.

Ginny nods. "Exactly," she says. She remembers the podcast she heard about the Golden State Killer, who snuck into houses when couples were sleeping. He tied the women up and raped them. He tied the men up and made them lie on their stomachs. He balanced teacups and saucers on the men's backs and if he heard the teacup fall he killed the couple. She doesn't know what else to say.

Matt looks at her. "Exactly? What do you mean, exactly?"

"Maybe he comes in the house to kill us? Maybe he's here right now." Ginny takes a sip of her water. Matt looks frustrated. Ginny's hands shake.

"The house isn't that big. There can't be someone in here right now that we don't know about."

"Maybe he comes in, goes down the stairs and out the front door. Or maybe he comes in and goes down to the basement and hides there?"

"Ha," Matt laughs. "Are you being funny?"

"I don't know, Matt. Why is anything happening in this house? Why is there a dead body in the backyard?"

"*Was*, not *is* – and there's no proof of that."

"Why is the ravine so creepy?"

"It's not that creepy, you just haven't gone down there."

"It's creepy. I saw that figure by the gate, didn't I? I keep seeing him. I know you think I'm lying but I keep seeing him. No one else has a gate down to the ravine, right? They said that at the dinner party. Just us. And you have seen someone walking, you've smelled a fire. So someone could be living there, right? And that man I keep seeing, he has no face."

"You're having nightmares, Ginny. You're just imagining things," Matt says. "I haven't seen him. He's not really there." Matt shrugs.

Ginny scowls at him.

"And no one is living in the ravine. There are no encampments, I never see anyone. The smoke is probably from the houses on the road. And everyone has a face, Ginny. His is just shadowed by his hood, by the light."

"Just because you haven't seen him . . ." Ginny's voice peters out.

They sit in silence and stare at each other. Matt looks sad. He looks at the time on his phone. He picks up the book on his lap. He sighs. He's always sighing these days. "I have to go. Class."

Ginny nods. Matt gets up, kisses her forehead, and goes

upstairs. Ginny boils a kettle for tea. "Fuckfuckfuck," she says, under her breath. And then she's quiet. The kettle turns off. She can hear Matt, far upstairs, a bit of a mumble. The heater goes on. Click. A rumble from the basement, air pushing through the house. And then something heavy drops. A thump. The sound is coming from the basement. Ginny is in the kitchen. She stands. Matt is upstairs in the guest room/office. The noise wasn't from him. Another thump. Her heart beats wildly.

And then the heat really comes on loudly – pushes through the vents and Ginny can hear that thump again, another one and another one, extra noise added to all the noises, all the failures, this house has. It sounds like someone pounding, a steady rhythm, someone trying to get out. Ginny breathes deeply. It's probably only the beginning of the heater breaking down, she thinks. Of course that's what it is. She sips her tea. What else could it be?

DECEMBER

CHAPTER 13

Ginny and Matt go with Ruby and Elton to a Christmas tree farm. They take turns with Ruby's saw and cut down trees they pick out. There is a horse-drawn wagon that brings them and the cut trees back to a firepit and they sit by the flames and drink hot chocolate while the trees are bound and placed by their cars. Elton entertains everyone with tales of school, of teachers and kids and confusion and tricks played on the librarian, and Ginny laughs so much she has to pee and almost does. After dragging the tree into their house Ginny waves goodbye to Ruby and Elton as Matt helps them drag their tree inside their house too.

"That's something you couldn't do in the city," Matt says. "Remember taking the subway with our tree that one year?" This has become their mantra. It cheers them up. If they get to the grocery store in five minutes, avoid all traffic, do all their shopping and get home within half an hour they look at each other and say, "That's something you couldn't do in the city," or "That's a Parkville moment."

When Matt needed to renew his driver's licence and there wasn't a line at the renewal office, and then when he realized he forgot his identification and had to go home and get it and then go back to the renewal office, and his parking spot was still miraculously there and there was still no one in line, he said, "That's something you couldn't do in the city."

They put up their tree and decorate it. They have strung it with bright coloured lights and ornaments collected over their few years together. The smell of spruce permeates the house. One year Matt's stepmother, Elaine, gave them about twenty boxes of ornaments from a closing-out ornament sale in the city. They can put them all on the tree this year. It's big enough.

At night Matt wakes, hearing a noise. A crinkly sound, light like wind chimes. He thinks about it for a bit and then falls back asleep. In the morning, when he bends down to water the tree, he notices that some of the ornaments have fallen off the tree and are broken, shattered below. Matt cleans them up quickly. He figures they were just hung wrong, balanced precariously on the small branches.

Ginny finds a shattered ornament in the dining room and a bit of broken glass in the kitchen but she says nothing to Matt, thinking that he was careless when he carried the empty boxes back down to the basement. However, each morning there are more ornaments off, and she begins to wonder.

Matt knows Ginny wants to show off her baby bump, which really isn't there yet. She's just thickening slightly everywhere. They're driving to the city to visit their relatives, or as many as they can see, and give them some of their Christmas presents. The rest they will mail. With Matt's parents divorced and remarried there are a lot of people to see.

Ginny's only two and a half months pregnant right now but, she tells Matt, she knows her mother will look at her disdainfully for drawing attention to herself before the three-month mark.

"I don't care," she says. "Just because Christine waited until exactly three months and then blurted it out to the world – like the perfect daughter she is."

"I hope they give us our presents now," Matt says. "So we don't have to come back for them after the holidays."

"I know Elaine got us a light fixture for the dining room. She said she'd give it to us today."

"We can put it up before the next dinner party."

As they get off the highway and drive through the tightly packed streets of the city Ginny says, "We are actually lucky we live where we do now. Don't you think? Even with all the noises and the strange things happening in our house, I can't bear the feeling I'm getting right now. It's a claustrophobic feeling, don't you think? Everything seems tight. The streets are narrow, the houses close together." She waves her arms around. "There are people everywhere. The smells too, gah – everything smells of fast food and oil frying. Diesel fuel too. My nose is very sensitive these days." She smiles.

Matt is actually thinking the opposite. He thought the country would make Ginny less anxious and he was excited to settle in, but with all the things happening he now looks at the city with new eyes. Today he looks at all the restaurants and stores – he could buy anything he wanted. Part of him forgets how convenient the city is. Especially around Christmas. And then he almost rear-ends a delivery truck and then forgets to stop when a streetcar's lights are blinking and remembers that he doesn't miss this crazy city driving, that's for sure. And he doesn't miss the prices of things – parking for one hour downtown is twenty dollars – and, of course, he doesn't miss the man in the alley.

They talk all the way down to the city about the house, about what more they need to do with it. He notices Ginny avoids talking about the basement or the hatch or the backyard or the attic. Matt talks about the windows but avoids conversation about the hallway one, which he still hasn't called anyone about. He did make it pretty stable though – it hasn't opened for a while. We'll see, he thinks.

But then Ginny says, "Maybe if we got rid of that old shed roof in the back, maybe if we got rid of it we wouldn't worry anymore about the window in the hallway because if it wasn't there no one could climb up."

"But then we'd get rained on when we barbeque," Matt says. "I was going to put the barbeque there in the summer, just under the overhang."

"It's not even in the right place for a barbeque, Matt, it's way too close to the house. And besides, it's short. You wouldn't be able to stand up under it," Ginny says. "Even I would find it tight. We don't need a roof for a barbeque anyway. We just won't barbeque when it rains." She pauses. "Why do you think they kept the roof after getting rid of the shed?"

"Maybe they had a barbeque?" Matt grumbles.

"Charles is tall, Matt, he wouldn't have fit under it either. Besides, do they seem like the type to barbeque?" Ginny pulls down the sun visor to fix her lipstick. Matt notices she only wears lipstick when she sees her mother. "Really. It was just a shed there at one point. For tools. A lawn mower, maybe. They tore the shed down, maybe it was rotting, but not the roof. Makes no sense but nothing in our house makes any sense. Everything's ridiculous."

Matt nods. He still can't figure out the locks everywhere. Since they've lived here Matt has had several odd dreams about locks – about being locked in or out of places, locked in the variety store near their old apartment in the city, or locked out of his parent's house, scrambling in the backyard, banging on their back door. He's taken most of the locks off, has filled in the holes and sanded and Ginny painted over their shadows. Much nicer now.

He glances at Ginny fixing her hair and makeup in the shade mirror. He noticed, when they left the house, that she was wearing very baggy clothes. She usually doesn't wear such loose-fitting clothing. He assumes she's trying to make herself look more pregnant than she is. Matt does notice that her face has filled out more, her hips and waist are slightly wider, but other than that no one would be able to tell she's pregnant – maybe just as if she ate one too many cookies. Funny that she wants her family to see her growing larger but if he mentions that she's thickening she will probably cry.

When they arrive, he sees that Christine is huge. All in the front. Her red hair is pulled back in a ponytail and her cheeks are flushed, almost as bright as her hair. She's normally as tiny as Ginny and so Matt is astonished and can't believe Ginny will get that big. But she will, won't she? Matt has never really been around pregnant women before. Working at home he's not surrounded by his colleagues, and seeing them on the monitor you never see the lower half of them. Pregnant colleagues look normal from the chest up. Maybe puffier faces, but that's it.

"You're huge," Ginny shouts and Christine blushes.

Since when, Matt thinks, did women react calmly and blissfully to "You're huge"? He sits down on his mother-in-law's baby-blue floral sofa. He removes the uncomfortable tufted pillow from behind his back and puts it on his lap. He takes the coffee she's offering, making sure the bottom of the cup is clean before he rests it on the pillow in his lap. The smell settles him. He can also smell something coming from the oven, something with oregano in it. Ginny and Christine disappear somewhere in the house, laughing and talking. Ginny always leaves him alone in her childhood house. He finds it awkward.

"So? How's the country life?" Ginny's mom, Joanne, asks.

"Not really the country," Matt says. "We live walking distance to the downtown."

"The downtown? Downtown?" Joanne laughs. "You don't even have a Starbucks. Or a Costco. Or anything really. Parkville doesn't have any good shopping."

"That's not what makes a town," Matt says.

"Of course it is. Stores make a town, Matt." Joanne laughs. She sees Matt's face fall. "But of course, dear." Joanne looks away. She sighs. "So how's everything else?"

"Great, fine. The house is wonderful," Matt says. "Really great."

"That's not what Ginny says. She says the house is a mess and terrifying. She says Parkville is small. She says you need to do a lot of renovations. She says there's a man bothering her." Joanne stares at Matt, and he feels her judging him. She's always done this – blame everything on Matt. Her grey hair has been styled so carefully it doesn't move, her blue eyes peer out at him from behind her thick glasses. She's wearing a dress that vaguely resembles the sofa – blue and floral.

"Well, you know Ginny. She exaggerates," Matt says. "Honestly, it just needs a bit of work. More than we thought. And, well, it's not scary. That's just her . . . her hormones talking." Matt shrugs. "We've had a couple of things happen, but nothing really to be worried about."

Joanne looks carefully at Matt. "I'm worried about Ginny," she says, quietly. "Aren't you?"

Matt shrugs.

"She's getting more and more anxious. She's talking in circles. I'm not sure your move to the country was a good idea."

"I –" Matt starts but Joanne gets up.

"But this has nothing to do with me," Joanne says. "I'm just her mother." She shrugs and then leaves to check on their lunch. Matt sits by himself in the living room with his coffee cup and his pillow. His father-in-law is in the TV room watching golf. Matt can hear the commentary from here. He wonders if he should go in and say hello but decides against it. This is going to be a long day.

At the next house, his father's, they have drinks and appetizers. Matt drinks more coffee because he's driving. He chews on a few crackers and salami pieces. He samples the red pepper jelly and cheese. Ginny sips on a soda water, burping slightly. His stepmother, Elaine, has given them a huge chandelier for the dining room. It's wild. Little balls of light, huge hanging pendants, silver and gold and brass. He wonders how many light bulbs it takes – and what kind? Matt is astonished at how big it is and wonders if he'll have to hire someone to put it up. He wonders if the old plaster in their dining-room ceiling will hold it – or the beam under the plaster? – or however you put chandeliers up. He has no idea. He should hire someone, actually. Ginny is gushing over it and Matt can't tell whether she loves it or hates it. He isn't sure, either, if he loves it or hates it. It's definitely unique. And huge. Matt wants to say "interesting," as, when he was a kid, that's what his mother used to say to him whenever she didn't like something. He would cook her dinner and she would say, "It's so interesting, Matt." He would buy her a Christmas present and she would open it and say, "So interesting!" Matt sometimes thinks he married Ginny because his mother didn't say she was interesting. Is the chandelier a bit gaudy? Matt doesn't know. But they both thank Elaine and finish their appetizers and kiss goodbye and move on to the last house, his mother's house, for dinner.

Matt's mother greets them with her hands folded on her chest. They were stuck in traffic and arrived late. She is wearing an apron over a business suit. She holds a spatula against her body. A few air kisses and she scoots them straight into the dining room where they settle into dinner. Matt gets into a long conversation about debt with his stepfather, Albert. They married when Matt was a teenager and so he feels he both knows Albert well and doesn't know him at all. Albert makes him uncomfortable most of the time. But then so does his mother. He watches Albert's thick eyebrows move up and down as he chews and talks. The conversation is about Matt and Ginny's mortgage and how Matt is going to renovate the house when he has such a large debt.

"How are you going to borrow more?" Albert shouts, well into his third scotch. "Did you think of that?"

His stepfather and mother have obviously been talking to Ginny, who smiles demurely at the table – she never knows what to say around Matt's mother, a daunting figure. Matt wishes Albert would just shut up or at least offer him some financial help. One or the other. Ginny tells them the story of the satellite image and Matt tries to fade out. He's tired of this story, hates what it says about his house, his life, his choice to move out of the city. He worries that with Ginny repeating it any chance she gets she won't ever be able to let it go. It will be the story of their life when they are on their deathbeds. And he knows what his stepfather will say.

"That's ridiculous," Albert says, holding his fork in the air, stabbing at the ceiling. "Are you two on drugs or something?"

Yep, Matt thinks, that's exactly what he thought his stepfather would say.

"Must have been your imagination, Ginny," Matt's mother says.

"But Matt saw it too, he saw it too, not just me."

"Matt wouldn't be that silly, Ginny. He doesn't have the imagination you have. Always thinking up ridiculous things." Matt's mother laughs and shakes her wineglass before swallowing. "Besides, you always exaggerate."

Ginny looks like she's going to cry. Matt stays silent.

"Ridiculous," Albert says again. "You two are just ridiculous." And then Matt's stepfather changes the conversation back to debt and mortgages and work, and then moves on to weather and directions – which way they came, which highways they took.

Matt has a headache.

⊗

They are both silent on the way home. Matt tries not to nod off. He drives carefully, his hands clutching the wheel. The food was rich and there was a lot of it. And he had so many coffees today that they are beginning to work the opposite way they should for him, they are making him sleepy. He tastes them on his tongue, coating it. Considering all the food they had today it's amazing that all he can taste is coffee.

Ginny falls asleep in the passenger seat and Matt listens to the radio. He has to shuffle the station when they get out of the city. He moves the numbers to the station from outside Parkville and listens to the farm reports and the weather.

⊗

When she wakes, just outside of Parkville, Ginny is startled. She doesn't know where she is for a minute. She rubs her eyes and straightens up in the seat.

"I had a nightmare," she says.

"You okay?"

"About the baby, Matt," Ginny says. "Maybe I shouldn't have told everyone I was pregnant – your mom, your dad, Elaine, Albert. Shit."

"No, of course you should have. They are family, Ginny, they are happy for us."

"It was horrible, Matt. I lost the baby. I could see it. There was blood. It wasn't fully formed." Ginny holds in a sob. "I know it was a dream but what if I lose the baby? I'm too old to have a baby, aren't I? I'm thirty-five. That's when it gets riskier." Ginny lets the sob out, almost a hiccup.

"You're so close to three months, Gin, you won't lose the baby. Besides –" Matt pulls into their driveway. "Shit."

"Matt –"

"What the hell?" Matt barely manages to put the car in park and gets out of the car quickly without even turning it off. He runs to the house. Ginny pulls out the key and follows behind.

"Stay back," he shouts at Ginny.

⊗

Ginny stops, puts her hand on her mouth and stares at her house, which is all lit up and glowing. It's lit up in every room. Every single light is on. She can see that even the Christmas tree lights are on. The front door is ajar. Matt runs through it and into the glow.

Ginny stands beside the car watching her husband disappear inside. And then she starts to scream and she can't stop.

CHAPTER 14

It isn't until later that they both realize Matt shouldn't have run into a house that had obviously just been broken into. They are lucky that there was no one in there, the police chastise him. What if the criminals had been inside waiting for him, ready to jump out and stab or shoot him?

Matt tells Ginny in bed that night that the scariest thing was her screaming. The fact that she couldn't stop. He stares up at the ceiling, lying on his back and he says, "Are you okay, Ginny?"

Nothing was stolen. Nothing was missing. Just the open door, and the lights were on.

⊗

At the Christmas dinner party Pierre says, "We were once broken into like that. All the lights in the house were on and all the windows and doors were open, just like yours."

"I wonder how long your doors were open," Ruby says. "Ours were open for hours. We lost a lot of heat. Our bill that month." Ruby rolls her eyes.

"It was our window," Ginny grumbles. "Our hallway window. That's how they got in."

"But the front door was open," Matt says. "It had nothing to do with the window."

"That window is broken, Matt," Ginny says. She sighs. She hates that he won't acknowledge the problem.

"What happened to you guys?" Matt asks, squirming in his seat, imagining the cost of the lost heat on his bill this month. Wondering how long the doors – and the window – were open.

"Just kids," Pierre says. "We think it might have been a couple of Erin's classmates. She was having problems with them; they were bullying her at school. Rumour got around that she was having a party. So we think some kids showed up thinking it was happening and then just left when it wasn't. Nothing was damaged or stolen."

"At least that's what we think," Ruby says. "We were lucky. The police were very helpful."

"I don't feel lucky," Ginny says. "In fact, I feel targeted. All the stuff that has happened to us in this house. Everything is so odd."

"At least we had nothing stolen or broken," Matt says.

Pat reaches across the table and holds Ginny's hand. She smiles at him. He heard her screaming the other night and told Michael he's never heard such a sound coming out of a person.

The Christmas tree looks lovely in the living room. They can see the reflection of it in the front window. The chandelier over the table is sparkling in the dining room. Matt called in a handyperson and he charged as much to install it as the chandelier originally cost. Rain is the only one not talking. She's wolfing down beetloaf again as if she's starving. It's as if Ginny's beetloaf has flipped a switch. Rain even had a glass of water during the appetizers. Ginny sees Ruby poke Pierre, they both look at Rain.

Ginny says, "Rain, there's a lot more."

Rain smiles. "It's so good. Doesn't anyone else want some?"

Everyone avoids Rain's question. Everyone looks away.

The rest of the guests are nibbling on Cornish hens, trying to take them apart delicately. Trying to look sophisticated. The only ones getting away with that are Michael and Pat. They've done this before. Matt and Ginny, Pierre and Ruby are tearing and jabbing at the little birds. She can see that Matt just wants to pick his hen up and suck on it but as he reaches for it he looks up and catches Ginny glaring at him.

Michael and Pat brought the dessert this time and it's on the hutch in the dining room. Something white and fluffy. Some kind of pudding cake. Rain brought appetizers and everyone tried one. Dry. Garlic. Really no taste. No one was sure what they were. Crackers? Pat surreptitiously spit into his napkin. Rain ate six pieces of the mysterious food and then drank some tap water to wash them down.

Ruby and Pierre brought wine. A lot of it. And Ginny and Matt cooked the Cornish hens, green beans steamed with slivered almonds on top and butter, and picked up crusty bread from the indoor market. Everyone is settling into their food, happily chewing, drinking too much wine, as usual. They've already discussed the break-in at the house in full detail and everyone compared break-in stories and said that it only happened because Matt and Ginny have a gate in their fence that leads to the ravine. It's all about the ravine. Matt and Ginny don't think that makes sense, someone could climb over a fence or a locked gate, but there's no use arguing. And they don't really care right now. Matt has had too much wine and Ginny is finally feeling less nauseous for the first time in a month. Ginny looks longingly at the wine and rubs her belly. Last month she was feeling so sick she didn't even want any wine, but this month she'd love a glass.

"I have some news," Ginny says when there's a break in the conversation.

Last week she and Matt went to the twelve-week ultrasound appointment and all is well. Ginny took the ultrasound picture off the fridge before everyone came and is holding it in her lap. She's about to lift it to show everyone when Rain says, "You're pregnant."

An ornament drops from the tree in the living room. Everyone looks up.

Ginny stares at her. "How do you know? Why would you say that before I could?"

"Sorry," Rain says. "It's just fairly obvious."

"Wonderful news," Pat and Michael shout.

Pierre and Ruby smile and raise their glasses in a toast. "Yes, wonderful. Kids are so amazing," Ruby says. "I can give you so much advice."

"When are you due?" asks Pierre. Finally, someone has said the right thing. He knows it and smiles.

"Thank you." Ginny looks at Matt. She fingers the ultrasound picture in her lap. "We're due early July."

She waited three months to announce and Rain steals the show. No one seemed surprised. Does she look that big already?

"Why was it obvious?" Ginny says. "That I was pregnant?"

Matt groans and makes his "here we go again" face.

"You aren't drinking," Rain says. "You've never refused wine. But last month you did. And tonight."

Ginny notices that Matt looks relieved. He must have thought Rain would mention the weight gain. Ginny knows she's a bit puffy. Every morning, she struggles with her clothes. And if Matt says, "You look great," Ginny starts to cry because she's swelling and she knows Matt is aware of it.

"Oh yes, wine," Ginny laughs. "Of course."

"And you've gained a little weight," Rain says. "Of course. Puffy in your face."

Ginny scowls and puts her fork down. Matt rolls his eyes.

"I think you look stupendous," Pat says. "Just marvellous. Glowing."

Ruby says, "You do!" and raises her glass to toast. "When I was pregnant I swelled up like a balloon."

"Dessert in the living room?" Matt says quickly and Ginny gets up and starts to clear the dishes. Matt follows, carrying plates.

"Don't listen to Rain," he whispers to Ginny when they are both in the kitchen.

"I am getting fat," Ginny says.

"First you wanted to be seen as pregnant and now you don't want to be seen as pregnant? I don't get it."

"True," Ginny says. If there's one thing she's figured out about pregnancy it's that she doesn't make any sense. Ginny has carried the dessert from the hutch in the dining room into the kitchen. She's looking at it – she has no idea what it is. Pudding? Cake? "Do you think I'm supposed to serve this in bowls?"

"Probably."

"It smells really good."

Matt bends to sniff. "Like vanilla and butterscotch."

Ginny licks the serving spoon as Matt carries the bowls to the living room. Everyone is sitting in their regular spots. There's become a certain routine to these dinner parties, as if everyone is learning a new dance. Pierre and Ruby on the sofa with Pat, Michael gets the recliner chair and Rain is on the floor. Ginny sits in the other recliner and Matt brings in a chair from the dining room for himself. Ginny has been wanting another sofa, a loveseat maybe, but Matt suggests they wait, they have to see what their finances look like after Christmas. Albert got to him with all the talk about money when they were in the city.

Ruby starts up with the local news. It's like she lives plugged-in to all the news channels. She always knows what's going on. She complains about the next town over and then talks about crime in the city and then narrows in on Parkville. Then she talks about true crime podcasts and climate change.

Michael chimes in with an article he read about what it called the crunchy alt-right pipeline.

Pat giggles.

"This is where people overly concerned about the control over their bodies follow more extreme actions in pursuit of health," Michael says. He talks about how these people will gradually move from an obsession with healthy food, to anti-vaccination, declining or spacing out childhood vaccinations, believing the false narrative that vaccinations cause autism. "People on this pipeline believe in alternative medicine with no scientific basis."

Everyone looks at Rain, she looks at the floor.

"And slowly these people," Michael says, "with their beliefs in independence and purity, slide easily into alt-right theories, blaming everything on anyone who is different from them. They move into 'back to living off the land,' into hoarding and prepping. It's a slow burn."

"Survivalists," Ruby says.

Michael and Pat nod.

The mood in the living room has changed. The neighbours look anxious. Ginny feels like everyone knows something she doesn't know; she feels like a kid again watching her parents talking. Listening. Michael's article seems to be about something they are all familiar with but Ginny's not quite sure what is being said. There are undertones to this conversation.

Ginny looks at Rain, who gulps more water, and looks at Ruby.

"You can eat healthily," Rain says, "and not be like that. This is ridiculous."

Everyone nods. Rain has broken the mood.

Michael says, "Yeah, that's true. These people, they are obsessed with having control over their lives," and everyone nods, looking uncomfortable again.

Pierre has definitely had too much wine and is partially falling asleep on the couch. He hasn't heard a word his neighbours have said.

"It's so interesting," Ruby says. "What people will get up to."

"Anything they don't understand, they view as inherently dangerous," Pat says.

"Not interesting really," Matt says, quietly. "Frightening."

Michael rambles on. Everyone nods along but no one really participates. Again, Ginny wonders what they are keeping inside. She has this feeling that she's missing something. But she doesn't know what. She feels the conversation is a bit too depressing, or real maybe, to focus on. And what does this have to do with Parkville? Or their baby? Michael moved from Ginny's pregnancy to the alt-right. He somehow missed the middle ground, the usual dinner-party conversations.

Matt is tired of this conversation. He looks over at Rain, sitting on the floor, and starts to wonder about her. She's sipping her tap water, which Matt suddenly realizes has fluoride in it – and didn't Michael just mention fluoridation and avoiding additives and government conspiracy? When Rain refused water at earlier dinner parties was that what she was doing? But, Matt thinks, Rain is drinking it now, gulping water furiously.

And then, just as suddenly as Michael started, he ends, the rehashed article is finished, and the conversation splits up. Everyone starts other topics and these topics travel throughout the room. Christmas holidays, decorations, the craft show in Parkville, carolling – supposedly that's a thing here. The tree glows in the room and the smell of spruce is warm and heady. There will be a Santa Claus parade down Main Street, Ruby says. Michael and Pat want to get a puppy, they've put an order in.

"You can order puppies?" Matt asks.

"From a breeder," Pat says. "There's a good one out on the 5th Line."

Another ornament drops from the tree and Ginny scowls at Matt, as if he was so careless placing them. It's true that he didn't bend the hook over each branch.

Rain settles back in and talks about how she needs more essential-oil bottles as she's running out. She has to order from China and doesn't know if she'll get them in time. The indoor market opened again, she says, when someone anonymously donated money to fix the heat. Rain thinks it was the mayor, she is always doing things anonymously. Rain likes her. She goes back to staring at the floor, finished with what she is saying.

Ruby and Pierre's kids both need new laptops so that's all they are getting for Christmas. "Not even stocking stuffers," Ruby says. "Laptops are so expensive. Kids are so expensive." Ruby sighs. They drove down to the city, she says, to get the laptops and Pierre got in a fender-bender. He curses the city now, holding his hand up to the ceiling in a drunken fist. Everyone laughs but Ginny looks alarmed, as if he's cursing her.

Matt thinks about his nightmares. When they aren't about locks, they are all about how expensive his kid will be – how they will afford the baby. And the house – the renovations. Clothes and food. What about another baby in the future? He asked Ginny one night if she thought they should stop these dinner parties, although at this one everyone brought something so it really didn't cost that much. Plus the parties give Ginny some purpose. Besides going to the market, shopping and fixing up the house, Matt knows Ginny doesn't have much of anything else going on – except worry and fear, of course.

Later, Matt overhears as Rain takes Ginny aside and whispers that she did have a child, a girl, when she was younger, she had to give her up for adoption, she says, because she was in the foster system and her foster parents didn't want a teenage girl and a baby. And, she says, that's always made her sad. She's always wondered where the baby went, who she lived with, what she's doing. Matt sees Ginny take Rain's hand and squeeze hard.

Matt and Michael graduate to the kitchen. Matt scoops up a handful of spruce needles and the fallen ornaments from under the tree as he passes.

"This thing sheds like mad," he says. Again, last night, more ornaments had come off and broken under the tree. Matt wonders if the branches are moving during the days and nights, adjusting, like flowers do – flowers droop and rotate, why wouldn't a tree? Or maybe there's a strong breeze in this leaky house.

Matt looks at the dirty dishes on the counter and starts making coffee. Michael is talking about their last jog, how slippery the sidewalks were, how he almost fell a few times.

"I might be getting too old to jog in winter, Matt," Michael says. "Sorry to say. I might have to wait to join you again until spring."

"No, really?" Matt grinds the espresso beans.

Michael waits until the grinder stops. "I just keep seeing myself falling, breaking something. I'm getting too nervous. I can't imagine being in our hospital these days. It's cram-packed with people. No doctors. I don't really enjoy jogging anymore because of that."

Matt nods. He's sad, of course, but maybe he can start jogging in the ravine again if he doesn't have Michael with him. No one would know. Ginny would probably rather he jogged on a wooded path instead of an icy sidewalk anyway, even if she knew about Michael saying there are dead animals down there. No one wants a new father to have a broken hip. There's more traction in the woods.

Matt makes three espressos: one for Pat, one for Michael and one for Ruby. The kitchen feels chilly after the living room full of people. Matt himself can't drink anything caffeinated after about 4:00 p.m. Maybe he is getting old too, he thinks. He and Michael carry the small cups into the living room. And then it hits him, something was wrong in the kitchen. Not just the chill, the cold air. Something else. He can't put his finger on it. Michael is following behind Matt with the tiny cups and Matt comes to a sudden stop and they both almost spill all the espressos. Michael bumps into Matt and they juggle the cups carefully.

"What's up? I almost spilled."

"Nothing, I . . ." Matt can't figure it out. He thinks hard. Stands still. Smells the coffee, the tree, the beetloaf garlic smell. He looks toward the living room, the tree lights glowing peacefully. He sees a car pass on the dark street outside, the curtains are open and the window is opaque. Something was off in the kitchen. The small, thin curtains were shut and the constantly open patio doors were too.

He gives everyone their espressos and sits again on his dining chair in the living room. Ginny looks at him. "Everything okay?" she asks.

"Yeah, fine," Matt says. But then he gets up again and rushes back into the kitchen. Ginny follows him.

"What's up, Matt?"

"Something's different in here. What's different?" Matt gazes all over the kitchen, looks at the stainless-steel appliances and the countertops, looks at the espresso machine and the leftovers, and then he sees it at the same time as Ginny.

The plates that Ginny and Matt had cleared from the dining room are still there, on the counter, but this time they are stacked whereas before they were side by side because on every plate (except Rain's, which is smeared with red sauce) there were little bones.

And now, every tiny bone of every tiny hen has been stacked in a pile on the counter. The plates are empty but on one side of the kitchen counter, beside the pile, spelled out with the rest of the bones, is the word "LEAVE."

Matt points. Ginny stands there, confused. Her mouth open.

"Leave this house?" he asks.

"No," Ginny says. "What's going on?"

CHAPTER 15

Later that night as they lie side by side in bed thinking about the tiny bones spelling out the word, Ginny turns toward Matt. "How?"

She's kept the light in the hallway on, too nervous now about the dark. Matt can see her face, he studies her lovely cheeks and her wide eyes, her soft ginger hair.

"There's got to be a reasonable explanation," Matt says, but he's not able to think of anything. They didn't tell the dinner-party guests about the hen bones. It was obvious to both of them that they'd scare them too much – first Charles staring in the patio doors, and the break-in where nothing was stolen but all the lights were on, and then this, the Cornish hen bones. The house feels haunted in some strange ridiculous way. And when everyone knows about the satellite image of the dead person too, well that just piles fear on top of more fear.

⊗

Earlier, when Ginny suggested a mid-January dinner party, no one seemed as excited as they usually did. Ginny thought it was from their scary house, but Matt thought it was because Ginny had said everyone could bring something again – he thinks they enjoy being fed more than contributing. But Ginny wonders if the neighbours are sensing all this bizarre stuff, if they are feeling uncomfortable here. Or maybe it's the neighbours who are doing things?

"Maybe one of our guests took the bones and put them like that. Maybe it was a joke," Matt says.

"No one went into the kitchen but you and Michael. You and I cleared the dinner plates from the dining-room table and then got the dessert. And what kind of a joke is that?"

"Didn't Rain disappear for a while?"

"She went upstairs to use the washroom. She didn't go through the kitchen."

In bed in the dim light Matt reaches out and touches Ginny's hair. She startles and slaps him by accident. He flinches.

"Sorry," she says.

She's so tense. She hasn't slept in so long. Neither has Matt. They both toss most nights as the house adjusts, creaks and cracks and thumps around them. When Ginny finally sleeps for an hour or so, the dark figure comes. Lately he's been laughing. Like the man in the alley in the city. Laughing at her. And she's so tired she can't tell if he's really there or in her dreams. Ginny always wakes wanting to reach out to Matt but she knows he thinks she's unhinged and maybe a bit ridiculous, so she lies there alone, her body twitching with fear, her hands crossed over her chest.

"Leave this house?" Ginny asks. "What if we did?"

Matt sighs.

⊗

Every day for a week Ginny thinks about the bones. She can't stop thinking about them. "Leave."

"I'm sure," Matt says, finally, "it must have been Pierre. Who else?"

"Why?" Ginny asks again and again. "Ask him why?"

"Maybe he was spelling 'love' but he was drunk?"

But Matt doesn't want to ask Pierre because he knows what the answer will be, and he soon forgets. There are other things on his mind.

It's a week before Christmas. Matt is off work now and has been rushing around buying gifts, mailing extra packages to their families, wrapping. He's disappointed at the choices he has in Parkville, things seem to be sold out or not available. Not like the city where there's an excess of things. Matt doesn't care, really, but he would like to get Ginny something special. He's been to all the baby stores in town but nothing unique is jumping out at him.

Ginny has been baking and eating what she's baked. Every day there is a different cookie, a loaf, a bar, on the kitchen counter. Her mood is up and down most days. Sad one day, happy the next. Matt blames the pregnancy. Or the cookies. Too much sugar. Or he blames not being around her family (although, Matt does know that Ginny is usually more depressed being around their families). But she does seem to be missing them more this year. Moving. Hormones. Nesting. She talks on the phone to Christine almost every day. Walking around the house holding the phone out, her earbuds on. They swap body stories – who is farting the most, who is swelling, whose sciatica is acting up, what the scale says. Matt will be in his office and hear nothing in the house and then suddenly laughter coming from the kitchen or the master bedroom or the living room. These sounds make him happy and slightly relieve him of his stress. He still has worries, lots of them, but hearing Ginny laugh is good. It's a normal sound. A sound she used to make frequently – laughter – before the attack in the city, before this house. A comfortable sound. This is the sound he married, this is the life he wanted. Before the other sounds start at night, the bad sounds, Matt begins again to hold his wife to him, touches her body, marvels at her beauty, at what she's doing to create their child, the way her body is building and forming. He's astonished.

If only they can have a good first Christmas in their own house. Things will get better in the new year, Matt thinks. He's sure of it. The house will settle around them, Ginny will calm, they will have the baby, they will figure it all out, they will be the family they want to be. That's all he can hope for.

"I'm going to pick up the turkey," Matt says and heads off in the car to the butcher shop.

Ginny decides to walk downtown and see if she can find a few gifts for Matt. She passes Michael and Pat's house and Pat is at the front window. He waves. Ginny waves back, but watches her step as there is black ice under the thin layer of snow. She's watching for dog crap too as the people in this town don't often pick that up, obviously. Everything these days is a potential threat – ice, dog shit, not paying attention to where you're walking and tripping and slipping. Ginny finds that being pregnant is a bit like carrying around a small bomb, you never know what'll make it go off. Everything makes her slightly nervous. Matt always says, "Parenthood is about guilt, worries, fear, there's danger around every corner." And then he quotes someone like Oscar Wilde: "Children begin by loving their parents; as they grow older they judge them; sometimes they forgive them." Something like that.

Head down, Ginny shuffles like a penguin to the town, past the convenience store on the corner, past the ice cream shop, pink and blue signage saying "Hot Enough For You?" – closed up for winter – past the bookstore that doubles as a pet store and is filled with aquariums, glowing with blue light, past an empty storefront for lease, and the one supposedly good restaurant, O'Rileys, and the odds and ends store that sells everything you need for kitchens and bathrooms, and straight past Truth and Beauty, stopping to wave in at Michael, who is standing looking out the front window with a strange expression on his face.

Ginny makes her way to the Running Store. She is surprised there is a running store in Parkville, but this gives her hope for other more interesting stores in the future. Things come and go so frequently she often doesn't know what she'll find from one week to the next. People are moving here from the city, like they did, so she assumes Parkville has to change in order to keep up with flow. Ginny enters the store and the bell above the door startles her. Everything startles her. There is one athletic-looking woman browsing the running shoes and a saleswoman behind the counter.

Ginny says, "Hello," and they both wave at her. She starts to look around.

The saleswoman and the other woman are in the middle of a conversation, which obviously stopped when Ginny came in. They resume and Ginny listens.

"He was holed up in the house for a bit with all kinds of things. And a gun," the shopper says, flipping through a rack of brightly coloured jogging bras.

"Oh god, what did she do?" the woman behind the counter asks. She's boxing something up and disappears occasionally below the counter, bending to the ground.

"Left him. Wouldn't you?" the shopper says, holding up a pink sports bra and studying it. "But then he wanted the kid."

"So scary," the saleswoman says. "What was he doing with a gun? What was happening?"

"Nothing. He was just paranoid. On the computer too much, I think. That's the thing about these guys. It's like a cult. A cult of terror. They want control. They get to each other on the internet and they make each other anxious and angry and everyone suffers," the shopper says. "Poor kid."

"Did she get to keep her son?"

"I don't know the end of the story. I just heard about it from Beth. I think they ended up back together and then they moved."

"With their kid? That's messed up."

The shopper nods her head. "Do you remember what they were like in high school? They were pretty normal, I thought. He was on the volleyball team. She was a cheerleader."

Then the saleswoman sees Ginny paused at the shoes and calls out, "Can I help you?"

Ginny has been deep in their conversation and is startled out of her thoughts. She shakes her head at the saleswoman, who smiles and goes on talking to the other shopper. Ginny thinks about her own high school friends. She thinks about her life in the city.

Lately she's realized that even if she's having trouble settling in this town, she won't ever be able to go back to the city. She's looked at the prices of houses in the city now. They've gone up considerably. Ridiculously. Even the house they bought here is probably worth a hundred thousand more than what they paid for it. Only four months ago. But that's not enough money to buy in the city. Ginny and Matt could never afford a house in the city anymore. They can never go back.

"Are you interested in shoes with spikes?" The saleswoman is standing right next to Ginny now and startles her. She jumps.

"Sorry, no, sorry." Ginny doesn't remember why she went into the store and so she rushes out and onto the sidewalk. She almost slips on the ice. Reaching out to steady herself, she grabs hold of a passing arm. The owner of the arm screams and Ginny lets go quickly and looks straight into the eyes of Marina who was shuffling past the store minding her own business when Ginny grabbed her.

"Oh, I'm so sorry."

Marina looks at Ginny. "You scared me." She stops walking. "Are you okay?" Marina asks.

Ginny is almost crying. Is she okay? Damn hormones. She rubs her belly. She can't help it. Marina notices and nods toward Ginny's flat stomach.

"Are you having a baby?"

"Yes. I'm just a bit . . ." Sad? Pregnant? Confused? Discombobulated? "Sorry."

Marina nods again. They look at each other.

"I have to sit down." Ginny walks over to a bench and wipes off the snow. There are cigarette butts under the bench and some garbage. Where is that idyllic little town she thought they were moving to? She thought they were moving to Stars Hollow but somehow they ended up in Amityville. She sighs.

Marina walks over and sits down. "Congratulations?"

"I'm sorry. I'm just confused. Tired, hormonal, you know."

"Sure," Marina says.

The two women sit beside each other. People pass on the street, a Christmas song is playing somewhere, it echoes out into the cold afternoon.

Marina says nothing. She isn't wearing mittens. She looks sad and tired. Ginny wants to ask her how she is, but suddenly feels like she shouldn't intrude. Just because she's living in the old woman's house doesn't mean they are friends.

"Aren't you cold?" Ginny asks.

Marina smiles and nods. "I have to get on with my shopping," she says. She's so stiff getting up but she manages it and starts to walk off. "Charles needs his things."

"I'm glad you found him," Ginny says.

Marina stops. "Found who?"

"Charles. You were looking for him on Halloween." Ginny pauses.

"I wish," Marina grumbles. "Sometimes I wish I lost him," Marina says and continues walking on, leaving Ginny on her bench.

Ginny stares at Marina, who turns back and walks to the corner toward the pharmacy. She disappears inside. And Ginny stands, confused, and begins to walk home. Halfway back, her head down, waddling carefully, thinking about Marina, past the row of churches, past the schoolyard, Ginny suddenly remembers she has no present for Matt. She was going to get him spikes for his running shoes so he could run in the snow and ice.

And then she sees someone up ahead, around the corner. That figure, her figure, that man. Dressed all in black. He's moving quickly toward her. She spins around, turns back to town, wanting to get away, but then she takes a deep breath and rotates back, she blinks her eyes rapidly – if she blinks will he be gone? Is he real or just a figment of her imagination like Matt thinks? The closer he gets the more she's trying hard not to scream. But suddenly he passes her, quite close. Her heart feels like it stops for a minute. She tries to get a look at his face. She wants to reach out and touch him but is too afraid. But it's as if there's nothing there, inside his hoodie it is dark, he is like a shadow. How can that be? Ginny can't even see the whites of his eyes. She can't see his teeth, the shape of his face. She sees nothing. And then he's gone. Is it a trick of the setting sun, of the gathering dusk?

All the way home she's shaking. She wants to scream. Instead, she swallows the force, swallows the sound, keeps it all inside, until her lungs ache, until she's about to burst.

And then her breath comes out in one huge whoosh.

Late at night Ginny leaves the bedroom. She heard something. It sounded like the patio door in the kitchen, sliding open. Waking Matt is not an option anymore. Too many nights she's woken him. It will cause a scene. He thinks she's crazy anyway. And she's starting to wonder if he's right.

In the hallway she sees and feels the open window. Again. She closes it and tiptoes down the stairs to the hallway and then she enters the kitchen.

The patio doors are open. Her feet are wet, there are puddles on the floor. The door to the basement is open. The light is on in the basement. Ginny turns and runs as fast as she can up the stairs and into their bedroom. "Matt," she whispers strongly, shaking him. "There's someone in the house."

"Oh my god, Ginny. You can't be serious!" Matt pulls his pillow over his face.

When the police finally come, an hour later, they see footprints in the snow leading to the overhang and up onto the roof and straight to the hallway window. The footprints then continue in the opposite direction out the patio door and down into the ravine. When Ginny called the police they said they would come in the morning and Matt listened to Ginny argue and scream. She screamed so loud and argued so forcefully that the police came right away. Matt worries that she's broken now as she sits, slumped, in the kitchen. Matt takes a hammer and a board from the basement and pounds it into the window in the hallway trying to keep the window shut. The police file a report and leave. Nothing was stolen, they say. Just like the last time. Just kids.

"Ginny's sanity," Matt wants to shout. "Ginny's sanity was stolen."

The next morning Matt calls a company to secure the patio door and replace the window. They will be there after Christmas. In the meantime, Ginny and Matt decide to put an alarm system in the house. The police tell them that's a good idea. And Matt will get rid of the shed below the window today. It makes it too convenient to get into the broken hall window. Ginny begins to discuss moving back into the city, staying at one of their parents' for Christmas and then looking for an apartment after Christmas. When she sees Matt's face fall, when she sees that he looks like he's going to cry, and she knows they could never afford the city now, she stops talking about it. "But one more thing happens," Ginny says, "and I'm getting out."

"How do we do that, Ginny? Sell a cursed house? And where will we live then? The city? Weren't you attacked in the city? Isn't the city too expensive?"

Ginny stops talking and looks at Matt. She doesn't know what to say. Her mind moves in circles. She shrugs.

Matt thinks about the ravine. Maybe it is the gate? Should he get rid of it? He says nothing to Ginny but he wonders if a gate lock would be enough to deter someone from getting in. But if someone wants in, they want in. Or out. If someone is in, they also want out.

JANUARY

CHAPTER 16

After Christmas, the alarm system is installed.

"We should have done this after we came back from the city that first time," Ginny says, even though she can't get used to it. She sets it off every couple of days by accident. It makes her extremely nervous. She runs from the front door, leaving it wide open, down the hall toward the alarm box and then panics that she won't remember the numbers – will she forget the hashtag or the "open" button? The front door remains open and sometimes snow blows in. Definitely cold air. The heat in the house escapes and Ginny dreams of the beeping noise.

Until the window and door installer comes, the upstairs hallway window mocks her every time she climbs the stairs. Matt has left the hammered board up for now. The installer is coming in a week. But at least the shed roof outside the window is gone now and that gives her some relief. Over Christmas Matt tore it down. Using a hammer and crowbar he smashed into it furiously. Glad to see it go. It amazes Ginny that, in the small town of Parkville, they are always on edge. It amazes her that a man holding a knife who punches her in the city seems to be the least of her worries now. Here, on a quiet street where they know their neighbours and everyone is looking out for each other, she's now scared all the time.

The police assumed it was a teenager who broke in again. Like the first time. Someone coming in the window and going through the house. They think it was someone who came up from the ravine. There have been many complaints in the last year about kids hanging out down there, about things missing in the backyards that border the ravine. The police questioned Ruby and Pierre's kids and Elton said he'd heard someone out back the night it happened. Erin, his older sister, was supposedly a bit nervous to talk to the police. Matt told Ginny he has smelled pot coming from their backyard lately so he assumes Erin has been smoking and thought the police were coming after her. She's only fifteen. He says he finds it amazing that Ruby thinks she has such control over her kids. It almost makes Matt laugh but then Ginny can see a change as he starts to worry about their own future kid and what he would do about a situation like this. Ginny wonders if she should tell Ruby? Would they want Ruby to tell them if it was their kid?

Ginny thinks it wasn't kids. This wasn't a prank. This was something else.

⊗

Matt's online classes are back in session, and conversation has almost died between Ginny and Matt now. They are both tiptoeing around each other.

Matt doesn't tell Ginny about the second satellite image. The one he saw last week. He assumes it was another computer glitch. He was checking Google Maps again, he's been checking it about once a week, and the other night the image they saw before they moved in had come back. Briefly. For only a few seconds, not even enough time to screenshot it. It startled him seeing it again. He wasn't prepared. What are the chances he would see another glitch?

Matt stared at it, without blinking, until it disappeared. Same image. A body, white, he now thinks it may have had clothes on, but he isn't sure because it was so blurry – lying on the ground beside the basement hatch, just in front of the old roof structure, on its stomach. Arms and legs skewed. Light spilling out of the patio doors, the whiteness of the body glowing. A small touch of red on the side of the stomach. A grey day. The hatch to the basement closed. He made sure it was a human body, not a prop or a doll. He looked for anything that would tell him what was happening. And then the image vanished. Matt was startled at first, the computer flashed, the image disappeared, back to a winter day. But then he felt reassured. This wasn't his imagination. It did happen.

He wishes he could tell Ginny.

Their marriage has become one of omission these days. He omits telling her anything that will scare her, he is protecting her. He knows she omits telling him when she is scared, he knows she doesn't want to worry him, that he thinks she's lost it, especially after her screaming fit before Christmas to the police. Matt feels as if they are balancing on a precipice, just on the edge – and any minute either one of them could fall. Ginny keeps everything bottled inside now, which has caused issues. He's noticed her hair is thinner, her neck is blotchy and red with rash. Hives. Stress hives. He feels she has no real friends, no real confidants, and she has told him that her family seems to have forgotten her since they moved.

Matt worries that Ginny should go back on her anti-anxiety medication. It's obvious that going off of it has really messed with her confidence and mental health. She keeps seeing things, and as he watches her scratching her neck, he thinks about ways to broach the subject. He knows how worried she is.

She tosses beside him in bed.

Matt and Ginny both thought that, by moving out of the city, they would become tighter, closer, become one. Not tiptoe around each other like they are now. By not having a huge mortgage in the city they would concentrate on family and on each other. But, instead, they have other concerns – not only the crimes that surround them and the ridiculously creepy house – but the cost of the renovations that they are looking at now. Matt sat down with a contractor over the holidays and the price he was quoted for what

Michelle Berry

they wanted was more terrifying than living here now with people creeping through the hallway window. And the thing Matt didn't realize about small-town living is that everyone knows everyone else, so when one contractor quotes you a crazy amount to fix your house, then everyone else does too. They all raise or lower their prices to match each other, give or take a few hundred dollars or a promise of finishing earlier. So the renovations end up costing more than they would in the city. He wonders if they all get on their phones at night and call each other. They are all booked up too. For months, years even. One contractor said he couldn't start work on their place for two years. Matt is also sure they give him a higher quote because he wasn't born here. They know he's moved in from the city and so they think he has money. But he doesn't. That's why he moved here.

Pat and Michael have been here for years but tell Matt that it doesn't matter. Matt has gone over to ask them who they would recommend for the work.

"You can live here for ninety years," Michael says, "and you'll still be from away, you'll still be from the city. Even if you aren't from the city."

"Unless your great-great-great-grandfather was born here you'll never be part of Parkville," Pat says. "And there's even a different price for people like us who have moved away for a bit and then come back to the town. We're the deserters who have come to our senses and seen the light."

They are right. He and Ginny will never fit in, no matter what they do. They will never belong. And right now they don't even seem to belong to each other. Not in the way they used to. Neither one of them starts a conversation, both wait for the other to speak. And Ginny seems so raw that he wonders if the baby will come out screaming and red with anger.

⊗

They are eating dinner in the kitchen.

During Christmas they went to Ikea, into the bargain section, and found a wooden kitchen island and two mismatched stools. "What a find!" Matt shouted. Ginny rolled her eyes. But they brought it home. Now they eat most of their meals on the island in the kitchen, saving the dining room for the neighbourhood dinners. They also bought thicker, bigger curtains for the patio sliding doors. Black ones. Now Ginny is looking at them, trying to see through them into the backyard, but she can't. They are velvety. She can't even see through them when the spotlight is on in the back. They are definitely not the look she was hoping for but they were the only curtains that completely covered the patio doors. Ginny worries every morning now when she opens them. Will there be someone there – Charles? – looking straight back at her? Tapping on the glass? Beckoning her? She shivers.

Every time Matt opens the patio doors the curtains get stuck in the sliding glass. He studies them now. He complains about it to her every day.

"I wonder about the decisions we have made, Matt," Ginny says, playing with her noodles. Her head is ducked down, she won't look at him. "Wasn't moving out of the city supposed to make things different? I can't imagine what it'll be like living here with a small child. I think we'll put our baby down for a nap and then the alarm will trigger and the baby will wake. I am convinced we'll have a child who will have insomnia."

"Things will get better," Matt says. "I'm sure of it." He has cut up his noodles and is shovelling them into his mouth. His never-ending optimism is getting hard to pull off. She can tell he's tired.

"What more can we do to stop all of this?" Ginny asks. "Surely we can do something."

"We took all the advice the police gave us, Ginny. We opened a file on the break-in even if the cops didn't call it a break-in. And we now have a direct line with a file number to give to the police if it happens again. The cops seemed interested in this case, perhaps because it was something new in a very dull town?"

They are sitting on their stools and both of their brains are moving a mile a minute. Ginny can feel the movement from Matt, the way he tenses his shoulders and stares vacantly around. They just have nothing much to say to each other right now. Ginny feels indigestion rising up her throat. She swallows it down. She thinks back to New Year's Eve when, glass of sparkling apple cider in hand, she silently swore to herself that she would stop catastrophizing and how that resolution has already been broken many times. It was broken the minute after she thought it. Maybe, she thinks, maybe she'll take up knitting instead?

Matt always thinks he doesn't want to have another dinner party but then another one gets planned and here he is again. And he always thinks he's tired or too worried about things and doesn't want to sit still anymore after he has taught all day, and then the party night comes and he enjoys it. Ginny, however, has told him she's starting to get uncomfortable sitting all night with her growing belly and she complains that there isn't much she can eat anymore. The smell of certain foods makes her feel nauseous so she says it's hard to cook. Matt has taken over some of the cooking and planning. Lately Ginny has been silent all day and night and only wants to watch TV before bed. She says she's tired and can't focus. Each day she seems to sink more into herself, to disappear. Matt hopes the company will pull her out of herself.

Ruby offered to bring all the food for this dinner party but Matt refused.

"Just bring the wine," he said. "And I'll get Michael and Pat to bring the dessert. We'll be totally fine and that will be a real help."

Ruby agreed. "How many bottles?" she asked. "Ten?"

Matt nodded slowly, and then closed his mouth.

So when the guests start to arrive Rain is a bit put out that no one asked her to bring anything.

"I could have brought the main course." She pouts. "Or at least the appetizers again. I could have tried bread. I explained to Ginny that I couldn't understand the sourdough starter instructions. But there are other types of bread, right? I don't really eat bread. Carbs. But I'm great at making vegan, gluten-free, organic carrot loaf. You can eat it for dessert or for dinner. It has no sugar."

Matt stares at Rain. He clears his throat. "No, no, seriously, it doesn't seem right to make you bring something only you can eat," Matt says. "I mean –"

"No, I get it. My stuff is usually so unusual. It does put people off."

"No, really, it's great. I just meant –"

Rain turns from Matt and walks into the house. "I smell the beetloaf," she says, happily. "I love that beetloaf."

Matt takes her coat and hangs it in the closet under the stairs. He notices some dirt on the floor of the closet, a little pile of it, and wonders how that got there. They put their boots and shoes in the front hallway, not in here. Matt scratches his head and follows Rain into the kitchen where Ginny is leaning at the island and holding her breath, obviously trying not to inhale the beetloaf and its huge amount of garlic. She's leaning on the island slightly, clutching her side like she's going to vomit. Matt gives her a quizzical look but she straightens up when Rain comes into the room.

"You okay?"

"Yes, of course. Hi, Rain," Ginny says.

"You're getting huge," Rain says, admiringly. "You look great."

Ginny smiles and stands straight. "Thanks." She pats her stomach. "Too bad about the nausea. It comes and goes," she says. Matt touches her.

Michael and Pat ring the doorbell and come in full of cold air. They are bickering about the store, about a silver lamp, Pat wants to polish it but Michael says it looks better tarnished. Pat smacks

Michael's arm and Michael laughs. They talk and snitch the cheese and crackers. Everyone is waiting for Ruby and Pierre and the wine.

And then Ruby and Pierre knock and rush in carrying wine boxes. They don't wait for anyone to open the door for them, but turn the knob and barge right in – not even taking off their boots or coats (Ginny cringes at her floor and Ruby sees her). They both run back into the hall and pull off their boots. They immediately start talking rapidly about some damage that was done to a few stores downtown last night, about graffiti and broken glass and theft. Groups of men, they say, all moving together.

"That's what Donna says," Ruby comments. "She says they were all together, lots of them."

"Who's Donna?"

Pierre says, "Owns Dreams and Coffee," and then he goes on about teenagers and wonders if it's teenagers, not men. Everyone listens carefully and Michael and Pat exclaim at the right places and say nothing happened to their store, thankfully, and Rain opens her eyes wider and gasps at times.

Matt feels as if he couldn't care less. He cares about the stores, the store owners, their property, but he doesn't really care, like you would if it was something that personally affected you. You'd really care then. The only thing he really cares about right now is Ginny's mental health. And he looks at her and sees the light in her eyes dull, he sees her mouth sag, her hand twitch.

But then, as always, the conversation moves quickly away from downtown and focuses suddenly on Pierre and Ruby's kids, on Pierre's job – what does he do again? – on Ruby's shopping trips and on interrupting Rain during her spiel about organic cauliflower at the market and how ridiculously expensive it is. Michael begins discussing the weather and tells Pat he wants to go to Bermuda again this year.

Ginny holds a blue pot holder and wanders around aimlessly, as though she doesn't know what to do with it. Matt watches as she moves to the dishwasher and puts the pot holder inside.

"Let's go have a glass of wine in the living room," Matt says, looking at the two big boxes of bottles Ruby and Pierre brought.

Matt pours the wine and they sit in the living room with the crackers and cheese. Ginny starts stuffing them in her mouth as she listens to Ruby and Pierre ramble on.

More news about the town, about a new bylaw that was just passed, and about winter fishing spots and the breakfast club at the high school.

"They are running out of banana bread," Ruby exclaims.

Today Matt spent two hours listening to all the gossip about the town from the window installer. Who was having an affair, which kid was busted for drugs, where the garbage from the corner store was really going, how the streetlight on the corner of Javis and King shuts down at 4:00 a.m. and just doesn't work again until 6:00 a.m. and no one knows why. Now he has to listen to Ruby and Pierre ramble on about their boring lives. Matt sighs. He wishes he had a scotch instead of all this wine. Right now he'd like to down a glass or two of scotch, get drunk quickly.

⊗

Ginny bites hard into her cracker and bites her cheek where the stitches were. "Ouch."

"Are you okay, Ginny?" Michael asks.

Ruby is waving her hands in the air as she speaks and wiggling her bum on the couch. It looks a bit like she has to pee. Ginny tastes blood on her tongue. She studies Ruby's waving hands and moving bum.

"More wine?" Matt says and everyone looks at him and nods. "Ruby and Pierre brought a lot of it."

Ginny can't wait to stop being pregnant.

Rain says, "I'd like more water if you're getting up."

Matt pours more wine for the people who are drinking.

Ginny has a super-strong sense of smell now and suddenly notices that her dinner is burning.

"Come help me," she says as she rushes to the kitchen. Everyone sits in the living room and stares at each other. Then they realize they are letting Ginny do everything so they all get up to help. Carrying dishes into the dining room, lighting candles, Matt puts on some music, and soon they are sitting together at the table and digging in. Rain has her beetloaf right beside her and is shovelling it on her plate. Everyone else is eating steak and asparagus and couscous with mushrooms. Everyone is silent for a minute while they chew and swallow, while they sip their drinks.

There is a sudden noise from upstairs, a whooshing noise, a thump, a rattle. And then it's gone.

Everyone looks up at the ceiling and then out the back windows at the dark backyard. They can see nothing, just their reflections in the glass, the fire from the living room, the dimmed lights in the chandelier. They are all looking back at themselves, a little confused. Faces flushed. Ginny jumps up and runs into the kitchen and immediately looks out the curtains on the back patio doors. She checks the lock and stares down the dark grass at the gate. That's when she sees him, the figure, running through their yard and down into the ravine. When she rushes back into the dining room in a panic everyone stares at her, and she feels like she's the intruder, she feels like she's the one sprinting through the backyard.

"Are you okay?" Rain says, giggling nervously.

No one else saw him.

CHAPTER 17

The day after the dinner party, the police knock on the front door. Matt answers. Ginny is unloading the dishwasher, and her gaze keeps floating to the backyard. She can hear them talking to Matt down the hall. They step into the hallway and shut the front door. Matt's quiet voice mumbles, the police say "teenagers" and "playing in the ravine." They keep their voices down.

Ginny uses her tongue to poke the canker sore that has formed in her cheek where she bit the skin last night, just on top of the scar from the attack in the alley.

She sighs and dries her hands and walks to the front door. She catches the tail end of the officer's question: ". . . have you lived here?"

Matt says, "Four and a half months."

Ginny introduces herself. The two men are large and beefy. They stand at the door with their big boots on.

"We're just checking around the neighbourhood and we've heard you've had some problems?"

"Some problems? That's an understatement," Ginny says.

Matt looks at her.

"So you wouldn't have known the previous owners then, the

Smythes? Were there problems that you knew of when you bought the house?"

"No, we met them when we closed," Ginny says, "but no, we don't know them. It was a really fast deal. They didn't say anything to us. They had just put the house up for sale and we scooped it up. We've seen them around though. In Parkville."

And then, for some reason, Ginny opens up and starts to tell the police everything. "We've seen Charles in our backyard, and at the market he shouted at me. And we've had the two break-ins you know about. And we hear noises all night. And then there was the satellite image, before we even moved, an image of a dead body in the backyard."

"Well not –" Matt tries to cut her off, but Ginny continues.

"And the locks on the doors everywhere here. So many locks. And the window was always open before we fixed it, always, no matter how many times we shut it. And there were the wet footprints, snowy ones, on the kitchen floor. And a man in my bed, lights on in the house, the figure I keep seeing." Ginny starts to cry. When she's done she catches her breath and sits down on the staircase.

Matt and the police officers look at her. Matt reaches out a hand and pats Ginny on the top of her head.

"There's no figure," he says to the police. "That's just Ginny's nightmare." He looks at the police and shrugs. The police look at each other and then at Ginny again.

"You okay?" one cop asks.

"Well, that's all interesting," the other officer says. "Sounds like a crazy house." He's writing notes in his pad. Probably writing, "Insane woman. Look into her."

The first officer tries not to smile. He clears his throat and looks at his phone. "Yes, we do have your file for the complaints about the two break-ins and about the window. That's why we're here. We think it was kids from the ravine. Not sure what you mean about a satellite image and a dead body and the figure? Would you like to expand on that?"

Ginny shrugs while Matt takes the cops through what they saw. He tones it all down, of course, doesn't really talk about the locks or the sounds in the house, and then the cops use their phones to look up the satellite image and they see nothing, of course, just the snowy image, no body on the ground. Ginny sighs.

The cops look around a bit, wander around the living room. "I see you've put in an alarm system. Any more break-ins since the kitchen one?" one officer asks.

"We had a new window installed where they were getting in," Matt says. "And the back patio doors are finally fixed."

"Of course not," Ginny mumbles from the stairs. She starts to cry again, she can't help herself. "We would have called you if we had had another break-in."

The cop nods and then he, too, pats her head like she's a dog. Ginny knows the police don't believe her. Hysterical woman. They are smiling in a demeaning way and are suddenly exceedingly polite. She can't stand it. It's like they are talking to a child. Which makes her act like a child, of course. Ginny knows she's close to the edge, she's losing control. She looks up at Matt and he looks embarrassed. He's been through all of this with her, all the things Ginny just mentioned to the cops, and yet he is pretending everything is fine. Ginny doesn't know what's right anymore. Is she crazy?

"We've heard Charles Smythe didn't want to move," one of the officers says. He's ignoring everything Ginny just blurted out. "His wife made him. So that could make him angry, I guess?"

"Yes," Matt says.

The officers and Matt nod their heads. Some sort of silent agreement that Ginny can't understand.

"We'll keep our ears open for any news about those teenagers breaking in," the cop says.

Ginny stares at her hands. She can't stop them from shaking. She can't help pulling at her hair slightly. Matt is watching her. The cops are watching her. The house is deathly silent around her.

"It's okay, it's okay, it's okay," Ginny whispers to herself. But it's not. Nothing is okay.

⊗

Two days later the same two police officers come back to their house. Matt is upstairs teaching and Ginny is in the living room trying to knit. She fulfilled one New Year's resolution and took it up recently, but she can't get the hang of it. She tends to make these long rectangular pieces that slowly become wavy, no straight lines. But it calms her. It gives her hands something to do. She answers the door.

"Ah, a scarf," one cop says.

"For a cat?" The other laughs. "It's so small." They both smile.

"Do you mind," the first cop says, "if we take a look inside your house?"

Ginny stares at him. Why would they need to look around her house? She looks at her knitting. He's right, it does look like a very uneven cat scarf. If she makes it a little longer she could use it to strangle him.

"We talked to some of your neighbours the other day," he says, "and they confirmed that things were stolen from this neighbourhood last year. If these kids are getting inside all these houses we thought we'd look around to make sure there isn't anything we are missing."

Ginny nods and steps back and watches the two men in their large boots start to tromp all over her house, leaving wet streaks. Ginny sighs loudly. Why can't they take their boots off? Is it a safety hazard to be a cop in someone's house without your boots on? They search the main floor, the kitchen, and go upstairs to Matt's office (waving at his students on the screen of his computer – who think the whole thing is fantastic) and then through the master bedroom, the soon-to-be baby's room, the bathroom and up to the attic. Ginny follows them down from the attic and lets them into the basement. She won't go down there. She waits in the kitchen.

When they come up, she mentions the locks, the sealed-up hatch, the sounds that come out of the basement. Then she walks with them to the front door.

"What do you think?"

"All looks good," one cop says.

Ginny groans, more to herself than to them. "And the satellite image?" she asks, aggressively. "What about that?"

The cops look confused. They've forgotten about that. "I'm sure you just imagined that," one says, when he remembers what she is talking about.

"And the figure I keep seeing?" Ginny is about to start listing everything again. Why won't anyone listen to her? But the cop interrupts. He holds his hand up to stop her. He looks at his notes.

"Your husband says that's your imagination, from your nightmares," he says. "Maybe just stress?"

"No," she says, almost to herself. "Everything about this place is so suspicious. It's like it's haunted."

The cops laugh again and then immediately become sullen when they realize she's not joking.

"Maybe," the second says, "maybe it's just the baby hormones." He looks down at Ginny's stomach. "When my wife was pregnant she was suspicious of everything too."

"Or maybe the house is really possessed," the other cop says through a chuckle.

Ginny glares at them both.

"You have no idea," she hisses.

Matt comes down the stairs then and the three men turn from her and talk and compare notes. They update Matt on everything. Everyone stops talking to Ginny. Even Matt doesn't turn her way as he talks. She's been erased from the all-male conference. Ginny feels ill. She sinks down on the staircase again, like she did the other day when they came, and she puts her chin in her hands and holds her head up. If she didn't hold her head this way she is sure it would fall off. In fact, she's waiting for her head to spin in circles. Everything feels so tentative and fragile. One wrong move and Ginny will burst. Half of her wants to just go back into the living room and continue making cat scarves. Enough cat scarves to strangle everyone. The other half of her wants to stand up and punch the cops.

Matt gives her the side-eye and she realizes she has been groaning quietly, mumbling to herself. The cops leave, both of them looking at Ginny as if she has horns coming out of her head.

"What the fuck?" Matt says, loudly, when they are gone. "What's wrong with you? They're going to think you're crazy." Ginny looks up at him from the stairs. "What if they tell social services you're a freak and take our kid away from us? Have you thought about that?"

She has no idea what to say. It's as if she's physically sick and doesn't have a doctor. There's no one who will take care of her. Not Matt, not her friends, not her mother or sister or father. No one.

"This house," she whispers. "This house."

Matt storms past her and goes back up the stairs to his office. "You have to get a hold of yourself, Ginny," he says when he reaches the top. "You need help." He shuts the door quietly and disappears inside.

Yes, Ginny thinks. For once, he might be right. Maybe she does need help. Ginny kind of wishes he hadn't shut the office door quietly. She wishes he had slammed it so hard it made her jump. That would have been impactful.

FEBRUARY

CHAPTER 18

Ginny is wearing maternity pants and baggy sweaters. She can feel the baby hiccup and move, kick and roll a bit. Or at least she thinks she can feel these things – or maybe the feelings are just more indigestion. No one explains to you what having a baby will feel like. No one tells you anything useful. Just books and advice on what not to do. Nothing on what will be done to you – your hormones, the shape of your body, your feelings and emotions. What food tastes like, the rashes on your skin, the way your bones shift, the way your hair dries out or becomes more silky or starts to curl – either way, every day something is different. The whole pregnancy thing is knocking Ginny for a loop; she has no idea what's real and what's imagined, she can't imagine the baby inside her at all, no matter how many pictures and diagrams she looks at. No matter how hard she stares at the ultrasound. The whole thing is incomprehensible.

And on top of all this is the memory of the knife attack, the move, the house, the break-ins, the figure she sees. The open doors and windows, Charles, the weird neighbours. On top of it is everything.

Ginny thinks she might be going crazy. She knows Matt thinks so too.

Matt rubs her belly at night, pets it like you would a cat, and falls asleep with his hand warming her over her belly button. He's still treating Ginny like glass, like something breakable, easily shattered. Any minute she'll shatter.

But right now, this day, this minute, this second, Ginny is actually in a good mood.

Lately she's been trying to enjoy fixing the house up a bit more and trying not to worry about everything else – like money. Matt has convinced Ginny to stay here for a little bit longer, to do some renovations so that if they have to sell later the house will be worth more. Do some renovations to make the house safer. New windows everywhere, for example. New doors. They will start the big overhaul in the spring. In May or even April. Fix it all up before the baby comes in July. They finally booked a contractor. But for now Ginny is painting the occasional room and has spent two weeks sanding the staircase (with a full construction mask on and a special sander that sucked in the dust). She painted a bit of the trim, the worst job of all, all the large baseboards and doors and doorframes. Occasionally Matt takes over for her when she's tired and frustrated. When her back aches.

In spite of Matt's complaining, they are having another dinner party soon, next week, and Ginny has found a new vegan dish for Rain. Ginny can finally smell garlic again without getting nauseous, but she still doesn't want to have that beetloaf in her house anymore, it almost made her vomit last month.

The best thing is that Charles hasn't been around at all lately. Not for at least a month. It's like he's disappeared. Ginny hopes he's okay, but it's so nice not worrying about his scary face pressed up against the glass at night. It's nice having a new window in the hallway and not worrying about someone climbing onto the old shed roof to sneak in upstairs. And the patio door locks tight. The alarm system is easy now, Ginny finally figured it out and there have been no false alarms for a while.

Ginny's mom and dad and sister came up for a visit a few days ago. Christine is so large, almost ready to pop. Ginny used to be jealous that Christine was showing so much. Now she's terrified. Will she get that huge? Their mom bought Christine some pull-on boots because she can't bend down to tie up her old boots anymore. She's due in May but thinks it'll be earlier. They had dinner and admired the house and then left by nine in order to beat the weather that was coming through the region, the mass of snow that dumped down the next day, blocking highways and roads.

And Matt's family came up for a couple of hours on their way to the ski hill. His mother and her husband and then, about a day later, his father and his wife. So Ginny has been showing off the house and remembering how much she enjoys living far from the relatives. Elaine loved the chandelier over the dining-room table and has promised another stand-up lamp for the living room the next time she comes. "It's so dark in here," she said.

⊗

Matt comes into the kitchen. He's been up for a while, outside jogging in the snow. He hasn't slipped yet. Ginny is terrified he will break something before the baby comes. If he does, she doesn't know what she'll do. He tells her she's being paranoid, that he has a good grasp of the footing, but Ginny doesn't believe him. He's out of breath and bright red. He reaches out to her, standing in the kitchen, leaning on the island, and kisses her. She groans. He's so cold. His nose is frosty, his lips are ice.

"Yikes, fuck, you're freezing."

"Yep, it's wild out there. Really cold."

Ginny nods and pulls out bagels and cream cheese. She's got the coffee on. A nice Saturday morning breakfast in February with her cold husband.

He kisses Ginny again and pours orange juice and coffee. She sits at the island. They look at each other.

Ginny is becoming a little more comfortable with the sounds the house makes now. The snow seems to muffle a lot of the creaks and groans, the cars on the street, there are no birds perched on their roof anymore cooing and calling. The clanging of the furnace is becoming background noise. She also hasn't seen that figure in a couple of weeks now and is starting to wonder if Matt's right, if he's just a figment of her imagination, a nightmare.

"We should open up the stairs into the basement from outside," Matt suddenly says. "So we can use them to get out back more easily."

"Good idea," Ginny says. "It's dangerous not having an exit down there."

"It would be nice to be able to get into the basement from outside, wouldn't it?" Matt looks down at his socked feet and looks out at the patio and his snowy running shoes.

"We could put our bikes down there, and maybe all the toys for the kid – a sandbox? I don't know," Ginny says.

"There's a lot of stuff we could store in the basement and not have to drag it through the house. Bikes, toys, tools. What about a kiddie pool? It's actually amazing we even got insurance for the house without a basement exit."

Ginny agrees. "Let's get a treadmill down there too so you don't have to jog outside next winter."

Matt sits down next to her with his coffee and bagel. Everything in the kitchen, right now, feels cozy and warm and contained. It feels to Ginny like she's got Matt back suddenly, he feels less nervous around her. As if she is finally acting as he expects. She's not the crazy, anxious, nervous, riled-up, teary woman suddenly. Things are becoming calm now. She can tell he's hopeful.

But then Ginny thinks of "the calm before the storm," she thinks of the coming Valentine's Day and worries about her expectations. She knows they are always bigger than they should be, flowers, chocolate. This year she's just hoping he'll remember. Her stomach lurches slightly. She twists on her seat and groans a little. She can't help it. Matt looks at her curiously. His shoulders fall. His defenses are back up again.

⊗

Matt is racing through the ravine again. Jogging hard. Almost sprinting, more like a race. He's getting out his frustrations and even though there is snow on the ground the weather is balmy. It feels good to push himself. He is thinking about the past Valentine's Day. It was a disaster. Almost one and a half years married and he just can't figure out how to be romantic. Although, to be honest, he wasn't very romantic before they got married either. Or ever. And Ginny is in such a hormonally charged mood. Up and down. Either in a great mood or bitter and sad or terrified and anxious. He can't figure her out. He's worried she'll fall off the deep end and maybe hurt herself or the baby. She seems amped up and manic. And he knows she's not sleeping. Matt hopes this all stops when the baby comes in July.

Matt runs. The path disappears and reappears. Some of the snow is packed down where others must have walked, some of it is deep and dangerous. He's being careful but he's also going fast. As always, there is no one down here. He slid down toward the path out of his gate, the ground underneath icy at times. Thought twice about jogging but when he hit the bottom he felt safe. He was hoping for jogging spikes to put on his shoes for Christmas but he didn't get them and they were sold out in town after the holidays. Ginny had said that she was buying them but instead he opened a box with new pyjamas in it. He doesn't even wear pyjamas. He hasn't worn them since his "Just Married" pair on the night of his wedding. And those he donated to a charity the week after he got back from his honeymoon. He wears sweatpants or boxing shorts and a T-shirt. That's why he thought a Valentine's Day gift didn't really matter. Ginny wasn't obviously focused on presents this year, right?

But he should have at least bought her flowers. Or chocolate. She does have a craving for sweets these days.

He runs over a dead log and almost trips but catches himself soon enough and keeps going. Breathing hard, spitting occasionally. His hat is stuck to his forehead with sweat and ice. His lungs feel good.

Okay, so he forgot Valentine's Day. What did she expect? They are having a baby, he's working hard, she's up and down emotionally all the time, slowly going insane with worry about the noises, her nightmares, sleepwalking occasionally, the house is falling apart around them and has so many secrets – so much to do to fix it up, so much to do to just keep it standing, it seems. Plus a couple of days before Valentine's Day the basement started to leak. A freezing/thawing situation outside. Hot sun melted the snow quickly. It leaked into the basement, a horrible, foul-smelling odour accompanying it. Right at the back near the boarded-up hatch. When Matt went into the backyard and pried open the hatch doors he saw that the entire staircase was full of snow. It had come in through the gaps in the doors and then it went down the stairs and leaked through the new brick at the bottom into the basement. All of that snow, so many steps down, was melting now and soaking into his basement. Matt dug as much snow as he could out of the stairs but there is still about half an inch of runoff spread around on the floor inside. He's got summer fans going, drying it out.

These are problems he and Ginny never had in the apartment in the city. There was always a landlord to take care of disasters. Now it's all up to them.

Matt runs on, fast and furious. If he didn't have the ability to jog, he thinks, he would be so frustrated all the time. He is sure of that. He's so glad he can burn off his anger. He doesn't know what he would do if he couldn't jog.

And just when he thinks this, just at the exact moment he thinks it, Matt catches his foot on a fallen branch and slips and falls. Hard. His left ankle twists in a gap in the deep snow, he slips on the ice underneath and that branch on the path under the snow snags him. He's down. Badly.

He hears two noises. First a laugh. Someone is there. In the bushes near the path, within the trees.

And second, he hears a loud snapping crack and hopes to hell it is the branch.

But it isn't.

⊗

Pat and Michael walk carefully down the ravine, trying not to slip. Pat has spikes on his boots, he holds Michael's hand. After they called 911 they drove down the street to the entrance from the park. They could have walked there but weren't sure if Matt would need a car. Michael is talking to Matt on the phone the whole time they are making their way into the ravine, he is trying to keep him calm. No one has thought to call Ginny, not Matt or Michael or Pat, and later they ask each other why they didn't call her first, before calling 911? Especially when, in the hospital later, she yells at Matt in front of all of them and screams, "Why didn't you call me right away?"

"Take it easy, Matt," Michael says on the phone. "We're almost there."

"I think I can see my bone," Matt cries. "Oh god, I can see my bone. Is that my bone?"

"Stop looking," Pat shouts back. "You'll pass out."

"I'm sure it's not your bone," Michael says loudly. They are on speaker. He shouts into the phone he is holding out. And he clutches Pat's arm for support. "I'm sure it's not."

"I heard a laugh," Matt says. "Someone is down here. I'm sure I heard a laugh."

Michael and Pat look at each other.

"We're coming."

The two men suddenly hear the sirens from the fire truck and ambulance back at the park. And then Pat waves frantically at the men and women he sees coming down into the ravine with a stretcher. They manoeuvre themselves down the icy path toward Pat and Michael and overtake them and continue on.

"We're all coming," says Michael. "Just hold on."

"It really hurts."

They find Matt curled up on the path surrounded by paramedics. He's shaking, crying, shouting as they move him. Michael and Pat comfort him and then the paramedics stabilize his ankle and bundle him onto a stretcher and wrap a silver blanket around him.

"His bone isn't showing," a paramedic says to Pat. "But it's a really bad break."

They all walk out of the ravine; the paramedics are skilled and make carrying Matt look easy. They get into their separate vehicles. The fire truck, not needed now, goes left into Parkville and the ambulance heads right toward the hospital. Pat and Michael get in their car and start to follow the ambulance.

"What was he doing jogging in the ravine?" Pat asks.

Michael shrugs. "I told him not to go in there. I told him about the dead animals. Plus it's so icy."

"I didn't see any dead animals today, did you?"

Michael shakes his head. "But there was snow everywhere, the animals are probably buried below it."

"True." Pat shivers. "Yuck."

"Matt did tell me that he hadn't seen any animal parts in the fall either so maybe that has stopped happening? Maybe it's better down there now?"

"What about the laugh he heard?"

"Yeah, that's eerie. Maybe he was just imagining it. Who would be in the ravine this time of year? I didn't see anyone, did you?"

Pat shakes his head. "I think I'll wait a bit longer before going into the ravine again, though. Just in case."

As they start their turn to follow the ambulance, Pat sees something move on the path into the ravine. But he looks again and there is nothing there and so he doesn't say anything to Michael and they drive on to the hospital.

CHAPTER 19

Matt is X-rayed and wheeled into a cubicle. "You'll need surgery," the doctor says. "We have a surgeon available now. The break is in your ankle."

Matt braces himself and finally phones Ginny. She comes barrelling into the hospital half an hour later with his overnight bag and a look on her face he's never seen before. Her hands are shaking wildly, she's shaking wildly. She can't stop scowling. Matt thinks she might collapse. He can't get off the bed to comfort her. Pat stands and hugs Ginny. Michael pats her back. Ginny is still obviously mad but she slowly calms.

"You were jogging in the ravine? In this weather?" she says, clearing her throat. Pat and Michael sit again in their chairs by Matt's bed and watch. Ginny perches on the bed. Matt can feel her shaking through the sheets.

"I didn't think it would be icy down there," slurs Matt. The painkillers are starting to work. "I thought the streets were icier."

Michael is nodding his head. "I stopped running a while ago," he says. "I'm too old to take a chance in this weather."

"See," Ginny says. "Michael is smart. He knew it wasn't safe."

Matt sighs. "Yes, Michael did warn me. But I don't feel old, I feel safe and comfortable in my body. I'm not old yet. I feel secure.

Now I just feel stupid. I feel really dumb." He looks at Ginny and she looks back at him.

"And the baby, Matt." Ginny puts her hands over her eyes and stands up. "Also, staying in the hospital tonight means I'll be alone in the house, you know. I'll be all fucking alone."

"You can stay at our house," Pat says.

Michael agrees. "We have a guest room. We have two actually. One in the basement. One on the second floor."

Ginny says, "I'm okay. I think I'm okay. The thought of being alone in the house is almost as bad as the thought of Matt on crutches when I'm hugely pregnant and need him to help me." She sits back on the bed. "But I have to do it. I have to start facing my fears. Especially if I can't count on my husband. How can I take care of a tiny human being when I can't even take care of myself?" She says, "This is horrible," and starts to cry a bit. "Why would you jog in this weather, Matt? And why didn't you call me? Do you think you can't rely on me? Do you not trust that I can take care of things anymore?"

Matt looks at her but with all the drugs in his system right now he can't even open his mouth to say anything.

A little later Matt goes in for surgery. Ginny waits until they wheel Matt back into a room where he'll stay the night. He's asleep and his mouth is open and he's drooling. She kisses him and talks to the doctor and then heads home. Pat and Michael go home and cook dinner and bring it over for Ginny. They tell her to call them if she needs anything. Ruby and Pierre check on her just after dinner and Rain calls her.

Ginny lies in bed for two hours with all the lights on clutching Matt's old sweatshirt to her chest and thinks she hears noises. She thinks that every creak is someone breaking in. The fridge shudders downstairs and she jumps. Her stomach rumbles and she jerks awake. At one point Ginny sleeps again but then startles awake dreaming about Matt, a nightmare where he leaves her. She isn't sure if he is dead or has just walked out on their marriage. But he is gone. And when she wakes she is sad. She thinks about how everything she is now, everything she lives for, is Matt – what would she do without him? And then she goes to the washroom and, on the way back to bed, she thinks she sees something move down the hall, a shadow on the wall, a reflection from the closed hallway window. That is enough.

And so, at two in the morning, Ginny leaves out the front of the house and walks over to Pat and Michael's and knocks on their door. She's carrying a blanket and a pillow. She's in her pyjamas, her large belly sticking out, unlaced boots on her feet. She is crying.

She's alone in the dark, cold night, walking outside by herself – and she's asking them for help.

"I'm not okay in that house alone," she says. "I keep hearing things."

Pat brings her in. He walks her through the dining room and up the stairs to the guest bedroom. The lights are off but Ginny is amazed at all the antiques and knickknacks in this house. Everywhere she turns looks like a nightmare for dusting. Gold and silver and glass and mirrored things, breakable things, chairs that look extremely uncomfortable. Pat sets her up in the guest room on the second floor on a huge ornate brass bed. He is wearing a gold bathrobe and he brings her some warm milk and sits on the edge of the bed talking to her until she falls asleep.

"My dad would give me hot milk before bed," he says. "But sometimes he'd give me boiled banana skin." Pat laughs.

"What?" Ginny sits up and sips the milk.

"Supposedly the skin of bananas has melatonin and tryptophan in it. And that puts you to sleep. Or at least makes you sleep well. He would put the skin in a pot of water and boil it for a while and then take it out. It was disgusting, Ginny. Don't ever try it. Boiled banana skin." Pat makes a face.

Ginny falls asleep wondering what that would taste like and

figures it would probably be bitter. Maybe, she thinks, just as her eyes close, that would be something Rain would like?

⊗

In their bedroom Michael and Pat look at each other. "That house," Michael says. "What's with that house?" He is putting cream on his hands and his feet, rubbing it into his heels. Might as well take advantage of being woken up at 2:00 a.m., he thinks. Moisturize.

"Haunted? Cursed?" Pat climbs into bed and gathers the duvet around his neck. Michael watches him point his toes a few times, easing out the tension.

"It was scary when Marina and Charles lived there too if you think about it. All the curtains were always closed, remember? And they were never around, never answered the door and never went out. It was as if no one was living there. Sometimes I would see someone moving in the windows of the attic or the living room and it would startle me because I would forget there were people in that house. Or when they got all those deliveries, that would remind me. Ruby said that she felt the same way. They were bizarre. They made everything about that house strange. Remember the arguing we'd hear? Marina shouting and Charles growling. So many fights."

"Shhh," Pat says. "Whisper. She might hear you." He lowers his own voice. "It's not only the house that's scary, it's what might have gone on in that house that is scary," Pat whispers. "Those men dressed in black, remember them? Visiting Charles."

Michael nods.

"All those packages. Two or three a day." Pat pulls his quilt up to his neck. "But before, years ago, they weren't like that. They were just quiet and older and we ignored them and they ignored us."

"Yes," Michael says quietly. "And then it all began. Something went on in there. I'm sure of it. The satellite image Matt and Ginny saw. What was that?" Michael climbs in beside Pat.

"You believe that? About the image?" Pat whispers as he rolls toward Michael for his kiss goodnight.

"I don't know," Michael says, softly. "I don't know what to believe in this town anymore. Anything is possible."

Pat says, "We never did anything; we never went over to see if they were okay. We never even said hello to them. I feel like shit about that now. We watched things change over there and we just ignored it."

Pat wraps his arms around Michael.

They both fall slowly into a scattered dream-filled night.

Michael dreams that he is searching for something, hunting for it. He has a rifle and is in the ravine. He doesn't know what he's looking for but he needs it desperately. He wakes from the nightmare and sneaks out of bed. He heads down to the kitchen to drink some milk and is startled to see Ginny there, sitting at the kitchen table, her head in her hands.

"Are you okay?" Michael whispers and hugs her.

Ginny keeps her head in her hands and says quietly, "I think I'm going insane." Then she laughs, sadly.

CHAPTER 20

Drugs. Matt's system is full of them. Oxycontin in particular.

He's nursing his ankle in the living room. He has a week off work to recover, to get these drugs out of his system. In the meantime there is a substitute teacher filling in for him that his students seem to like better than him. He checked in once and they were all smiling and they frowned and groaned when they saw him suddenly appear on their screens.

But thankfully Ginny has been taking good care of him. She has made a lot of notes about his drugs, when to take them, when not to take them, how to slowly wean himself from them, but he hasn't looked at any of the lists. He just pops a pill in his mouth whenever he can. The pain is ridiculous.

There goes the work he was going to do on the house in the spring. He figures that in March he will be limping around with a cast and crutches, in April he should be down to just crutches. But what about May? Will he be better in May? How long does an ankle take to heal? And the baby is coming in July, that's probably enough time to heal. But Matt might not be able to start preparing anything before the baby arrives. It's a good thing Ginny painted the baby's room before she was even pregnant but who is going to put together the crib that they haven't even bought yet, or strap in the car seat when Ginny can't even bend over to tie her shoes. He remembers Christine, huge and awkward last month, unable to bend forward. Ginny's not quite there yet, but he should maybe encourage her to get everything done soon, like this week? Finish it all off before she's feeling too big? Matt doesn't even know if that will happen, he's pretty sure Ginny's going to be capable of moving freely up until the very end. But then there's the actual taking care of the baby after the birth. Getting up at night, changing all those diapers, bathing the kid. Is Ginny going to have to do all that alone? Will he be out of commission? He figures that he'll be able to walk without crutches by that time, so he should be able to carry the baby around. Right?

Right?

Right?

Matt pulls at his hair. He is lying down on the sofa, his foot up on a pillow, his head on another, a blanket wrapped around his body. He feels so guilty about his jogging. If he could turn back time . . .

"I'm going to get groceries," Ginny says, coming into the living room. She smooths Matt's hair down. "Are you craving anything in particular?"

"I can't think of anything. The Oxy makes me feel a bit nauseous."

"We'll get you off of it as soon as you can handle it. I'll get some ginger ale in the meantime." She kisses him and heads out the door. "Oh, here. I'll leave your phone right here beside you," she says, coming back to him, "just in case you need anything when I'm gone. You can always phone one of the neighbours if it's an emergency."

"Thanks."

Was that a subtle hint that Ginny is still upset that he didn't call her first when he fell? She's been saying stuff all week about how he doesn't really need her help. She's still angry. Matt doesn't know why he didn't call her first. He guesses it was because he knew she'd be mad at him for going down to the ravine. For a month at least she had been asking him not to jog anymore on the snow and ice, to get that treadmill he'd been excited about and set it up in the basement. But he didn't get that treadmill because the basement was still damp from the melting snow that had seeped in and it stunk badly, and so he continued to jog outside over the ice and snow. He ignored her warnings. And then he tried the ravine. He knows how close to the edge she is with stress. That's another reason he didn't phone her. He wasn't ready to deal with her drama when he was in so much pain. Michael and Pat were much easier.

Ginny turns and heads back to the front door. She has her keys in her hand and she leaves.

Matt wakes and the sun has gone behind a cloud and it feels like snow outside. That dark, grey, thick feeling, overcast. Clouds scudding across the sky. From his position on the sofa Matt can see out the front window. There are a few kids walking down the street on the way home from school. One throws a snowball at the other. Matt closes his eyes again and then he opens them.

And suddenly Charles is standing there, right at the window, staring in. Matt jerks and as he moves his ankle, he screams in pain. Charles is staring straight at him, his grey hair blowing in the wind. He is looking at Matt but his eyes don't seem focused. He is much thinner than he was the last time Matt saw him. And what is that? Is there something coming out of his mouth? Some kind of liquid? Is it red? Blood? Are there words floating above his head, little captions like in the cartoons, bubbles of words? Matt shakes his head, he feels dull and dizzy. This must be the medication.

He tries to stand but falls back. Is that blood dripping down Charles's mouth and nose? It can't be. And now Matt sees Marina standing next to the old man. Matt can't see Marina's face, it is blurred out. The kids on the street still walk home from school in the background, behind Charles and his wife. They don't seem to notice what's going on in front of them.

Matt starts to sweat. Cold sweat, he's so cold. Charles is saying something and begins pounding on the window, shaking his fists at Matt. He starts shouting and Matt can suddenly hear him. "Get out of my house, get out of my house, get out of my house," over and over and over. And then, "Leave this house. Leave."

Matt thinks he sees Marina move behind Charles and pull him away and drag him down the snowy lawn toward the sidewalk, toward the kids who aren't noticing anything. She is crying. The snow is suddenly covered in blood. Drops of red from Charles's mouth, which is copiously leaking blood. She drags him with one hand as if he doesn't weigh anything, as if he were a rag doll. And then Marina is Ginny. Her face has changed. She isn't crying anymore, she isn't pregnant anymore, and she drags Charles down to the street. She is wearing all black – black pants, hoodie. The black hood covers her head.

Matt's heart is beating rapidly. He closes his eyes again and when he opens them there is no one there. Everyone is gone. No Marina or Charles or Ginny, no bloody path to the curb, nothing. Just the children still walking on the street and laughing and throwing snowballs. There is a ginger ale on the table beside him fizzing slightly, popping. It's much later. He can hear Ginny cooking in the kitchen.

His heart is pounding in his chest. He has to get off these drugs.

⊗

While Matt is sleeping Ginny is in the grocery store. She is annoyed at Matt for his injury but she also feels sorry for him. He takes out his frustrations by jogging and she worries now that he'll have nowhere to put his feelings. What if he starts to behave like her? What if he starts to get anxious and paranoid and frustrated? She reaches for the orange juice and sees Marina standing over by the milk. Marina looks up and sees Ginny and then turns and quickly starts walking away.

Ginny is so tired. She puts a hand on her forehead, leans on the cart. She lay in bed at night without Matt – he was on the sofa downstairs – and she heard things moving around her, she heard creaks and clicks and snaps and the wind in the ravine. She heard water dripping from the roof and the call of birds – haunting and piercing. Ginny spent all night convincing herself not to go downstairs and climb in beside Matt on the faux-leather sofa. She worried, no, she knew that her presence would disturb him. And he needs to sleep in order to heal quickly.

She buys the ginger ale and the orange juice and then she sees Marina in the lineup. They don't look at each other, they don't even acknowledge that the other is there.

A week later, when Matt's walking with his cast and crutches a little bit, when he's finally only taking half a dose of his Oxy, he hobbles outside, over to the living room window, and looks at the ground below it. It hasn't snowed in a while and there is one set of footprints in the snow there. Just below the window, exactly where his drug-induced vision of Charles was standing, blood running down his face. Matt shivers. The rest of the lawn is clear, no footprints, no blood, no drag marks, but under the window are the one set of prints, the feet facing in as if someone was peering through the glass. There are also handprints on the window but Matt can only see them from one angle and they look small, like a child's handprints. The footprints are large and look like they came from nowhere, as if they just appeared there or came out of the sky. Matt looks around, looks up and looks all over the front lawn. He shakes his head, confused and worried. He knows this was a drug-induced hallucination, but he can't understand how the footprints got there.

MARCH

CHAPTER 21

Matt stands in the kitchen with his cast and crutches and tries to help but really gets in the way.

"Scuse me," Ginny says, "steaming colander filled with noodles coming through."

Almost six months pregnant now, Ginny has popped: the baby bump is pushing out and making it hard to get around Matt and his crutches and his large plastic boot. She tries to look down and over her stomach to see where she's stepping. Matt pats Ginny as she passes. His baby, inside his wife, more obvious now. It's still such a strange concept.

"I can't wait until July," Matt says. "I can't wait. Especially now that Pat and Michael and Ruby and Pierre came over last week and put together the crib and the changing table and put the car seat in our car. They are amazing."

Pat and Michael finally got their puppy, a border collie crossed with an Australian shepherd and Lab. They've been waiting since just after Christmas when Michael found a breeder whose pups would be ready to go in March. His name is Noodle, hence the dinner Ginny's making: fettuccine with cream sauce and meatballs. Noodle came over with everyone last week to put together all the furniture. Tonight is his celebratory adoption dinner, even though he's not at the party. Everyone was in a great mood in the house last week; Ruby took charge and gave orders, Pat and Michael were confused by the furniture. They have no Ikea in their house and had no idea how to put it together.

"What's an Allen key?" Michael asked. "Why do they call it that? Is it named after someone called Allen?"

Erin, Ruby's daughter, also came over to see Noodle and the girl and dog rolled all over the floor together and everyone had tea and coffee in the baby's yellow room when they were done – all sitting on the floor around Noodle who was getting up to no good (almost swallowing the Allen key). Ginny was amazed at the kindness of her neighbours. It makes her think that maybe Matt is right and all the strange stuff happening around here is just growing pains, just getting used to the environment, maybe going off the Xanax. Nothing nefarious is going on. It can't be. Matt was so grateful for all the help. There is no way he could have put all that furniture together with his leg the way it is now. He has such a hard time even lowering himself to the floor. "I feel a bit teary," he told Ginny later, when they all left.

Tonight Noodle is home alone, although Michael thinks they might have to go get him later, as he does start to howl the longer he's left in his kennel. Ruby has brought over some of her kids' baby clothes, onesies that are still in good condition – some of them not even worn.

"Elton was the wrong size at the wrong season for some of these. They were gifts that were never used. I thought you could use them."

Ginny is excited to wash them and put them in the baby's room. Her first baby clothes. She wants the dinner party to end right away so she can start organizing.

Rain arrives with some baby blankets she has bartered for her oils at the market, and everyone agrees that this is now officially Ginny's first baby shower. Since she's convinced that her mother and sister have forgotten about her, Ginny says this will be her first and last baby shower. Sad, but expected. Ginny knows she'll get a cheque or an e-Transfer when they remember. That's okay because Ginny and Matt can spend it on the renovations. They've decided they are going to get second-hand clothes and Ikea furniture for the baby until their finances are better. Babies don't know the difference. They will get a loan for the renovations. Ginny and Matt are going to make a conscious effort to stop worrying about their finances, they've decided. At least that's one worry Ginny thinks she can control.

The guests have all settled around the table, the overhead light is on dim, the music is on, candles are glowing. Rain has the new vegan dish beside her, something Ginny found online. A tempeh bake that tastes, Ginny thinks, like mouldy nuts. But then Ginny's taste buds are completely crazy right now. The others are looking at it, kind of interested. Should Ginny have made more?

The rest of the guests are eating the homemade fettuccine noodles, which were draped all over the kitchen all afternoon drying out. Matt hobbled around a pot of cream sauce for a couple of hours, stirring occasionally. Ginny made meatballs. The kitchen smelled wonderful and still does. Red wine. Italian bread from the market. Arugula salad with pecorino and apples and walnuts. Ginny looks around at everyone as they dig in. Pat and Michael groan with delight at the same time and then laugh. Pierre is already red-faced from the wine and Ruby is chewing thoughtfully. She smiles.

"You're such a good cook, Ginny," Ruby says.

"I didn't use to be." Ginny blushes. "I used to burn everything. But I'm really enjoying cooking these days. It's something to do while I wait." She points to her belly.

The men brought dessert again and Ruby and Pierre stocked everyone up on wine. They brought over a bottle of Perrier for Ginny and Rain. Seven dinner parties they've had already since they moved here and Ginny is starting to feel like she's sitting with family. With a family she trusts and really likes. It's odd, all their weirdness seems normal now, Ginny doesn't even remember why she thought they were strange anymore. She feels a bit teary. After all the worrying about these people and all the suspicions, now Ginny's happy hormones are bleeding through her veins – she can almost taste them. Pregnancy certainly gets easier before it gets harder, Ginny thinks.

"There are moving pains," Matt says aloud and Ginny thinks, yes, that's it! But he means his ankle. "Moving all over the leg and hip. I guess I'm just standing and walking awkwardly because of the crutch and the boot. So now everything hurts. My hip, my back, even my arms. But I'm definitely not going back on the Oxy. That was crazy. I had such strange, violent dreams. Wild ones."

"Glad you aren't addicted," Rain says. "I knew this boy in my foster home who was so addicted to Oxy. He couldn't get off it." She takes a bite of her vegan dish. "He died."

Ginny often forgets about Rain's foster life. Rain's parents died when she was young and Rain was raised in the foster system. Her parents' inheritance bought Rain's house and lifestyle. She doesn't have to work full time but supplements her parents' money with her essential oil business. And she had to give her baby away when she was a teenager. Ginny reaches out her hand and takes Rain's hand and squeezes. Rain looks shocked but squeezes back. Rain's life has been hard.

Ruby asks, "Any more Charles sightings?"

"No," Matt says, awkwardly, as if he's lying. "We haven't seen him in a while. In fact, all has been calm for a couple of weeks."

"I see him sometimes from afar," Ginny says as she looks at Matt and wonders, has he seen Charles? "And I saw Marina at the grocery store and then again walking around here the other day. She came up the street and then turned and headed down the dead end and then up the street again. It was as if she's trying to find something. Maybe Charles?"

"I saw that too," Ruby says. "It was like she was desperate. She kept walking around in circles."

"I also saw another man wandering around here," Ginny says

but then she sees Matt's expression – as though he's telling her silently to stop.

Ruby shakes her head. "I just see Charles driving and Marina walking," she says. "Sometimes he is yelling at her but I can't tell what he's saying."

"He looks skinnier too," Pat says. "I've seen him downtown. He wears all-black now."

"Shhhh," Michael says. "Let's talk about something else."

Everyone looks at Ginny and Matt and then Pierre snorts, like he always does. As if someone has told a joke.

Ginny is not sure that she has really ever connected to Pierre. Matt says he's just socially awkward, but Ginny thinks it's the wine, and she doesn't see Pierre connecting with Matt either. Or anyone else, for that matter. Sometimes not even Ruby. Pierre did install the car seat, though. Ginny knows that Matt appreciates that. So Pierre is, in some ways, useful, if strange.

"From your experiences here, Ginny, everyone would think this town was possessed," Pierre slurs, sipping his wine. "Wouldn't they?"

"Pat and I were thinking," Michael says, quickly changing the conversation, "what about the next time we have a dinner party we all go out for dinner? Instead of coming here? Ginny, you need a huge break, especially now" – he gestures to her stomach – "and we'd like to treat you and Matt. Everyone else can pay for themselves."

Matt smiles. "That would be amazing, thanks. We haven't gone out for dinner since we moved here."

Ginny smiles. "We used to go out for dinner all the time in the city," she says. "It's just that the house takes all our money now."

"And our kitchen is nicer here," Matt says. "Bigger. So it's fun to cook in it."

"But I could use a break," Ginny says. She scowls at Matt.

"Yes," Pat says. "We'll miss your food the next time, Ginny, but you need a rest."

"That's lovely," Ginny says. "Thank you."

Ruby clears her throat again. And here it comes, Ginny can see Matt thinking, more Ruby news hour. Her kids, Pierre's job. Just a pause, a commercial break, and we're back to this again.

"How are the kids?" Matt asks. Earlier, he told Ginny that he's starting to realize that if he just lets Ruby talk about what she wants for a while and doesn't fight it, doesn't try to change the conversation, Ruby will move on to something else quickly. If he ignores her and switches the conversation she'll butt in for a couple of hours with more stories. Ginny watches as he pours more wine and more Perrier. "How is your daughter?" It's clear that all of a sudden he can't remember her name.

"Erin –" And off she goes.

Michael tears off a hunk of bread and butters it and then dips it in his sauce. He starts to say something about Noodle but Ruby doesn't let him butt in.

Matt rolls his eyes. He looks at Ginny and she smiles slightly.

When Ruby is finally done there is silence for a bit, everyone looks full and tired, and then Pierre begins to talk about hockey. It turns out Elton is playing this year at the local arena. Pierre is certain he's going to make it to the big leagues.

"He has skill," Pierre says. Ruby nods her head. "And he's big."

Ginny thinks of little Elton, on the Christmas tree farm just two months ago, ten years old. He seemed so small. And delicate.

"He'll be big and strong and talented like his father," Ruby says. And everyone looks at Pierre. Pierre drinks his wine and puffs up his chest. Rain tries not to laugh. She catches Ginny's eye and they both look away quickly. There is nothing about Pierre that they would call big and strong.

"I have to pee," Ginny says, and quickly rushes out of the room. She hopes no one can hear her snort, she's got the giggles, as she makes her way up to the bathroom. She passes the hall window and it's shut tight.

At night, after doing all the dishes and helping Matt take a shower, holding him up, making sure he doesn't slip, Ginny sits in the living room with the one lamp on and a blanket on her legs. Matt is up in bed reading. Once Ginny gets him up the stairs it's almost impossible to bring him down again. That's a chore for the morning. Ginny is tired. It's a cold night tonight and there are more cold nights to come before the weather changes back to spring. She wishes the seasons were faster. Or that winter was, at least. Ginny thinks that she'll have to get Matt to bring up their spring and summer clothes from the basement when he can. She'll go through them and give away the old items.

⊗

A week later Matt makes it down to the basement. He limps down, carrying one crutch, holding tightly to the banister on the creaky old stairs. He has their laundry in a backpack. One thumping step at a time. They've been living in the house since September and he still hasn't gotten around to unpacking his basement boxes – tools, old documents. Ginny asked him to get her summer clothes and that gave him the idea of clearing a lot of stuff out, just like they've talked about. There was a lot of laundry that needed doing too. It's not the greatest time to do this, it's hard enough to bend and reach anything on the ground, but Matt is bored and it's a cold, wet Saturday, snow melting outside, everything muddy and dirty, all the garbage thrown on the streets coming up out of hibernation. He has always hated March, even when in good shape. Running is always so gross outside after the thaw. Melting dog shit, decomposing takeout containers, cigarette butts and all the waste of winter. It's no better here than in the city. If anything, the garbage is worse. Probably because in the city there are garbage bins on every street.

Matt puts the laundry in and then shuffles around, looking at everything. The boxes he put down here when they moved in are all off the floor on broken, old pallets. Good thing he used them when they moved in as The Hatch Staircase Flood, as it has come to be called in Matt's mind, would have seeped into everything. But the puddles of snowmelt flood didn't damage any of his things because of the pallets he found behind a store in town, and a summer fan he turned on. The flood didn't ruin Ginny's stuff either. He doesn't exactly know what she has in these boxes but there are quite a few of them. Matt and Ginny took everything from their apartment storage unit in the city and also from their parents' house – yes, they both still had boxes at their parents' houses – and brought it all here and dumped it in the basement. Now is the time to sort it, to dump it, to keep it, to store it in practical ways and get rid of the broken pallets.

Ginny is off doing the grocery shopping and said she wanted to read and nap when she got home. The pregnancy is progressing. She gets tired quickly lately. Matt thought that by disappearing into the basement he would give her a break from waiting on him, from worrying about him hobbling around.

He looks at the walls. Some empty ones. Some with shelves attached to them. A workbench, handmade. It looks like a wooden door on legs. A few old doors and windows from the house leaning up against a wall or two. There is the furnace – an old clunker. There is a hot water tank. The fuse box. The basement covers the whole of the footprint of the house. It's quite large. The wall at the back, with the leaking from the hatch, is a bit mouldy. He can smell it, a dusty, rotten sulfur-egg smell. Matt will have to scrub at that, maybe buy a dehumidifier, use bleach. The foul smell of mould and old soil makes him worry about his unborn child. Should you live in a house with mould? Matt decides he won't bring the baby down here until he's sure everything is cleaned up.

He opens one box. One of Ginny's. There are papers and old yearbooks inside. From high school. He rifles through one of the books. It's signed all over. Silly things like, "Gin-Gin, thanks for 'sharing' that Math quiz!" and "Prettiest girl in phys. ed!" and "I'll always remember dissecting the fetal pig with you and Mandy!!!" Lots of exclamation points. Teenagers. Matt smiles. It's hard to believe Ginny had an entire life he knows nothing about. It's hard to believe he will one day have a teenager. He puts the book back inside the box and seals the box and labels it "Ginny High School" and places it on the shelf. One box done.

Matt works on labelling and shelving the boxes for a bit. He makes a pile of garbage, of things they won't want and don't need to keep anymore. The lease for the apartment in the city, the old carrier for groceries that they would lug down the city streets. He sits on the stairs for a while and looks around. Those windows and doors. What will he do with them? They are at the back of the basement, to the left side, near the hatch disaster mouldy area. The doors are large and with mottled glass, probably once used between the front hall and the living room to block the air from outside coming in. The windows are small ones, maybe once used at the sides of the house or maybe even down here in the basement? Matt limps over to them and starts riffling through.

When he gets to the end of flicking through the pile he feels something is odd, something is off. He can't put his finger on it. Matt slowly starts moving all the doors and windows over toward the workbench. It's hard work, hobbling along, terrified he's going to hit his ankle or drop a window on his toes, but he manages slowly. And then he stands there staring at the space left empty from the rearranging.

There, at the back of the basement, is a wooden door. It has been hidden behind the stacked doors and windows and painted the same colour as the walls – it blended in. A room under the patio. A dry cellar? Isn't this a common nightmare? Finding a room in your house that you didn't know was there before? An image of the satellite body flashes into his mind. He shakes his head.

Matt moves over to the door and puts his hand on it. He steadies his breathing. His heart is beating fast. He listens for

Ginny's arrival and takes the handle and twists it. Matt's ankle is aching and pulsing and beating. He needs to sit down soon.

The handle turns but the door doesn't open. It has a lock on it. Matt grabs a crowbar and hammer and goes at it. He works hard and yanks it open. The sweat is pouring down his face. His ankle, his ankle, his ankle, that's all he can think about. And Ginny – he is listening so intently for her that every squeak and thump in the house makes him jump. The furnace goes on, a drip outside sounds like a volley of gunshots. Everything is heightened. What if he finds something inside? What if the body from the satellite image is in here? Behind this door? Or more bodies? Or . . . ?

Matt stops and shakes his head. What the hell is he thinking about? He's turning into Ginny. Paranoid, suspicious, freaking out.

Matt hobbles over to the stairs and grabs his phone, which he left there when he came down. He jumps back to the door and finally opens it fully. The room is dark and smells musty. All the smell from the basement seems to be gathered in this room. Mould, dust, trapped air. He flips on his phone flashlight and takes a deep breath and holds the light up in front of him.

CHAPTER 22

Full. The room is stuffed full. Floor to ceiling.

With food. Cans, jars, buckets, candles, sealed packets, bags. Tupperware containers, large bins, suitcases, patio cushions. Everything stacked and orderly, everything labelled. "Long-Term Food Number 1," "Long-Term Food Number 25," "Toiletries," "Chemical Cleaners," "Waste Bags." Matt opens a bin. Cans of tuna, soups, canned vegetables and buckets of dried meats. Spam, nuts, grains, oats. And on the floor: bottles and jugs of water with dates on them. A tool box. In another bin: puzzles and board games, loads of batteries – car batteries and boat batteries and flashlight batteries. Shelves of flashlights – shampoos and soaps and creams. T-shirts and shorts, big and small. Pharmaceuticals, pills and creams and bandages and hot water bottles and tampons. An entire bin of ripped cloth. Another full of noodles. A huge barrel of rice. Cake mix and canned coconut milk. Everything sitting there, in its place, waiting to be used.

For what?

Matt stands back. His mouth open.

There are spiderwebs and there is dust. But it's actually kind of clean and very organized. There are some fingerprints in the dust. A footprint or two. It's dry, the hatch flood didn't make it this far.

Matt walks out of the room, then walks back in and shoots his flashlight all around, looking again and again at everything. A few spiders scurry when the light hits them.

He doesn't know what to make of this. A bomb shelter? A storage room that was forgotten? A prepper's paradise? A survivalist's bank?

From what Matt can see, the walls are panelled. The floor here is concrete, painted blue. There is a light socket in the ceiling, but no bulb. Of course. Once again the Smythes didn't forget to take their bulb. Not even from their secret room.

Sitting on the stairs again Matt thinks, this, this is why Charles is mad. Mad both ways – furious and crazy. He wants his stuff back. Why didn't he take everything with him when he moved? Maybe Marina didn't know about this room? Maybe Charles had no chance to take it all? It was a fast move. Or maybe, just maybe, he didn't want all of this anymore.

Matt stares at the door across the room and then gets up. He tries to seal the broken lock but gives up and leaves it hanging from the door. He quickly starts to pile up all the doors and windows as before, attempting to make it look the way it looked when he came down to the basement. Ginny never comes down to the basement, of course, they didn't do laundry for weeks when he first wrecked his ankle, but he still isn't taking any chances. He is sure that if she saw this she would – what? What would she do? She'd imagine the worst, he's sure, probably start talking about torture and kidnapping and murder – not just storage. He is 100 percent sure it wouldn't be something innocent like . . . well . . . just a room full of supplies for the end of the world. Matt shakes his head. He pushes the last window up to the wall covering the door, and just then he hears the front door open upstairs and Ginny is home.

Matt stuffs the finished laundry into his backpack, picks up his crutch and his phone and climbs carefully back up the stairs to greet Ginny. He places his backpack on the couch and breathes deeply and moves into the kitchen where they talk about nothing as they unpack groceries. Matt sits down at the kitchen island and looks at his pregnant wife. He studies her while she moves around the kitchen fixing lunch, giving him odd jobs, like cutting the cheese and opening the pickles. He's cold now from the sweat drying on his back, his face. His ankle aches. Matt looks out at the back patio and thinks of the full room underneath it.

What was going on here?

Why was it locked and hidden?

Why, when they moved, did they forget everything inside?

And, most of all, has Ginny been right all along? Something strange was going on in this house.

Ginny is upstairs in the bedroom going through a box of her summer clothes. Matt went down into the basement after lunch and got her a box. He said he'll get the rest another day. Everything smells stale. She's looking for her capris and wondering if they might still fit. They were elasticized so maybe she can stretch them out when it's warmer? Ginny is piling the things she wants to wash and keep on their bed. Matt is downstairs watching TV in the living room, his ankle up on pillows on the sofa.

She gathers everything together when she's done and heads downstairs, her arms full. "I'm not going into the basement. Sorry. But I need this stuff washed when you go down the next time." She looks at Matt.

She notices Matt looks nervous. Uncomfortable.

He clears his throat. "I'll go down to the basement again next weekend. I still have more stuff to organize."

"I just want this pile washed before I give birth."

"That's months away, Gin. I'm sure I'll be down there doing laundry before then." Matt laughs.

Ginny nods. He's right.

"Spring is coming," Ginny says. "Next week is April, right?"

"I know." He shrugs. She puts the pile of clothes next to him on the sofa. Matt goes back to the TV. He's watching golf.

Ginny heads upstairs. She holds the banister and her stomach. She feels slightly nauseous from the smell of the dusty clothes and she rushes quickly into the bathroom and turns on the water to mute the sounds as she tries not to gag.

⊗

Ruby and Pierre, Elton and Erin are in the ravine. Ruby insisted Ginny come down with them. Ginny is scared and she is tiptoeing through the mud, being so careful not to slip and fall.

"Mom, this is ridiculous. It's cold, windy and muddy." Erin smacks her boots on a tree and then fixes her ponytail. Her long dark hair is blowing in the wind. She picks at her fingernail polish. "God, it's gross here. And Ginny's pregnant, Mom."

Ginny nods and says, "I have to agree, Ruby. Why are we doing this?"

"You haven't been down in the ravine yet and you've lived here seven months."

"But there's a reason for that. I never wanted to come down here," Ginny says and Erin grins.

Ginny and the family have walked into the ravine through the park down the street. Ruby was insistent and Pierre agreed. And then they practically forced Ginny to come. Pierre says he's tired of seeing his kids sitting on their computers and phones all day long. He's tired of sitting on his computer all day himself. Ruby says she goes for walks every day on the streets, but Pierre sits at his computer and works: his ass is spreading, his back hurting. She says she has noticed he has a hump in his neck. It's time to get out and do something. Pierre rolls his eyes and groans.

It seems most of the ice has melted.

"It's not as if we are afraid of the ravine," Ruby says. "Right, Pierre?"

"More disgusted than afraid," Pierre says. "All the garbage piling up, the dog poop on the path, the odd animal bone decomposing."

Ruby tells Ginny in confidence, "Erin is getting to that age where we worry about her sneaking out at night and heading down into the ravine to party. So the whole place makes us both nervous. But now I think it's time to clean it up. Don't you? This is a place our family used to enjoy when the kids were young. I want to take it back."

Last summer Ruby and Pierre said they replaced the gate from their backyard with more wooden fencing and blocked themselves out of the ravine because of the thefts (and, probably, because of Erin too, Ginny thinks, looking at the girl). Ruby tells Ginny that the ravine was the number one reason they moved into their house in the first place.

Ginny tries to smile.

"Stop whining," Ruby says to Erin. "It's not so bad down here." Ginny is looking around at the trees, the mud, the branches strewn on the path. At no path. There is no path here. There is also a lot of garbage. How does it get covered with garbage when no one uses it? Paper and cans and bottles strewn everywhere. It's certainly not the ravine she thought it would be when she moved from the city. She can't believe Matt jogged down here.

Ruth tells Ginny, "There used to be a wood-chip path here, quite wide, and garbage cans, and there were containers nailed to the occasional tree for dog poop bags. Everything was kept up nicely. There used to be a few lights down here too, just some so-lar ones but at dusk it was lovely walking in here. And now, it's a mess." Ruby scowls.

Only Elton is having fun. Ginny thinks his legs have stretched this winter and it seems as if he can't stop running. He is running ahead and then running back, playing his own internal game with the trees. Tagging them and then running around in strange pat-terns and then tagging his parents. His sister keeps trying to hit him hard when he passes but he manages to avoid her blows.

"Stop it, you two," Pierre says. "Let's just try to enjoy this."

"Stop touching everything," Ruby says.

"Enjoy what?" Erin says. "Mud? Cold? Garbage? It stinks here. It's so creepy."

Ginny nods at Erin. She agrees. She trudges along holding her stomach, being so careful, looking around, careful not to step in anything.

"Trees," shouts Elton, his mouth wide.

Ginny looks at him, she thinks he may need braces and then she wonders if her kid will need braces and thinks, how will we afford that?

"I can smell a fire," says Ruby. "It must be coming from one of the houses."

They all smell fire now. It begins as a fireplace smell and then slowly starts to smell like cooking chicken. All four look up toward the houses. Pierre scans the chimneys but sees no smoke.

"Chicken," Elton says.

"I guess our cooking smells must come down to the ravine," Pierre says.

Erin smacks out at her brother as he rushes past her again, but he ducks her hand and takes off again. He trips on a branch lying over the path.

"Down for the count," Ruby says. She laughs but then rushes to her son and helps him up. "Last thing I need is for Elton to break an ankle like Matt did. I take care of him enough, I don't have the energy to do more."

Ruby brushes off her son and the family and Ginny all stop and look around. There is a line of grey smoke misting through the air far away. They can't see anything but the smoke and trees and bushes.

"This place," Pierre says, "it's really gone downhill."

Then Pierre turns and starts walking back. Erin looks relieved. Elton spins around and then continues back to where they came from and touches every tree on the way back. Ruby looks at the sky, looks at the line of smoke, looks at the garbage all around and the unclear path.

"I want to fix up the ravine," she says. "Maybe if we – the neighbours, the townspeople – fix it up we could have a gate again out of the back fence down to the path. Or if we start with it clean, it might stay clean. Who knows? I know that Elton is more likely to keep his room clean if it starts out tidy. Erin, on the other hand, well . . ."

Ginny rolls her eyes. The amount of work it would take to clean this place up is hard to comprehend.

"The cooking food smells good," Elton says.

"It's time for lunch," Pierre grumbles.

The family and Ginny walk the rest of the hidden path back until they come out of the ravine and are in the park. Then they walk on the road home. Quietly. Even Elton is quiet. Ginny hears birds cawing and singing, and realizes there were no bird sounds in the ravine.

But as they come closer to their houses Ginny sees Charles and points. He is on the sidewalk and then he runs down the side of her house and slips into her backyard. He's so fast for his age. And dressed in military gear? Ginny groans. Pierre starts to walk quickly toward him. Ginny follows.

Charles has disappeared down the side of the house. When Pierre and Ginny get to the backyard Charles is gone, down through the gate to the ravine. Pierre walks to the gate, looks into the ravine, sees nothing and closes the gate. Ginny stands on the lawn. They turn and look at the back of the house and the kitchen window. Matt is standing there, drinking coffee. He sees Pierre and Ginny and waves. Pierre and Ginny wave back and Matt turns and hobbles away from the window. He limps to the patio door and opens it and calls out.

"What are you two up to?"

"We were following Charles. I was going to ask him what he's doing." Pierre walks up to the patio and talks with Matt for a bit. Ginny stays a bit farther away.

"He was here?"

"You didn't see him?"

"No, I was just getting a coffee to take up to class."

"Charles is fast," Pierre says. "It's amazing really. He doesn't look that healthy yet he runs so fast, like he's been training. And he was wearing military clothing. Camouflage." Pierre looks back to the gate. "Funny, when he was working, when he was a realtor, he always dressed so professionally. Suits and all. But now –"

When Pierre gets back to his family they are all waiting at their front door, and they begin to remove their shoes on the stoop, leaving them outside to dry the mud. Ginny has come around the front of her house and she can see them. She hears Erin say, "You think he's fast? Maybe you're just slow for your age, Dad."

"That's not nice, Erin," Ruby says. "Your dad's in great shape." Ruby looks at Pierre and then over at Ginny. She shrugs. Pierre looks hurt. "You're still a young man," she says, poking him. "Very athletic."

Ginny waves goodbye and heads toward her front door. She fiddles in her pocket for her keys but Matt opens the door for her and lets her in.

"I don't like that place," Elton whispers. It's the last thing Ginny hears before Matt closes the door behind them. "I don't like the ravine. I don't like the people in there."

APRIL

CHAPTER 23

Matt comes downstairs. Still hobbling. He's in the boot, dragging his crutch behind him for support. He's exhausted because he's still not sleeping well, his ankle is aching and stiff. Because he isn't mobile most of the days, he's not as tired at night anymore, his body is used to being exhausted at bedtime. Instead he now tosses and turns and every toss wakes him up with the pain.

"Good morning," Ginny says. She puts down a plate of pancakes. She's been baking so much lately, anything bread-like. Cakes, bread, muffins, cornbread, biscuits. She can't get enough carbohydrates. Matt is starting to think their baby will be made out of carbs. Matt smiles and sits. He pours syrup on his cornbread and takes a big bite. He doesn't say anything. He just keeps eating. Last night he woke to go pee and when he passed the hallway window he looked out into the backyard. There was no one there. Of course. No matter what Ginny says, there is never anyone there.

"Thanks," he says when he's done with his breakfast. "That was a nice treat. Should I make coffee?"

"I did already." Ginny places a cup in front of him. She settles down beside him at the island. "Can you wash my summer clothes today?"

To avoid answering, Matt takes a sip from the cup. It's hot. He blows on it.

Matt's been afraid to go back into the basement. He doesn't want to confront that room and all the supplies that are in it. He assumes he should get in touch with Charles and ask him what to do with it all. He guesses it's all gone bad by now. Matt's not sure you can eat cans of food that have gone through a winter season, that have frozen and thawed. Or even through the heat of summer. The room isn't insulated, it shouldn't be used for food. But he hasn't thought all this through quite yet. He really just wants to talk to his wife about what to do, but Ginny isn't the same wife he married. He can't tell her what's down there, she'll freak out.

Matt wonders if he should be freaking out. Is it really that bad for Charles and Marina to have forgotten a bunch of things when they moved out? Even food? The room is hidden behind doors and windows, and was locked.

But why? Why is everything locked up like a nuclear war bunker? And why isn't Charles just saying something? Knocking on their door, asking them if he can collect his things? Instead, the thefts, the anger, the racing toward the house. It all makes no sense. Is Charles the one breaking into their house? Leaving the lights on, the doors and windows open? Was he the one laughing in the ravine when Matt broke his ankle?

Matt nurses his coffee. He pulls over another stool and puts his ankle up on it. Ginny holds her breath and then opens the curtains to the backyard and they both look out. The grass is slowly growing, starting to dry up from the winter of snow and ice and slush.

"Can you get the other boxes too? I just want to see if some of my summer clothes will fit," Ginny says. "They are mostly baggy. I don't want to buy any clothes to get me through the last couple of months."

Matt nods. "Sure. I get it." Although Matt would much rather not have to hobble down the stairs in his boot.

⊗

Ginny gets up and starts to clean the kitchen. When she's done she goes to the living room to open the blinds. Matt limps up to the second floor to wash up, get dressed and work on his computer a bit, to prepare for next week's classes.

The window blinds open to sunlight and a fuzzy glow, the trees look blurry as they start to wake up after the long winter. Everything seems to glimmer. There is still mud on the ground and the temperature is cool, but Ginny can feel spring coming.

Suddenly she sees movement. It's Charles again – he looks dirtier than usual, he's limping slightly. As if he's fallen. He's on their front lawn coming from behind their house, and he heads out to the street and half-walks, half-jogs toward downtown. He's wearing black pants, rain boots and a large puffy jacket. No hat, no gloves.

What's going on? Why does Charles use their lawn? Why is he always around here? Once he's gone Ginny continues to look out the front window. And then she sees the Smythes' truck parked out in front of Pierre and Ruby's house. Marina is sitting inside it. She's watching her dirty husband move fast down the street. She's staring at him. She hasn't started the truck. She doesn't follow him or even reveal that she is there. Occasionally she looks toward Ginny but she doesn't wave or signal with her eyes. The whole thing is so confusing. If Ginny were dressed she would go out and confront the older woman. Ask some questions. But she's wearing a nightgown and a bathrobe. Instead, Ginny looks out the window, watches the truck and watches as Marina watches her husband disappear around a corner. She stares. Then Marina sits up suddenly, as if she's thinking. Eventually she starts the truck and drives off down the road, toward the town, toward Charles.

"What are they doing?" Ginny says to herself. Marina said he liked to walk down in the ravine when they lived at this house. But there are so many other places to walk in the town. Why does he have to walk behind their house? What about the lake? There's a path down by the lake, a boardwalk. Instead, he walks the overgrown, dirty, dark ravine and he comes up into their backyard and peers into her patio doors. There are all kinds of things lurking in the undergrowth of the ravine, Ginny muses.

Ginny wonders if they should get a restraining order. Or get something legal to stop him from trespassing? Even a sign on the gate out back? When they bought the house they didn't think they would be getting the previous owners in the deal.

Ginny heads up the stairs to Matt who is sitting on the side of their bed putting on his one sock.

"Let's go back to bed for a bit," Ginny says and lies back into the quilt, onto the pillows. Matt's ankle boot is on the bed, Ginny's stomach is large. They are awkwardly placed. Ginny rolls toward him, her belly between them. They both look down at the large bulge.

Ginny tries to smile. Her heart slows down, it stops pounding so heavily. She thinks about how every time her heart speeds up, every time she thinks she might explode with fear or frustration, Matt's presence calms her down. Even when he's sometimes the cause of her fear – with his broken ankle in the ravine or his nervous coddling – he still makes her feel safe. What would she do if she didn't have Matt?

Matt looks at her.

"Baby's coming soon," Ginny says softly and rubs her belly.

"Soon," says Matt, and he kisses her.

Ginny's a bit chilly as she walks with all the neighbours downtown to have dinner at O'Rileys. The only "good" restaurant in Parkville, they say; serving mashed potatoes, baked potatoes, turkey, steak, fish, french fries, frozen peas and carrot mix. Caesar salad. Jell-O and whipped cream out of a spray can for dessert. At least that's what Ginny assumes. That's what everyone has led her to expect.

Bench seats in booths, the TV on to sports, waitresses wearing uniforms (skirts and aprons, hospital shoes). Like something from another era.

But someone is cooking for Matt and Ginny. And someone is paying for them. She'll take anything.

They walk in pairs. Ginny and Pierre are at the back. How did she end up walking with Pierre? Matt is setting the pace with his crutches, and Pat is with him in the front, then Rain and Ruby, then Ginny and Pierre. Michael is meeting them all down there after he closes up the antique store for the night. Ginny shivers, trying to warm up.

"The weather is slowly changing," Pierre says. He notices her shivering but doesn't offer help in any way. Couldn't he lend her his jacket? Although he is only wearing a spring jacket, he's got his hands in his pockets and looks cold too.

"Yeah, not fast enough."

"You've never had a summer here, have you? Of course you haven't." Pierre laughs. "It gets really hot. Humid. And the bugs. Oh god, the bugs."

Ginny grimaces. "It got hot in the city too."

"But not like this. So humid it's like you're walking in water. And you can't go outside without being attacked by mosquitoes or blackflies."

"Blackflies?"

"More near the lake than in our backyards. The mosquitoes are bad, though."

"Thanks for telling me," Ginny sighs. Now she'll have to buy a newborn-safe insect repellent.

"I'm just saying that you'll appreciate being a little chilly now when the summer comes."

That makes no sense, Ginny thinks. You don't get to a hot summer day and think back to a cold winter day and wish you were back there. Brains don't work that way. But Ginny does wonder what she'll do about the baby with mosquitoes everywhere. And now she's wondering if they will need air conditioning in the house. God, how much will that cost? Ginny is also figuring out right now why Ruby is so paranoid about her kids. Maybe Pierre is part of the reason? Both of them seem to need to discuss all the bad things that could happen to people in life – kidnapping, mosquitoes, blackflies, overwhelming heat, girls in boxes under your bed. If you're surrounded by negative things, if you immerse yourself in dread all the time, then maybe you can't step back and appreciate the things that aren't actually happening to you, Ginny thinks. But then she knows she's been doing this since they moved here, actually before that. Since the knife attack in the city. She's become paranoid. Like Pierre and Ruby. Ginny thinks about this while Pierre continues talking about the lake and the hiking trails around the area.

She definitely feels that this has been her problem with the house. It's overwhelmed everything else, all the good stuff. It has made her wary and suspicious and nervous about everything. It contributed to the anxiety she was feeling when she left the city. The man in the alley. He laughed, he hurt her, he terrified her. For a minute she thought she had become a statistic – another girl dead in an alley. Ginny still can't sleep through the night without dreaming about him, although that could be the uncomfortable baby bulge, and every noise in the house does make her jump. At least she hasn't dreamt of the figure in the house since they've had the window fixed.

Pat and Matt are talking conspiratorially up front. Matt uses his crutches like a pro. Ginny tries to hear what they are saying but can't hear past Ruby and Rain, who are nattering on about what they are going to order at the restaurant.

"What can you eat there?" Ruby says.

"Potatoes, I guess, unless they use milk to mash them. Or butter. French fries, I guess? If they are fried in vegetable oil? Not lard." Rain thinks. "I hope there's something I can eat. I haven't been out in a long time. Not since I became vegan."

"Why did you become vegan?" Ginny cuts in. "What made you?"

"No one made me." Rain sulks. "I just want to be healthy and save the environment."

"Save the environment? Really?" Ruby laughs.

"Not by myself," Rain grumbles. "All those pamphlets on the poles. I read them."

Ginny looks at Ruby.

Ruby says, "That was advertising for a cult, Rain. You shouldn't have changed your diet for a cult."

Rain looks down at her shoes. "I just want to be healthy."

"What cult?" Ginny asks.

But Ruby quickly changes the subject. "So you could order Caesar salad if you just ask for lettuce and croutons."

"It's not a cult, Ruby," Pierre says quietly. "That's not what it is."

Ginny stares at them.

Ruby says, "Whatever," and laughs, as if Pierre has told a joke.

"I ate something before we left. I had rice and tempeh."

Ruby says, "Of course you did."

Pierre rolls his eyes.

Ginny listens and watches all this as if she's in a movie. Her eyes and her head go back and forth. Like a tennis match, actually, not the movies. Her brain wants to process what they are saying but, for some reason, it can't. She's tired. She's pregnant. There are so many things happening. Ginny stops listening and looks down the street at Matt and Pat. Why has she never noticed that they have rhyming names? Matt and Pat. Like a little kid's book. Matt and Pat own a cat and sit on a mat and each have a hat and are frightened by a bat. Ginny smiles to herself. Is this pregnancy brain, she wonders?

When they reach the restaurant they have to wait outside for their booth to be cleaned. Ginny is amazed that on a Tuesday night in mid-April the place is so busy. Pat said he made a reservation. A reservation? For this place? But the restaurant is hopping and their booth has just been evacuated by a family of four and the wait staff basically have to do a deep clean. There are french fries and crayons on the floor, ketchup smeared on the tabletop and on the back of the bench. Ginny can smell frying onions.

She wants to sit down, her back is aching. Matt must want to sit with his crutches. Ginny watches the wait staff clean and feels sorry for them. They don't get paid enough for this kind of mess.

They finally all settle into the booth. Matt and Ginny across from each other by the window, Rain and Pat next to them, then Pierre and Ruby – and Michael will be at the end when he arrives.

"This is really nice of you, Pat, thank you." Ginny wants to be clear, to remind him he's paying for it. Money has been so tight.

"No problem at all, you two have been taking care of all of us for how many months now?"

"Eight," Matt says a little too quickly. He's been counting down the dinner parties all the way through. Adding up the expense, getting slightly weighed down by it. Although when everyone started bringing things, that lightened the load a lot. Especially all the wine. Now they have a pretty good wine selection thanks to Ruby and Pierre. And Matt has a dessert gut thanks to Michael and Pat's creations. Rain doesn't eat much either, so there's that.

Michael arrives and plops down at the end of the table.

"Did you all see?" he says, loudly, when he can get their attention.

"What?" Ginny asks.

"Out the window." Michael points out to the street. They all look. Nothing, just some evening traffic and pedestrians heading home from downtown. "Well, they were just there."

"Who?" Pat asks.

"Marina and Charles. In their truck. Waiting at the lights."

They all look again. No truck there.

"So?"

"Charles was driving and he was stopped at the light and he was staring into the restaurant. I couldn't figure out why until I saw Ginny and Matt here, by the window."

"Yes, so?" Pat asks again.

"It's just the way he was looking. The truck was stopped through two changes of lights. Charles seemed as if he didn't even know the lights had changed and there was no one behind him, so he just sat there and stared at you two. If looks could kill," Michael says, laughing. But no one else laughs.

Ginny feels cold. She can see Michael thinking that maybe that was not a great thing to say.

"Sorry, I didn't mean that. Just that he was mesmerized by you all."

Matt rubs his good ankle on Ginny's leg under the table. Ginny jumps a bit, not expecting it.

"Those two certainly don't make me think that aging will be a relaxing time of life," Pierre says. "They seem so angry all the time."

Ruby sighs. "I've never thought aging would be a fun thing. Did you?"

"Retirement?" Pierre says. "I'm looking forward to retirement."

The server comes by to take their orders. They all order something different and Rain ends up ordering french fries (fried in canola oil) and lettuce. Beers all around. Ginny gets a glass of lemonade, hoping it'll make her think of summer. Rain goes for her old standby, bottled water.

How can a notice stuck to a hydro pole make Rain so paranoid? What did the notice say? Ginny wants to ask but she doesn't want to start up the whole discussion of food and health again. She wants to chow down on the greasy shit this restaurant is serving.

Ruby starts to talk about the ravine, about how they all went down there, the kids and Ginny, at the end of March and about how, if anyone is interested, she's been thinking of talking to the town council about fixing it up. She says they can apply for a grant from the town and use it to do most of the work themselves. Then Matt starts to talk about the renovations they've scheduled for the house, the new windows everywhere and putting the basement door to outside back in. Ginny discusses the baby situation with

Pat. He has a few nieces and nephews so he remembers a bit of what she's in for and warns her about sleeping whenever the baby sleeps and lets her know about a diaper service if she wants to use non-disposable. Michael shouts across the booth to Ginny about how they'd love to babysit but they'd have to bring Noodle with them because Noodle is still like a baby himself. He needs lots of love, Michael says. He whines if he isn't in bed with them at night and has to watch TV with them spread out on their laps. Michael and Pat beam like new fathers.

"Will you be sleeping with your baby?" Rain asks Ginny.

She hasn't thought about this. She knows some people sleep with their kids, but Ginny can't imagine doing that. She thinks she would keep the baby up or the baby would keep her up. How would her baby learn to be independent? To sleep on its own? What if she rolled over and crushed it? She looks at Matt. Matt shakes his head at her, No. She agrees.

"Doubt it," Ginny says. "But who knows?"

"Good answer," Matt says. "We have no idea what we're going to do."

The food comes, everyone digs in. Ginny is happily surprised at how good it is. She ordered spareribs and french fries. Comfort food. Coleslaw too. She is determined to make tonight feel like summer. No matter what Pierre says about the bugs, Ginny can't wait until then. The baby, the hot weather, the lake – which Ginny has been told is good for swimming. No weeds. But the baby, really. She can't wait to meet their baby. And she can't wait to be able to bend down to her toes again, to put on her shoes, to take a shower and actually fit in the shower stall.

Ginny always wondered how women approached having a baby, how they were so courageous and where that courage came from. But now she knows, it's not courage, it's a desperate need to have that child out of you – so you can meet it, yes, but also so you can move around and be comfortable in your own body again. Any pain or fear is worth that, she thinks. Bodies weren't made to carry watermelons inside of them.

There is a sudden noise. The table all looks up from their food. There is a commotion on the street outside.

"Oh my god," Pat says. "We can't get away from him during any of our dinner parties, can we?"

And there he is again. Charles. His face pressed against the glass, right near Matt's shoulder. Scowling, angry Charles. Matt jumps. The older man is shouting, saying something they can't understand but Ginny assumes he's screaming about their house again, about how they stole it. The glass blocks his voice. They hear a few scattered words, "home" and "you," but nothing solid. He starts to pound on the glass and Matt moves away as far as he can get, pushing Rain aside. Ginny pushes down on the bench a bit too, forcing Pat and Ruby to get up. That's when a few of the boys busing the tables go outside and shuffle Charles down the street. When he is gone they come over to the booth and apologize to everyone. Free fries all around, perhaps? More wine? Beer?

Ginny watches Charles walk away, watches as he turns a corner. She is scared of him. He's obviously violent. Ginny worries about Marina. Even though she doesn't know the woman, she wishes Marina well and hopes she is safe with this man. He's a menace and should probably be in prison.

A thought that is echoed around the table.

"Well," says Michael. "You can't say our dinner parties aren't exciting." He laughs.

"Let's see what happens at the next one," Matt says. "How long do you think we can carry on with him showing up at every single party? Any bets?"

Pierre is on his third beer and ready to bet. He pulls out his wallet and holds it in the air. They all laugh.

More beer. More wine. Fries all around. Ginny gobbles them up. She's always so hungry now. And she's eating from stress too. She's gained a lot of weight in the last month. She's not sure what is the baby and what is just extra weight. And, frankly, Ginny doesn't care anymore. She just has to get through the next two and a half months.

The neighbours walk home in the dark. It's strangely warmer now. Or maybe it's all the rich food inside Ginny's gut – warming her up. They all part at their houses and it's agreed that next month should be the last dinner at Ginny and Matt's house for a while. After that someone else will host the next party and then someone else. They'll take turns. And they will occasionally go to the restaurant too. Maybe when it's Rain's turn, Michael and Pierre say at the same time. Everyone laughs. Even Rain.

⊗

"That was a good night," Matt says to Ginny as they are readying for bed. He says his ankle is a bit sore from all the walking, from keeping it down all night, but nothing like before. He's healing. Getting better.

Ginny lies on her side beside him on the bed. She rubs her stomach.

"I've got such indigestion now," she says.

Matt laughs. "Guess the baby doesn't like french fries and spareribs?"

"No, the baby does like french fries. Too much. I don't like french fries, I guess."

They kiss, they say, "I love you." And they both toss until they fall asleep.

In the middle of the night Ginny wakes with horrible pains. More indigestion. She burps. She tiptoes to the washroom to get a Tums. She takes three after reading the label and then begins to head back to bed. She's half-asleep, her eyes barely open. She passes the hallway window and looks down into the night. The moon is lighting up the lawn. There, in the middle of the lawn, is the figure in dark clothing. Her nightmare. Is she asleep or awake? He is standing there looking up at their house, straight into this window. Ginny ducks down quickly. Her knees crack. She's sure he saw her. When she stretches back up will she see him right there in front of her? Staring back? But then she remembers the roof is gone. There is no way he could get up to the window to peer in at her. She takes a deep breath and stands.

She looks quickly out the window and he is gone. There's no one there. Ginny rubs her eyes. Was she dreaming again?

Why does this keep happening?

Is Matt right? Has there never been anyone there?

CHAPTER 24

Matt is driving. It's a sunny day, warmer than usual. Ginny's window is partly open, the late April air whipping her hair. It smells green like cut grass and sunshine and budding trees. She is holding the seat belt away from her belly. The tightness of the belt rubs against her. Matt has the music on loud and is humming along with it, tapping his fingers on the steering wheel. They drive from their house through farmland, down the highway, which slowly becomes congested. From farmland, fields that stretch straight to the sky, and the occasional gas station to suddenly the outskirts of the city with factories and huge glass buildings. And then into the city where the streets are packed with Saturday cars, people out to shop, or go for lunch, or visit family. Ginny observes everything, pointing things out to Matt. She says she feels like an alien here now. As if she doesn't belong here anymore. Matt's music begins to match his heartbeat, which speeds up as he gets more into the traffic and the sky feels smaller.

It's amazing, Matt thinks, how big the sky seems where they live. With no high-rises, no tunnels of darkness, no crowds of people on the street, no mass of cars and trucks, everything is wide open in Parkville and the sky always seems so large and full. He's always aware of the sky at their home. He watches the clouds when he jogs (when he could jog), notices when the sky is brilliant blue or streaked with sunset pinks. He never noticed the sky when he lived in the city. Each time Matt comes back to the city now he knows he is less likely to ever live here again. He loved living in the city, but now he knows he could never afford to move back and, actually, he likes the space he has in their new home. He feels less claustrophobic. Even with the town lacking all that the city has to offer he is now more comfortable where he is. If only he could get rid of all the bad things. Get rid of the stuff in the basement room. Get rid of the Smythes – surely they will die someday? And Ginny will have the baby and be so busy that she'll forget how worried she is. Things will work out. The blue sky, the yellow sun, the song on the radio, "sun keeps on shining" by almost monday, the radio DJ says – life will be normal soon.

Besides, he thinks, keeping beat with the song on the steering wheel, he can always come visit the city whenever he wants.

They are driving into the city to have lunch with everyone. All the relatives. Ginny's sister and her husband, their new baby, which was two weeks early just as Christine predicted. Ginny has yet to meet the baby and is excited. They are having lunch with her mother and father and some relatives and they might visit Matt's parents on the way home. Everyone is meeting at Christine's house so she can put the baby in her crib if she falls asleep. Christine has had the lunch catered. Ginny seems fairly happy, Matt thinks. Even though she hasn't been sleeping very much. The weather and getting away from the house seem to make her less anxious. Matt is hungry and stiff from the drive. He is grateful that he can drive now and that he doesn't have a stick shift. There's no way he can put pressure on his left ankle. Not yet. But he is stiff from keeping completely still as he drives, making sure his left ankle doesn't touch anything.

Ginny is humming now, hanging her hand out the window and making it ride on the wind. Humming to the music.

"Nice day," she shouts over the music.

Mat nods. He smiles. The car slows down in the traffic. Soon they are at a crawl. Matt turns the music down.

"Aren't you glad we don't live here anymore?" he says. "Even with all the issues and the house problems I'm really glad we live where we do."

Ginny smiles and reaches over and ruffles his hair. "I'd like it better without a couple of demented previous owners, but yes. I'm glad too."

"It will hopefully be a good place to have a kid," Matt says.

"Hopefully?"

"It will be."

Ginny smiles at Matt and he takes note of the black bags under her eyes.

Matt pulls into Christine's driveway. He can see the other family members' cars on the street. Seems like everyone is here.

They walk up the front steps, Ginny cradling her belly, Matt using his crutches. It took him a minute to straighten up after the drive but now he's limber. They knock and Christine, holding her newborn, opens the door to a surprise baby shower. Of course. Of course that's what this was, Matt thinks. There are streamers hanging from the ceiling and balloons. Ginny seems stunned. Matt, after catching his balance, realizes that of course the family wasn't going to forget about them just because they left the city. They are family, after all. Even both of his parents and step-parents are here. He waves at them, sitting on the sofa with Ginny's mother.

He sees a few of Ginny's old work friends and friends from university sitting on the other sofa in the living room. Ginny settles into a huge gaggle of these women who coo at her. She looks both nervous and proud. Anxious and happy. Matt watches her trying to get a word in edgewise. These women are so assured and aggressive. They keep interrupting each other, talking over each other. Matt wonders if that has something to do with living in the city – you have to be confident to even drive here. He leaves Ginny and walks through the house to the kitchen where the men are gathered. The barbeque is smoking on the porch. A caterer is tending to it. There are kids in the backyard and the kitchen. He doesn't know whose. He's careful to keep his ankle away from any kid running by.

"Hey, Matt." His brother-in-law, John, offers him a beer but he's driving home in a couple of hours so he grabs a ginger ale from a cooler and settles on the back porch with all the men. He can hear squeals of delight coming from the living room and the occasional cry from the new baby. The houses beside this house are close, so close, Matt's not used to that anymore – and he can see some of the neighbours through their windows moving about inside.

There are presents in the living room with Ginny and the women and Christine and the new baby. Presents that, later, Matt will help open. Things that make having a baby more real. Clothes, blankets, a rocking chair, a breastfeeding pillow, a baby monitor, the list goes on and on. Matt didn't realize that they would need all these things and, by the look on Ginny's face, she didn't either. Neither of them has really done much research. The baby has been that thing in the background that they will deal with when it comes. They've been too worried about the house. But both of them have always approached life this way. Matt and Ginny haven't talked about it, but they both know now that this approach won't always be possible anymore. They have to start being adults, start planning and thinking ahead.

After lunch and present-opening there is the required conversation about why Ginny and Matt moved.

"So there's only one restaurant there?" Christine says. "Is that true?" She's nursing the baby, a blanket thrown over her shoulder and breast.

"Sort of," Ginny says. "Only one good restaurant, the rest are takeouts. No movie theatre, a few stores, a little library where you mostly have to order your books in, a lake, a ravine." She thinks it does sound ridiculous when she says it out loud. "We have a running store, though, oddly."

Christine laughs.

"But there's sky," Matt says. "Huge swaths of sky."

The men laugh. The women look confused.

"What do you do with sky?" his father-in-law asks.

"I stare at it. I watch it. I follow the patterns. I feel more connected to the world when I'm there. Here, I feel like a machine."

"Ah, he's gone all soft," his father says. "Hippy."

His stepmother laughs with her mouth open but then covers her mouth with her hand. "Sorry."

"Seriously, Dad. It's different living outside of the city. You have more of a sense that you belong to some bigger pattern."

"Oh god, are you religious now, Matt?"

Ginny rolls her eyes. "Matt's right. The sky is huge. And getting things done, grocery shopping or even going out for dinner is –"

"To the one restaurant!" Christine shouts. The baby under the blanket whimpers.

"– is easier." Ginny sticks her tongue out at Christine.

"How can going out for dinner be hard?" Ginny's mother says. "I don't get it."

"Well, you don't need a reservation," Ginny lies. Of course they did have to make a reservation. "There's also no choice of the place. Just one place, Christine. It makes decisions easier." She laughs.

"But what I mean is," Matt interrupts, "I mean that there's space. Everything feels wider and larger and more connected."

The conversation peters out – no one knows how to respond to Matt. No one is really interested in Parkville except to tease them. Matt and Ginny look at each other. They both shrug. Maybe it's not where they live, maybe it's more about them together. What they share. History and laughter and fear and sadness and just being together. No one seems to understand exactly what they are saying. Ginny understands completely what Matt is saying. But it's not just about the city vs. the town, after all, the dinner parties always seem to go this way too. No one understands who Matt and Ginny are. Just them. This thought makes Ginny feel warm inside. She looks carefully at Matt, studies his face. She wishes she wasn't such a traumatic mess. She wants to be a pregnant woman who is strong and unafraid, not nervous. She wants her anxiety to disappear for good, and she thought moving to the country would do that. Make it vanish.

Instead moving made it worse.

And going off the medication, that was a problem too. She was calmer just after the attack in the city when she was taking Xanax. It's all a loop – attack, anxiety, meds, move, anxiety, stop meds, pregnancy, anxiety. What comes first? What comes last? She looks down at her hands holding baby slippers, soft green with bows. Her hands are shaking.

⊗

On the way home this time, their car is loaded with gifts – the rocking chair is tied to the roof. Ginny and Matt breathe deeply when they creep their car off the main highway and onto the back roads.

"Look at that sky," Matt says. They both look up. It looks like rain. Ginny's window is still open. She laughs loudly.

"I'm glad you think the way I do," Matt says to Ginny. "I wasn't sure. After all that has gone on in that house, I thought you might want to move back."

"I can't say I don't think about it. All the time. But no. This is home for now. We'll figure it out later. We're having a baby soon."

As they pull into their driveway he asks, "So you're okay with all the renovations then? Because if we ever needed to sell the ren-ovations would increase the value."

"Yep. I'm ready."

Ginny walks up the front walk. This time their front door is closed. The lights in the house are off, just as they left them. She opens the door, enters the house and rushes to turn off the alarm. She flips on the light switch in the hallway. Matt is behind her, struggling with the bags of gifts and his crutches. The rocking chair on the roof of their car will take two people to carry it so Matt dumps down the first bags in the front hall and then turns to go back for it, limping in his ankle boot. "Ginny, can you help with the chair? It's not too heavy."

Ginny nods and comes out again. They walk back to the car and then, in the mild darkness, they both see the Smythes' truck idling around the corner of the dead-end street. Charles is sitting in the driver's seat staring straight ahead. He won't even look toward them. He won't acknowledge them. Marina is nowhere to be seen.

Ginny starts walking toward the truck, shouting, "Hey, hey!"

Matt grabs her arm and says, "Just leave it."

But Ginny pulls away from him and moves as fast as she can toward Charles. She has almost reached the truck when Charles starts it, not even looking at Ginny, puts it in gear and pulls quickly away. He almost hits Ginny. She pounds on the trunk.

Matt runs up beside her and they watch the truck drive off.

"What were you going to do?" Matt says. "Punch him?" He laughs slightly, nervously.

"I was going to talk to him, Matt," Ginny says. "And then maybe punch him." Ginny tries to smile but can't.

"It's like we have ghosts, like we are being haunted by these people all the time," she says as she comes back to their car and begins to lug one side of the rocking chair awkwardly off the roof and onto the driveway. Matt is limping and balancing the other side of it beside her.

"It's like Shirley Jackson's *The Haunting of Hill House*," Matt says. "'No live organism can continue for long to exist sanely under conditions of absolute reality . . .'" and Ginny looks over at him and rolls her eyes.

MAY

CHAPTER 25

Ginny is up in the baby's room. Lately they've been talking about names. They both agree they don't really care, as long as they don't call a boy Charles or a girl Marina.

It's a beautiful May day, the sun is shining and warm, everything outside is budding, the grass is growing. She has the hallway window open to the air. This is the first time the window has been open on purpose. There is no action in their backyard today. Ginny hasn't seen Charles for a week or two and when she got up last night to pee her nightmare man wasn't there. She hasn't seen *him* for a while either, come to think of it. Ginny's hoping her brain has finally flipped that switch off. With the window fixed and the roof of the shed gone all she has left is the rest of the new windows. She can't wait until they get them installed so she can open all of them up to the air during the day and close them tight and lock them at night.

Supposedly they will be installed in the next couple of weeks. The hall window is lovely and feels safe, but that's not enough. And only another week until the basement renovations start. Matt has been down there a lot lately. She assumes he's organizing all their boxes and his tools. He comes up and down the stairs all day carrying huge black bags that look very heavy. He puts the bags in the car and then takes them to the dump. She has no idea what he's getting rid of and she doesn't remember taking that many things down to the basement when they moved in. But anytime Matt tries to clean something up, that pleases her. She feels if she asks any questions he'll stop. So she says nothing and sits around a lot watching him come and go and thinking of her baby.

And then one day he shows Ginny the room under the porch. An empty room he just found, a room they both knew nothing about. Ginny feels a shiver go down her spine. But she agrees with Matt about how it'll stretch the footprint of the basement. Perhaps they can ask the contractor to winterize it and move Matt's tool room here. Matt is nervous showing her the room and she tries to make him more comfortable.

"There's nothing in here, Matt," Ginny says. "Nothing to worry about. It's just an unused and forgotten room. I imagine Marina and Charles just put these doors and windows in front of it and forgot all about it."

Ginny is trying, lately, to be kinder. To the contractor. To Matt. It's like her pregnancy hormones are at a stage where she's feeling almost mellow. She thinks of those Buddha statues people have in their gardens. That's what she feels like most days now. Content and calm. And large. She is attempting to forget everything about the house that freaks her out. And forgetting is easier each day of her pregnancy. Pregnancy brain. The other week she even forgot Rain's name when she ran into her at the market. Ginny kept thinking her name was Water instead of Rain. She knew it was something liquid but couldn't, for the life of her, remember what. Ice? Snow? Melt?

She can't believe she only has a month and a half left. She also can't believe she's still going to grow. Right now Ginny feels huge and lumbering, she has pushed out of almost all of her pregnancy clothes, her legs and back hurt all the time, she feels swollen. She can't do up her shoes anymore, or bend to get something from a lower cabinet. She has occasional sciatica that buckles her left leg.

Rain took her to a charity store in the next town the other day to drop off the bags of clothes Ginny had cobbled together to do-nate from her summer wardrobe, and she bought some large men's shirts. There was a pregnancy section in the store too and Ginny found some maternity shorts and leggings. But basically nothing fits and she's wearing the same thing almost every day now.

In the baby's room Ginny folds and puts away the tiny baby things. So cute. Everything is doll-like. Hard to believe that some-thing this size will be a human being. The size of a football. Hard to believe that something this size is in her body. Ginny can hear Matt in his office down the hall talking to his students. She knows he has his ankle up and is looking out the back window toward the ravine. Dreaming of running. He's been talking about it a lot lately. He's in a lot better shape with his ankle than they both thought he would be at this point. It's healing well. He limps a lot but often can get away without the crutches now, at least going up and down the stairs. He leaves the boot off during the day and only sleeps with it. This gives Ginny some confidence for when the baby is born.

The rocker is in the corner, a breastfeeding pillow that looks like half a donut is leaning up against the wall. A changing table and a crib are all set up and ready to go, the blankets are washed, the teddy bears are placed all around the sides of the crib. A mobile is up above and the walls are painted a cheery yellow.

Ginny spends most days going through the room, as if taking inventory. Again and again making sure everything is ready. In the evenings lately Ginny and Matt sit on the back porch on their dining room chairs and Matt has a beer and Ginny has water and they talk about their day, about what they need for the house (a patio set) and when the sun sets they drag the chairs back inside and read in bed. When they are outside, Ginny always keeps one eye on the gate to the ravine and the other on the side of the house for Charles. But Matt looks at the sky. Ginny is sure that one eve-ning Charles, or the figure in black, will pop through the gate and frighten both of them but, for now, they've been alone out here. Quiet and alone.

Ginny often feels as if someone is watching them from the ravine, but that can't be possible. The fence and gate are too high to see over from down below. But she feels fingertips down her back some nights as she looks out at the spindly, dark trees. And she shivers.

Spring is here and all should be better soon when the baby arrives.

⊗

Today Ginny finishes up in the baby's room and, as she waddles down the hallway, passes Matt's office room and asks him if he'd like a coffee. He nods and his class shouts, "There's the missus," with British accents. They are reading Shakespeare and have all decided to speak with British accents. Matt shuts them up and signals, yes, he'd like a coffee. Thumbs-up. He's standing up before his computer, acting something out. Ginny watches for a bit. His smile, his joy in reading Shakespeare to the kids. He should really be in a classroom in-person, she thinks. It's a waste of his talent to be stuck at home. Suddenly he limps to Ginny and pulls her over to the camera. He kisses her on the cheek in front of his class. They all hoot and holler and make kissy noises. Ginny blushes. She doesn't know that this is the last time for a long time that she'll see him like this, peaceful and happy and completely absorbed in what he's doing.

Suddenly one kid, Ginny can't see which one, shouts, "The course of true love never did run smooth," and Matt laughs.

Oh god, Ginny thinks, he's trained another boy to quote things.

Matt brushes loose hair out of Ginny's face, and he shrugs, "*A Midsummer Night's Dream*," he says to her and the class hoots and hollers.

So Ginny starts down the stairs feeling happy and content. She holds tight to the banister as her stomach is throwing her balance off and she worries about her left leg.

And that's when she sees it.

Through the window at the top of their front door, Charles and Marina's truck is going fast, too fast for this neighbourhood. It strikes her as odd and dangerous. Charles is driving. There is no one in the passenger seat. No Marina. She suddenly hears a lot of loud shouting and then a huge bang, a thump, as if the truck has hit something. It's a startling sound, louder than anything she's heard before, a wet sound, a massive thunk. Ginny almost falls down the stairs. The shouting sounds primal. More like wild animals, a feral sound. A howling and gurgling noise, a high-pitched squeal. Ginny can hear syllables all jumbled, words not making sense. And then violent screaming. Lots of screaming.

And, just like the visions of the man sitting at the end of her bed in her dreams, she wonders, as she runs down the stairs, if she really saw or heard anything at all. Time slows down. Time speeds up.

She moves faster to the door and she still hears the shrill screaming.

Something wasn't hit by the truck.

Someone was.

The door hits her belly as Ginny flings it open to see what's going on. She gasps. She sees Charles in his truck on the sidewalk in front of the house. His truck has gone over the curb and has come to a stop almost on top of a figure lying on the ground. As she holds her stomach and shuffles as quickly as she can, closer, closer, Ginny recognizes that the figure is Marina. Charles is out of the truck now and he is shouting nonsense, no words, just sounds, as he moves quickly around the front of it to his wife. Gibberish is coming out of his mouth and he leans over her. Her head is bleeding profusely and Charles kneels and then sits in the grass and grabs her body and pulls her into his lap. Ginny is still running awkwardly toward the scene, holding her belly. She is watching the grass as she runs, making sure she doesn't trip on a hole in the ground, when the shouting stops. The noise stops. Charles stops screaming. Suddenly there is dead silence. The silence is suddenly so loud that Ginny screams and puts her hands on her ears.

Matt comes outside quickly and limps as fast as he can to pass his wife. Even though she feels as though she is moving quickly, Ginny hasn't yet made it to the scene. He shouts, "Call 911."

Ruby and Pierre run out of their house and Michael comes out. Rain crosses the street. A few other neighbours Ginny doesn't know rush over. Ruby has a cellphone and calls for help and the ambulances and fire trucks and police cars begin to arrive in rapid succession. Marina is lying there, on Charles's lap, at an odd angle. Her short, thick body is bent out of shape. There is blood coming from her mouth, her nose and elsewhere on her head. She is on her back, her face twisted toward Ginny. Her eyes are open but blank, blue holes with nothing inside.

When the ambulance arrives she is carefully moved onto the stretcher and pushed quickly into the ambulance, which then rapidly picks up speed down the road. As it turns the corner the ambulance slows gradually and then the sirens turn off. Everything is happening around Ginny as if she's watching a movie. She can't seem to process it all. It makes no sense. Her hands are still covering her ears. Her mouth is open, her eyes wide. She's seeing everything and nothing all at once.

The police rapidly bundle up Charles and race off with him after the departing ambulance. He is covered in his wife's blood. He is crying. Everything is so fast. Ginny is in shock. There is a truck on the grass in front of her house. And bloodstains seeping into the lawn.

"What happened?" she keeps asking. "What happened?"

"I think she's dead," Ruby says. "Charles hit Marina with his truck."

"On purpose? No, that didn't happen. No," Ginny says and begins to cry. "That's not possible." She stands.

Matt holds Ginny. Ginny can't think and squirms out of his

arms. She can't even remember how she got here, to the front side-walk, how she got to this place. She is wearing her pink slippers and no coat. She looks down at tread marks that go up on the curb into the lawn, she looks at the truck and the group of police gathered around it. She looks at all her neighbours, at Matt. Everyone is standing strangely still, staring down the road.

Matt takes Ginny's hands. "We need to go to the police station," he says. "They are telling us to come down now."

Ginny nods. Everything sped up so quickly and she had her hands over her ears so she didn't hear anyone talking or asking questions or telling Matt to come. Even now she can barely hear the cops gathered by the truck. She heard nothing but Charles and his shouting, screeching, animal-like noises. She heard, "Call 911," from Matt, and then Ruby said something on her phone, but nothing after that. Complete silence as if her ears were underwater. She feels broken. She feels numb. Apparently, she and Matt have to leave now, go to the police, tell them what they saw. Tell them everything.

What did Ginny see, though? A woman was run over, her body shattered and squished and broken, by a man who presumably loves her?

She doesn't know. Did she see what she thought she saw? Or is she back upstairs going through the baby's room, folding the little clothes? Has she finally lost her mind?

It is such a beautiful May day, warm and fragrant, and the new window in the hallway is wide open to the spring breeze.

⊗

Matt and Ginny are finally in the same room in the police station, waiting to leave for home. The police have left the room to get some paperwork.

"Hey, are you okay?" Matt asks.

"Yes, I guess. I don't know. Are you okay? What time is it? How long have we been here?"

"I'm not sure. They took my phone," Matt says.

"Mine too. Why would they do that?"

"Something about distractions. They don't want us distracted while we talk to them. And they separated us earlier so we would tell them what we each saw without getting mixed up in each other's stories."

"They brought me some fruit and tea a while ago. Did you get anything?"

Matt looks down at the table. There are scratches and dents in it. The table has obviously been subjected to some violence and he wonders about all the people who have been left in this interview room at the police station in the past. How did this happen, he wonders.

"I wasn't offered anything. It's probably because you are pregnant." Matt tries to smile at Ginny. "We've been here a long time. I wonder what my students did?"

"Oh god, that's right. You were right in the middle of class."

"I'm sure they just logged off."

Ginny nods. "Have you seen Charles? Why would Charles . . . ? Or have you heard how Marina is doing?"

"Oh, honey. Marina —"

Ginny sighs. "Of course," she says. "Right in front of our house." Ginny puts her head in her hands. She is sitting down and resting her elbows on the table. "Charles then. Have you seen him?"

Matt shakes his head. "No. Oh hello." A police officer comes into the room. Matt says, "Can we go home now?"

"Where's Charles?" Ginny looks up.

"You can go soon," the police officer says. He is a tall man in a uniform, his dark hair is greasy and his large nose is red. "You've just got to sign these forms. We're getting the truck off your front lawn right now. Someone will give you a ride home."

"Okay." Matt nods. But he thinks about home and what that means. And Matt isn't sure if he wants to go there now. He heard that horrible thump, he heard the brakes squeal and he limped in his boot from his office, down the stairs, and out onto the lawn. He looks at Ginny. "Hey, it's okay. You have to stop crying. Oh, Ginny, it's okay. It's going to be okay. Everything will be okay. We'll be okay. Let's just go home and have dinner and go to bed. It's been a horrible day." Matt knows that Ginny mentioned everything about Charles to the police before, when they came to the house, about how he was bothering them, scaring them, threatening them. But Matt didn't tell the police much of anything today and now he wonders if he should have. He wasn't sure if this information was important or applicable to what happened on his lawn.

On the front lawn, outside of their house, are bloodstains. Dark liquid marks, marks that have seeped into the dirt. Marina's blood. Ginny stares at the lawn and then at her front door and seems to shrink considerably before going inside. Matt watches her whole body collapse upon itself, he watches her height shrink, her overall being shrink. It's as if she's melting in front of him. He sighs and follows her inside.

At night, in his dreams, Matt is at the hallway window, which is open again. He is watching as the satellite image of the body on the grass gets stiffly up and begins to limp awkwardly toward the ravine. He watches as it slides its legs to the gate and opens it and then disappears behind the fence. And he feels nothing, just interest and curiosity. He feels no fear, no terror. The figure just slithers away. As if nothing has happened.

JUNE

CHAPTER 26

It is now the middle of June and Ginny with her really big stomach and a limping Matt have gone for a walk down the street. No boot, no crutches. Matt says he feels like a new man. They both avoid the lawn in front of their house, Ginny won't even look at it. They have been discussing moving again; Ginny is sure they could get something very small in the city but Matt says he doesn't want something small with the baby coming. He mentions again how Ginny was the one who initially wanted to move from the city, he mentions the attack. She wonders why he always brings this up. Maybe he thinks by reminding her of the attack she'll remember what she was afraid of, she'll remember what it was like in their small apartment in the city. She'll remember the alley and she'll remember, more clearly, the laughter and why she wanted to move here.

"Before Charles hit Marina with his truck," Ginny says. "Before I saw what I thought was a dead body on a satellite image. That's when I wanted to move here, Matt. When the scariest thing in my life was a man with a knife in an alley. It almost seems tame now." Ginny says this but deep inside she knows Matt is right. "Don't think for a minute that I've forgotten the laughter. The attack."

Maybe with Marina's death and Charles being incarcerated

things will begin to be normal in this house, in this town. Maybe the town, the house, will suddenly be the peaceful, clean, safe country that Ginny imagined before she moved here. Maybe then Ginny will feel better. If she's not terrified by Charles twenty-four hours a day, maybe she'll adjust. She hasn't seen the dark figure lately either, maybe Matt was right and he was a figment of her imagination? Or maybe he moved away? Moved on to haunt someone else? Or maybe he was Charles all along?

She doesn't know what to do.

Matt mentions how they will never get back into the city again, how they don't have enough money anymore. Prices of houses have risen considerably in the last year. "And there isn't another house in Parkville that we like or a nicer neighbourhood we want to be in. You know that, Gin. We will be happy here once we get the renovations done. We will love living here now that everything is over. The baby, Ginny. Think of the baby. Besides, there is no space in the city, and the baby can have space here, in this house."

Ginny nods. She walks on. "You're right. I'm just waiting for you to mention the sky."

Matt laughs. They continue down the street.

There is also the fact that the renovations have already started and they really have no option to move right now. There is no time, the baby is due soon. And the contractors have promised them that the house will be worth more after they've finished the renovations. And so Ginny thinks she'll give it a year and see what happens. Maybe she'll go back on her anti-anxiety medication after she gives birth. That's what she'll do. Drown her fears with pills. And this thought calms her.

The contractors have already torn out most of the basement in order to make it all new. Matt and Ginny have watched as a workshop with a large workbench for Matt's tools was going in under the patio, and as they put in a new laundry room with a mud room entrance from the new back hatch and stairs. Ginny has gone down to the basement a lot lately to do the laundry and talk to the contractor. It has started to look like a new house, like their house now, not Charles and Marina's house.

The hatch doors are solid and thick. No leaks. The door at the bottom of the stairs is steel and comes with a large deadbolt. Nobody can come up from the ravine and break in. There are storage shelves going up all over the place and Matt says it will be so clean and fresh that Ginny will hardly recognize it. She likes the idea of a workshop for Matt – he'll be able to do more renovations himself, instead of hiring others. If he's all set up and he can find his tools, which will be all organized, he will be able to build things and fix things and keep the house up. No more broken latches on the windows, Ginny thinks.

In the last week of June Ginny reads the police notes she ordered from the lawyers. The trial won't be for a year, but they are getting their "ducks in order," they said, and compiling the police reports now. She received the notes in the mail so quickly. She can imagine how long all of this would have taken if she still lived in the city. She is in the kitchen, leaning on the island, her belly feeling heavy and full. The baby squirms and punches and kicks. Ginny's back aches.

ONGOING POLICE QUESTIONING:
(The witness states that she lives at 430 Ravine Drive, Parkville.)
Q. And you are the owner of Charles Smythe's previous house at 430 Ravine Drive, Ms. Miller-Jones?
A. Yes. Charles and Marina used to own the house. I think they lived there all their married life. They had no kids. We learned he was a survivalist. Is that what they are called? I'm not sure. We found things in the basement. A room for storage –
Q. Please just answer the questions, don't speculate and don't ramble, don't answer anything I didn't ask.
A. Yes. Sorry. I'm nervous.

Q. You were the first one outside the day of the accident, weren't you? The first one to see the accident?

A. Yes. But everyone else from the neighbourhood started coming out really quickly. The noise was awful. It was loud. Wait, you said accident? Do you think it was an accident? You don't think he intended to run her over?

Q. We have no proof it was anything else. That is what we are here for. Please tell me about your relationship with Charles Smythe.

A. Well, I didn't really have any relationship with him. Although he did keep bothering us, me and Matt. It was like he wanted his house back. He confronted me more than once. He kept using our backyard to get into the ravine. We would see him back there and . . . and I think he came into the upstairs window. The stuff Matt found in the basement was his, he left it there and he came through our window to get it –

Q. I'll interrupt you here, Ms. Miller-Jones. Are you saying that Charles Smythe was a thief? Are you saying he broke into your house?

A. Well, the window kept coming open all the time, the latch was broken, so I suppose he didn't really break in, he just came in, snuck in –

Q. May I remind you again that we are dealing with facts right now, we are not speculating. We are just trying to get everything written down so that we can give this information to the lawyers. Are you sure it was Mr. Smythe who broke in? Do you have proof? And you have no proof of the things left down in the basement, is that right?

A. The fact is there were things in a secret room. In our basement. I'm assuming he wanted those things back. Matt got rid of the items. That's why Charles kept the shed roof out back, so he could climb up to the window –

Q. As I've said, Ms. Miller-Jones, we are asking you for facts. This interview is not about assuming things. It is about stating the facts. Did you know the injured victim?

A. Injured? She was killed. A woman was killed. And yes, I sort of knew her. I knew her as much as I knew Charles . . .

Q. So you didn't know her very well at all. And you had no idea what was going on in their lives? You're speculating again.

A. I suppose I didn't know what they were going through. No
one really knows what anyone is going through. I –

On and on the transcript goes. The questions, her answers, several
other people meeting with the police. Matt's interview. Five, ten,
twenty more pages. At the end of Ginny's section it mentions that
she was asked to leave the room. Ginny remembers asking, "What
about the satellite image?" but the police transcript doesn't record
her saying that.

Rereading it now, Ginny feels that she never got to the point,
she didn't explain everything correctly. She was only allowed to
answer the police's prepared questions about what he assumed was
an accident, she didn't say everything she wanted to say, she didn't
ask everything she wanted to ask. About Charles, about the house,
about Marina, about the noises she would hear in the night and the
day, about the ravine, the figure sitting on the end of her bed, the
bird in the hall, the squirrel in the wall, the Christmas ornaments
falling from the tree, the house lit up and glowing. There was so
much she wanted to know.

After he was arrested Charles told the police his foot slipped
on the gas pedal but the police didn't fully believe him. Ginny
hopes her interview against his character – his anger, his stalking
– helped with that. But now that she reads it again she wonders if
she really helped with anything. Charles is awaiting his trial but
the police told Ginny and Matt it would be quick and clean and
Charles would most likely be sentenced and serve time. Not much
time, considering what happened, they said. A few years. There are
some mitigating circumstances, the police say. Ginny guesses that
being forced to move house by your wife is an excuse for murder.
Because that came out in the news – that Marina owned the house,
a wedding present from her parents, that she sold the house out
from under Charles. That he never wanted to move.

The police reassured Ginny that Charles would get a bigger
sentence than he would have if this whole thing had just been an

247

accident, or even careless driving. Everything he has said to the police, every strange thing that happened in the house, the locks on the cupboards so that Marina wouldn't use all the food, the shed roof he planned to escape from if he was attacked – attacked? By whom? – provided the police with motive and reason and made the case a lot more interesting.

Ginny thinks about Charles at the windows peering in, wanting his hidden supplies and his aluminum-lined closet, possibly for growing plants under the stairs? There were signs of his prepping, his survivalist lifestyle, everywhere. Signs of his panic and his paranoia about the end of the world. Matt managed to explain more to the police about the room in the basement stacked high with supplies, something Ginny was actually grateful she only knew about after. She thinks that if she had known about what was in the basement she would have fallen over the edge, gone completely insane. But, of course, Matt had cleared the stuff out, trying to protect Ginny, and so the police said he had no proof.

Supposedly, Charles stood at the police station and screamed about the government, about how the first rule of survival is to not let anyone know what you are doing.

"Not even your wife," he shouted. "Don't tell anyone. Don't take anyone into your confidence."

He told the police that when he started ordering new supplies to the new apartment and Marina caught on, "Because the damn apartment is so small," he said, she became furious with him, and was heading over that fateful day to talk to Matt and Ginny about it, to tell them what was hidden in the old room in the basement. That's when he got mad, he says, and accidentally ran into her.

"She was in the way," Charles shouted to the police. "I was just trying to stop her but she was in the way of the truck. The truck hit her."

The truck hit her, Ginny thinks, not Charles. The truck hit her. She wasn't even on the road.

Reading the transcript, she realizes she did change a few things.

She made the police ask Charles more questions. And asking him questions made him want to blurt everything out, defend himself, justify his reasons. Ginny hopes he'll blurt it all out at his trial too. Ginny sighs and stands taller. She rubs at her lower back.

But the satellite image, she thinks. What about the satellite image? Ginny still doesn't know if she and Matt actually saw that on her laptop the night before they moved. And even Matt didn't say anything about the second time he saw it. In fact, he only told Ginny about the second time a few days ago. When Ginny brought up the image no one really seemed interested in hearing anything about it. Was there actually a body in the backyard before Marina's body in their front yard?

Ginny guesses she might never know.

There is a small part of Ginny that wants to visit Charles in jail. Matt and the police tell her that would be the wrong thing for her to do right now. The baby is coming soon and the stress might be too much for her mental and physical health. But how can she live here every day and not ask Charles to clear up that satellite image for her? When Ginny said to Matt, "We saw a body. On the satellite image. Don't you want to know what happened?" Matt just shook his head. He told her he doesn't know what he thinks anymore. He told her that no one will believe them anyway. The image is gone. No matter how many times they told the police about the satellite image no one ever listened or cared. But Ginny still checks her computer all the time and Matt has confessed that he checks his occasionally too. With time, Matt reassures Ginny again and again, they will forget.

Ginny leaves the kitchen. She turns out the light and goes into the living room. She takes up her knitting, her cat-scarf, it's getting so long now, and puts a crime podcast on her phone and settles in. The early evening is fresh. She has the window open slightly to the spring breeze. Matt said they would go for a walk later. Without his boot and crutches his ankle is now feeling almost better. He's increasing his distance a little more every day. He's convinced he'll be all better by the time the baby comes.

⊗

Days later, a Saturday morning just before the baby comes, Matt and Ginny are out walking again. As they head past the park that attaches to the ravine, they see a bunch of their friends getting out of their cars. Ruby and Pierre are wearing long boots, their children, Erin and Elton, have ripped jeans and T-shirts on. They are all wearing gardening gloves. Then Rain is there behind them, she has walked up the street with a wheelbarrow and a shovel and her own gloves. And Michael and Pat and Noodle drive up in their car and jump out with work clothes on too. They pull all kinds of things out of their car. Leaf bags and shovels and rakes. And finally a large truck pulls up and a man climbs out and opens the back and the truck tilts and Ginny and Matt watch as wood chips come pouring out.

"What's happening?" Matt asks.

"Ruby's convinced us to fix up the ravine," Pat says. He rolls his eyes. But Ginny thinks he looks a little excited. "I'm just happy to get her to stop talking about Charles and Marina. Or the news and her kids. Or just stop talking, really." Pat laughs.

Ginny and Matt head down the path into the ravine a bit and look around. They look at the garbage strewn everywhere. "This will be amazing," Matt calls back to everyone. "We can help too after the baby comes." He imagines wearing the baby in a carrier on his back and raking the wood chips down here.

"We're all going to put the gates back in our fences again," Ruby calls back.

"It's like we're getting rid of the bad vibes," Rain says. She has come up beside Ginny. She smells strongly of peppermint. "We're going to make this a street we can be proud to live on, not terrified."

"But what about the thefts?" Ginny asks.

Rain shrugs. "Kids," she says.

Ginny keeps walking tentatively toward their own gate. She steps over the dead tree limb Matt fell over on the muddy path.

She climbs carefully up to the gate holding her stomach, opens it and looks at her house from the back. It's the first time she's seen it from there. She looks at their second-floor hallway window. It's not the only new window now. Most of the windows in the house have finally been replaced. She looks at the hatch door to the basement, now strong and leak-free. Now an entrance. She looks at Matt's crutches, which are leaning up against the side of the patio. He doesn't use them anymore but hasn't gotten around to storing them in the basement yet. She can suddenly see a child running around this yard and she can see patio furniture and an umbrella and a barbeque. Ginny can see a wading pool and a swing from the tree. She shuts the gate and goes back down into the ravine. Matt is watching her.

"You okay?"

"What a fucked-up year," Ginny says. And Elton, who has come running down the path with Noodle, giggles, shocked at her language. Noodle runs in circles chasing his tail.

"I don't really know what I'm doing here," Rain says. She comes up behind Ginny and begins to collect garbage by the fence. "I don't even live on the ravine."

"You can come down the side of our house and through our gate to get down here anytime you want," Matt says, looking at Ginny. "Right? She doesn't have to walk to the park to get in."

Ginny nods and laughs. "What's one more person in the huge scheme of things creeping through our backyard?"

AUGUST

CHAPTER 27

Timothy Felix was born on the sixth of July. Felix because Ginny always wanted a name with an "x" or a "z" in it. And because she was still high from the medication and the euphoria after she gave birth and kept spouting nonsense until Matt agreed with anything she said. At one point Ginny said she was going to name him Potato Man. After all, she pushed out an eight-pound, healthy child, she rationalized she could name him whatever she wanted and he did look a bit like an uncooked potato. Ginny constantly reminds Matt that he owes her a lot.

It is now the end of August and fall will be coming soon. Sadly. Fall and teaching again. Ginny will miss the full summer days with Matt. They've taken Tim to the lake these last few weeks, they have been out for walks in the newly developing ravine every day. They have frequented the outdoor market and have had barbeques outside with the neighbours and just alone with their child. Tim is easygoing. He's been a dream. So far. Christine says that's because he was eight pounds at birth.

"At eight pounds," she says to Ginny, "he's already so well-fed that he doesn't need you all the time."

She's jealous because her daughter was six pounds at birth and hungry every second of every day for the first two months. Christine still hasn't slept more than two hours at a time for months. In fact, Christine and her husband are thinking of moving to Parkville to be closer to Ginny and Matt, to live by the lake. They are considering it and have been looking at houses nearby. Christine says it's not as if they can go out for dinner anymore anyway so it doesn't matter that there's only one good restaurant in town. And supposedly a lot of people from the city are moving into towns like this. It's cheaper, easier, there's more space.

"And there's sky," Matt says. "Don't forget there's sky."

"It's an exodus," Christine says. "A pilgrimage."

Ginny wants to say, "Are you kidding? Haunted houses, crazy old people, survivalists, murder on your front lawn, theft by teens?" but Matt reminds her they were just unlucky, that not everyone who moves here has to deal with a year like they did.

"It has to be the country air," Matt says about Tim's appetite and about how large he was at birth. "The big sky. The fresh air."

Ginny says, "I think it was the french fries and pizza." Once there were contractors in their house every day and they had discovered the great pizza place downtown, Ginny and Matt almost fully gave up cooking in May and June. They indulged in pizza. Matt gained six pounds. But now their walks are slimming them down again. And soon Matt will hopefully be jogging. He has a treadmill in the basement now. In the winter, as soon as it's icy, he'll be down there running. And the basement is lovely now, fully refurbished.

Every day it gets easier.

⊗

It is late August and they are in the backyard with Tim. The gate to the ravine is open. They can hear the occasional hiker down there on the path that Ruby and her team created. Tim is sleeping on a blanket and they have a few lawn chairs out here that they borrowed from Michael and Pat. Matt thinks that, like everything else Michael and Pat own (and sell), the chairs are old-fashioned and very uncomfortable and tippy. Ginny gets up and lies down on the blanket with Tim. Her baby tucked in her arms. He grunts a bit, sleeping soundly. The umbrella is blue, and looking up through it Matt thinks it's the same colour as the sky. Everything blends together. It's hot. And humid. The air waves. But they don't mind. And there are no bugs, no mosquitoes. Ginny says she doesn't know what Pierre was complaining about. Although Pat says the bugs are better this year because they are now fixing up the ravine, getting rid of all the dead wood, the muddy and swampy areas. Every day one of their friends is down there adding to the ravine, making it solid and clear, making a path they want to walk on.

Their neighbours have all made gates through their fences again. Of course they've only fixed up a bit of it, there is a lot more to go, but every day they work on it more. Now they have to drive a long way to get to where they stopped the day before, with their shovels and bags and wheelbarrows and wood chips and garbage bags. Matt will get a good jog out of it soon. Now he jogs for about fifteen minutes before the path becomes awful again. But that's better than just yesterday or the day before or last week. It's getting there. And Matt has only seen two dead animals so far. Squirrels.

Matt and Ginny relax in the sun and Matt thinks about their year. How it started, with the man in the alley in the city, and how it ended – a murder/accident, whatever you want to call it, on their front lawn? The bad and the bad. But there has also been good.

The neighbours who have become friends, the tidying of the ravine and Tim here, their little potato. Their house – creepy, yes, but getting a makeover. And now that Charles is gone they will have nothing to worry about. Ginny and Matt, together no matter what. Ginny's a bit stronger now. He's proud that she has already lasted so long without her anti-anxiety medication.

But they moved here to escape Ginny's nightmare and, at times, their escape became a nightmare. The large figure, all in black, that Ginny is convinced was sliding through her days, her nights. Matt's ankle, his drug-induced nightmare of Charles at the window.

Matt thinks about that man in the alley in the city. How he pulled Ginny in and held a knife to her, how he punched her. And then how he let go. Laughing wildly. Why do people do the things they do? He can't understand it. Why would Charles drive his truck over his wife just because she was going to tell on him for his survivalist tactics? What is the real reason? Matt and Ginny are just trying to live their lives. So is Tim. Matt watches as Ginny grabs Tim's little feet and squeezes.

Ginny looks up at Matt as he stretches his legs out on the old chair. His ankle is completely healed and it only hurts now when it rains. He watches Ginny with his son. Yesterday he smelled smoke in the ravine, but, like the dead squirrels, it doesn't bother him anymore. Moments like this are perfect. The wind in the trees, the intense and humid heat, the sun beaming down on the top of the blue umbrella, the vast sky and their son asleep on a blanket on the lawn of a backyard that they own, that is theirs.

Matt thinks about the future here, in this house. He thinks about Tim and Ginny and he hopes it's finally okay. For now.

Ginny leans back again and closes her eyes. And then she hears a noise and opens them again and looks around. Over in the corner of the yard her eye catches on something moving by the open gate. A shadow? Was the gate open before? She thought it was closed. But it's too dark to see over there after she's been lying in the blinding sun. When she sits up and tilts her head, and when her eyes adjust to the light after the sun on her lids, she sees there is nothing there. And then she hears something in the distance, a crackle of footsteps on the twigs, coming from the ravine. People walking, she assumes. Right? Matt doesn't seem to hear it. He sits there, peacefully, on his chair, his eyes closed. But he senses her sitting up.

"You okay, Ginny?" Matt asks. He holds his hands up to shade his eyes. She can see the concern in his face. But then he says,

"'Keep your face to the sunshine and you cannot see a shadow.'"

Ginny looks at him curiously.

"Helen Keller," Matt says. "She said that."

"Of course she did." Ginny rolls her eyes and whispers to herself, "Helen Keller. Wasn't she blind?"

And then she looks at him, peaceful in his chair, the sun on his body, and she shrugs. She smiles and reaches up and squeezes his hand. She thinks of his big brain and how it's full of useless quotations and she hopes Tim avoids this gene. "I'm doing fine," she says. "Just fine."

What else can she say? There's nothing more to say.

Has she learned anything this year she could say about human fear or misunderstanding? About how we all see the world so differently? Or has she learned anything about how every single one of us interprets differently what is coming at them?

She looks over at the open gate and there he is, the faceless figure, wearing black, his hoodie up shadowing his face. He stands there, watching her.

She puts on her sunglasses and reaches down and grabs hold of her son. Tight. He squeaks in her arms. She looks again.

The gate swings in the breeze but there is nothing there.

There is never anybody there.

EPILOGUE

Charles

Charles Smythe doesn't know when it began. All these uncontrollable feelings. Probably sometime in his twentieth year of work. But he knows suddenly that he needs to take back control of his life. He has no control of his job or his wife or his taxes or how he spends his money or his private time. No control of anyone around him – the people who skip the lines in the grocery store, the man on the street begging for money, the ornery women at the government renewal office, the inquisitive, nosy neighbours. There is nothing Charles can do and he gets angrier and angrier, begins butting in line, yelling at the driver's licence clerks, scowling at the panhandler and the neighbours.

Everything in Charles's life is scheduled and full – cleaning days, beer days, sex days, weekends, workdays, holidays, meeting days, house-viewing days, on and on. Breakfast at 7:00 a.m., lunch at noon, dinner when he gets home from the office. Nothing spontaneous anymore, and no way to do his own thing, to take control of his life. Retiring would solve that, he thinks, and he looks forward to it. He dreams about it. But he isn't quite sure.

Each year these feelings get worse. They compound, magnify,

add on, increase. They pile on. Drowning him. Suffocating him. Choking him.

This isn't his life. This isn't what he wants.

And then Marina tells him to tear the old shed down.

He goes out back with his tools, his hammer, his crowbar, grumpy and angry. Marina scowls at him from the kitchen patio doors.

"Get rid of it," she orders. "It's useless."

It isn't until he has taken most of it down that, suddenly, he looks at it hard and thinks it would actually be a good idea to leave the roof attached to the house, use the covering for rain protection, for storage for his lawn mower, for his wife's plastic plant pots in the winter. He stops ripping it all apart and braces the legs, making everything holding the roof up solid again. And later he will fix any leaking and damaged black tiles on the roof.

Marina watches now from the upstairs hallway window. She doesn't say anything this time. She just stares. A day goes by. Two days. She still doesn't say anything. Charles finally does something that he wants to do without even asking his wife. And she says nothing.

But when he climbs out the upstairs hallway window three days later to fix the roof tiles – early morning in the white long johns he slept in, Marina still sleeping in bed – and he snags his white T-shirt on the window latch, ripping it clean off, cutting his waist, he falls wildly off the roof, his stomach bleeding, and he lands sprawled out in the yard wearing only his long johns, it is at that exact moment when everything in his life becomes clear to him.

Lying there, not sure if he's seriously hurt, watching the lights in the sky twinkle into dawn, watching a lone satellite moving above him, this is the moment he knows for certain that things have to change, that things need to change, that things will change. He knows then that if his life isn't in any way controllable, he will make it so.

ACKNOWLEDGEMENTS

The last few years have been quiet. Covid issues and health problems have kept me solitary. For the first time, I wasn't sharing my work or talking about it with many people. Although the people who did help me and listen to me were few, their patience, kindness and respect was phenomenal.

Paul Vermeersch has been my challenger for many years now. This is my third book published with his imprint, Buckrider Books, and he has been unfailingly supportive of me and my work. Our discussions about characters, plots, structure, ideas, about everything really, have always been thoughtful and thrilling. Thank you, Paul, for all you do for my work.

Suzanne Brandreth, my former agent, was another champion. For two years she worked hard, listened to me ceaselessly drone on and was incredibly patient and kind. I'm indebted to you, Suzanne, and I hope you find the strength to read this new version of *Satellite Image* again.

Emily Schultz, my editor. I've followed Emily's writing for years and when Paul suggested we work together I literally jumped with joy. Emily is a writer who balances the literary with the thriller, and she had just the talent I needed to take apart this book. Thank you, Emily, for seeing, hearing, reading, listening, thinking, inspiring.

Noelle Allen, publisher and owner of Wolsak & Wynn, you are such a beacon of light in this industry. Thank you for all your support. Ashley Hisson and Jamila Allidina, thank you both for all you've done to make this manuscript cleaner. And Jen Rawlinson for the stunning cover and interior design. And Sharon Caseburg, another beacon – just look at all the emails between us and you know what you mean to me and my work. Another person I have to thank for her time and thoughtfulness is Bhavna Chauhan, an early reader.

Thank you to my good friends and neighbours – my dinner party companions – Peter and Janet Harris, Jen Wales and Kevin Oickle and Karen Kretchman. Don't worry, you are not the dinner guests in this book.

My mother, Margaret, and my daughters, Abby and Zoe, three powerful, intelligent, motivating women, thank you for loving me. My father, Edward, always my first editor, your deep editing skills always astonish me. Moving through all of my books is a huge piece of you. I can never express my gratitude enough. And Stu, how many times have you read this book? How many walks have we done where I ramble on and on about this made-up world? I couldn't do it without you. I also can't forget my three-year-old dog, Maybe, who snores and dreams wild, squirrel-chasing dreams beside my desk every day.

A small, but formidable list.

Michelle Berry is the author of seven novels and three books of short stories. Her books have been shortlisted, longlisted and won awards. Her writing has been optioned for film several times and she has been published in the UK. Berry was a reviewer for the *Globe and Mail* for many years. She teaches at the University of Toronto in the Continuing Education department and has also taught at Toronto Metropolitan University, Humber College and Trent University. She has been on the board of PEN Canada and the Writers' Union of Canada and on the Authors' Advisory Group of the Writers' Trust of Canada. For five years Berry owned and operated her own independent bookstore in Peterborough, Ontario, called Hunter Street Books.